D1631933

k3

BEST LEGAL STORIES

by the same author

★

RUN FOR COVER
STOP AT NOTHING
BEWARE OF MIDNIGHT

edited by the author

BEST MOTORING STORIES
BEST SECRET SERVICE STORIES
BEST GAMBLING STORIES

edited by the author and Vincent Orchard

BEST HUNTING STORIES

BEST LEGAL STORIES

Edited with an introduction by

JOHN WELCOME

FABER AND FABER LIMITED
24 Russell Square
London

First published in mcmlxii
by Faber and Faber Limited
24 *Russell Square, London, W.C.*1
Printed in Great Britain by
Purnell and Sons, Ltd.,
Paulton (Somerset) and London
All rights reserved

© *This collection John Welcome*
1962

CONTENTS

★

INTRODUCTION

★

Stories about the law, lawyers and legal cases appear to have maintained their popularity from one generation to another and in and out of the changing fashions in books and authorship. This popularity may very well spring from the fascination all of us feel in listening to the shop of another man's profession, to the drama inherent in the clash of wills and characters in a courtroom, and to the dark secrets lawyers are believed to carry with them and which they can sometimes—under a suitable cloak of disguised names and places—be enticed into telling.

But writing fiction about the law has its pitfalls even for those qualified to do so. For those not qualified the pitfalls become yawning chasms of disaster. Because of its dramatic possibilities the legal story exercises a *Lorelei*-like fascination for writers of all sorts and kinds—especially, it sometimes seems, for those without any legal knowledge at all who are thus lured to their own destruction amongst the rocks and shoals of technicalities and procedure. How many so-called 'deadly' cross-examinations has one read (or witnessed on the screen) containing questions no lawyer would have dared to ask and answers no witness would have been permitted to give; how often has one's willing suspension of disbelief been jolted into frank incredulity by the author's ignorance of what goes on in a solicitor's office or a barrister's chambers, or of the steps which have to be taken before ever a case comes on for hearing?

Even Trollope, careful as he almost invariably was to write with authority and exactness upon whatever subject he touched, did not escape falling into this trap. His trial scene in *Orley Farm* is a tissue of mistakes and improbabilities. It indeed drew down upon his head a ferocious attack by a leading barrister in a *Law Times* article of long ago. It has always been a mystery—at least to me—why Surtees included a trial scene in *Handley Cross* unless, like many another, he wanted to try his hand at it to see how it would come off. It doesn't, in fact, come off at all, and is one of the few tedious pieces of writing in the whole Surtees canon.

Lawyers themselves, who, naturally enough, are best qualified to write about their esoteric trade, are, by and large, a fairly prolific lot. Their output is, however, mostly concentrated on the factual aspects of the business—personal reminiscences, lives of other lawyers, examinations of great cases and the like. Mr. Edgar Lustgarten, for instance, who in *A Case to Answer* has written a novel about a murder case which is almost certainly a minor classic (why, incidentally, has it never been reprinted?), tells me that he has written no short stories with a legal background at all. The fact of the matter is that few lawyers write fiction and few laymen when they write about the law do so convincingly. That was the first and greatest hurdle to be surmounted in compiling this book.

The task has been made simpler in that in recent years two writers of fiction who are lawyers themselves have been steadily making their way further and further into literary prominence. Michael Gilbert is a practising solicitor and Henry Cecil was a practising barrister for many years. *Mr. Portway's Practice*, which I have now rescued—for ever, I hope—from the obscurity of magazine publication, is a little masterpiece, though probably only lawyers will be able truly to appreciate the delicacies of the scheme for perpetual wealth therein propounded. It is fortunate for our clients perhaps that the art of Florentine engraving is one not to be lightly learnt and that a search for a sufficiently skilled employee would certainly be both expensive and unrewarding. Henry Cecil needs no introduction from me. The upward graph of his sales discloses one of the literary success stories of our times. But in *Painswick v. Gloster* the reader will find, what he will be hard put to find elsewhere, legal accuracy concerning all aspects of the profession combined with wit and point. Henry Cecil is an original; the only talent which comes to mind comparable with his is that of Theobald Matthew who wrote the series of *Forensic Fables* before the war. It had been my intention, because one generation seemed largely to have forgotten these brilliant squibs and another never to have heard of them, to include one or two in this book. As, however, I finished my work on this collection the news came that the *Fables* were being reprinted in an omnibus edition and will again be readily available to those wise enough to wish to make their acquaintance. It seemed therefore supererogatory to reprint them here, so I had to deny myself the pleasure of meeting once again *The Young Solicitor and the Sagacious Old Buffer* and, that cautionary tale indeed, *The Prudent Counsel, the New Client and the Strident Person.*

Lawyers, take them as a whole, are not intellectuals. Birkenhead's recreations were hunting, yachting and good living; the first Lord Russell of Killowen had a passion for racing which led him in the end into the purple of the Jockey Club; Patrick Hastings loved the theatre, but it was the theatre of Agate and Rattigan, not of Anouilh, Brecht and John Osborne. These, therefore, are not stories to excite the interest of the intelligentsia. The lawyers here represented deal, as they do in their profession, with the basic facts of human nature—so do the laymen.

For, despite the difficulties I have pointed out in writing about the law, there are, of course, laymen represented here. But Maugham and Agatha Christie, to take but two of them, wisely confine themselves to writing about the law as outsiders looking in. They do not attempt to take on lawyers on their own ground. The Christie story is, of course, that on which the wholly satisfying film about a law case has been based; the Maugham is the Master *à choix*, dry, astringent, worldly and, some would say, unlikeable. Posterity, presumably, will judge Maugham's standing as a writer. He has been much exposed to the slings and arrows of criticism, most of it, surely, unfair. He is an entertainer and a storyteller and thus unfashionable today. His enormous sales, too, seem somehow to rankle in the critics' bosoms and they have failed even to pay him the respect due to his refusal to allow his talent to be corrupted by success. He is often spoken of in the same breath as Maupassant whom he read devotedly as a young man and with whose work his, undoubtedly, has much in common. But Maupassant is the greater of the two. Both of them are storytellers, both use contrivance and plot in order to obtain their effects. But Maugham uses them, perhaps, too much. Even *Cakes and Ale*, the best of all his books, has something of the appearance of literary sleight of hand. Maupassant subdued contrivance to character: with Maugham it is the other way round. He cannot resist the ironic twist, the chuckle of the puppet master, and, so far as literature is concerned, these are fatal weaknesses. Nevertheless, place his work beside that of some of the fashionable overblown literary reputations of today and it will be seen how near to greatness he is.

Maugham's story is about a judge, Galsworthy's about a juryman. It was my original intention in making this collection to attempt to show in each story a different aspect of the law and lawyers in action; to have, for instance, one story about a solicitor, one about a junior barrister, another concerning a silk, a witness, a magistrate and so on. To a certain extent this intention failed, for stories such as *The Witness for the Prosecution* and *Legal Aid*, which fit into no particular category, put up their heads and cried aloud for inclusion. Also, for good value, I felt I should include a picture of an independent tribunal, in this instance a court-martial.

Colonel Henriques' story shows soldiers at work administering military law and doing it very well. If a personal note may be very briefly sounded, they are doing it much better than ever this editor saw them doing it. Years ago, during the early days of the war, it was my duty and privilege to appear as defending officer before many and varied boards of senior officers, and I am bound to confess that I found (as did those of my fellows with legal experience with whom I compared notes) their procedure astonishing and their verdicts incomprehensible. "There is all the difference," a saddened subaltern was once heard by me to remark as he left the impromptu courtroom, having been savaged by a red-tabbed president, "which these chaps don't seem to be able to grasp, between knowing a man is guilty and knowing that there is sufficient evidence to find him so."

There is indeed, and that again is something which many laymen find difficult to understand. But it is because of that fact and many like it that the law makes probably more demands on the integrity of its practitioners than does any other profession. Some—the cynics, the careless, or the hard-boiled eggs—ignore those demands; some—the vast majority, I suppose—compromise with them as most of us compromise with life; others, like the unfortunate Timothy Colt, try to meet them in full.

That the law is a hard taskmaster is a truism. Two essentials in the make-up of anyone who essays to practise it are mental and physical toughness. Lacking them, the lawyer, beset by problems on all sides not only of his own but of his clients, by personal and delegated responsibilities, by the complexities and physical strain of running a solicitor's office or pursuing the practice of a busy barrister, is likely to find himself in early middle age the possessor of a flourishing crop of ulcers or a medical history sheet marked with the dread word *coronary*.

That there are rewards dedicated lawyers at least will aver. Certainly victory in a hard-fought case can bring some of the same satisfaction as a race well-ridden and won. Sound advice, too, seen working out its effect through correspondence to ultimate success can carry with it its own glow of satisfaction; the steering of a client away from danger and into safety, the solving of a particularly trying point in conveyancing or company law carry their own particular solaces. It is well that they do, for one thing is certain, and that is that, with some very few and much to be cherished exceptions, gratitude is seldom the emotion uppermost in the minds of those who leave their lawyers' offices. It is also true that, save in the case of the very fortunate few, the financial compensation is not commensurate with the energy expended, the work done, the responsibility shouldered. That alone is a reason for the reduction in numbers entering the profession, and the draining off of some of its best brains to business, commerce, or authorship, where the heat and burden of the day are not so oppressive, the labour less frustrating and the rewards more in accordance with the effort.

Those who remain struggle on as best they can, some for money, some for security, some for love of the thing, some for the knowledge that they have at least once in a while well and truly served their clients and the rule of law.

JOHN WELCOME

Michael Gilbert

MR. PORTWAY'S PRACTICE

★

I qualified as a solicitor before the war, and in 1937 I bought a share in a small partnership in the City. Then the war came along and I joined the Infantry. I was already thirty-five and it didn't look as if I was going to see much active service, so I cashed in on my knowledge of German and joined the Intelligence Corps. That was fun, too.

When the war finished I got back to London and found our old office bombed and the other partner dead. As far as a legal practice can do, it had disappeared. I got a job without any difficulty in a firm in Bedford Row, but I didn't enjoy it. The work was easy enough but there was no real future in it. So I quit and joined the Legal Branch of Inland Revenue.

This may seem even duller than private practice, but in fact it wasn't. As soon as I had finished the subsidiary training in accountancy that all Revenue officials have to take, I was invited to join a very select outfit known as I.B.A. or Investigation Branch (Active).

If you ask a Revenue official about I.B.A. he'll tell you it doesn't exist. This may simply mean that he hasn't heard of it. Most ordinary Revenue investigation is done by accountants who examine balance sheets and profit and loss accounts and vouchers and receipts and ask questions and go on asking questions until the truth emerges.

Some cases can't be treated like that. They need active investigation. Someone has got to go and find out the facts. That's where I.B.A. comes in.

It isn't all big cases involving millions of pounds. The Revenue reckons to achieve the best results by making a few shrewd examples in the right places. One of our most spectacular coups was achieved when a member of the department opened a greengrocer's shop in Crouch End—but that's by the way.

When the name of Mr. Portway cropped up in I.B.A. records it was natural that the dossier should get pushed across to me. For Mr. Portway was a solicitor. I can't remember precisely how he first came to our notice. You'd be surprised what casual items can set I.B.A. in motion. A conversation in a railway carriage; a hint from an insurance assessor; a bit of loud-voiced boasting in a pub. We don't go in for phone tapping. It's inefficient, and, from our point of view, quite unnecessary.

The thing about Mr. Portway was simply this. That he seemed to make a very substantial amount of money without working for it.

The first real confirmation came from a disgruntled girl who had been hired to look after his books and fired for inefficiency. Mr. Portway ran a good car, she said. Dressed well. Spent hundreds of pounds at the wine merchant (she'd seen one of his bills) and conducted an old-fashioned one-man practice which, by every law of economics, should have left him broke.

Some days he had no clients at all, she said, and spent the morning in his room reading a book (detective stories chiefly); then took two hours for lunch, snoozed a little on his return, had a cup of tea, and went home. Other days, a client or two would trickle in. The business was almost entirely buying and selling of houses and leases and mortgages and sale agreements. Mr. Portway did it all himself. He had one girl to do the typing and look after the outer office, and another (our informant) to keep the books.

I don't suppose you know anything about solicitors' accounting, and I'm not proposing to give you a dissertation on it, but the fact is that solicitors are bound by very strict rules indeed. Rules imposed by Act of Parliament and jealously enforced by the Law Society. And quite right, too. Solicitors handle a lot of other people's money.

When we'd made a quiet check to see if Mr. Portway had any private means of his own (he didn't), we decided that this was the sort of case we ought to have a look at. It wasn't difficult. Mr. Portway knew nothing about figures. However small his staff, he had to have someone with the rudiments of accountancy, or he couldn't have got through his annual audit. We watched the periodicals until we saw his advertisement, and I applied for the job.

I don't know if there were any other applicants, but I'm sure I was the only one who professed both law and book-keeping and who was prepared to accept the mouse-like salary that he was offering.

Mr. Portway was a small, round, pink-cheeked, white-haired man. One would have said Pickwickian, except that he didn't wear glasses, nor was there anything in the least owl-like about his face. So far as any comparison suggested itself he looked like a tortoise. It was a sardonic, leathery, indestructible face, with the long upper lip of a philosopher.

He greeted me warmly and showed me my room. The office occupied the ground floor and basement of the house. On the right as you came in, and overlooking the paved courtyard and fountain which is all that remains of the old Lombards Inn, was Mr. Portway's sanctum, a very nice room on the small side, and made smaller by the rows of bookcases full of bound reports. In fact, the whole suite of offices was tiny, a box-like affair.

I have given you some idea of the scale of things so that you can gather how easy I thought my job was going to be. My guess was that a week would be quite enough for me to detect any funny business that was going on.

I was quite wrong.

A week was enough to convince me that something was wrong. But by the end of a month I hadn't got a step nearer to finding out what it was.

My predecessor hadn't kept the books awfully well, but that was inefficiency, not dishonesty.

I reported my findings to my superiors.

"Mr. Portway," I said, "has a business which appears to produce, in costs, just about enough to pay the salaries of his two assistants, the rent, rates, lighting and other outgoings, and to leave him no personal profit at all. Indeed, in some instances, he has had to make up, from his own pocket, small deficiencies in the office account. Nor does this money come from private means. It is part of my duty as accountant to make Mr. Portway's own private tax returns"—(this, it is fair to him to say, was at his own suggestion)—"and apart from a very small holding in War Stock and occasional casual earnings for articles on wine, on which he is an acknowledged expert, he has—or at least declares—no outside resources at all. Nevertheless, enjoying as he does a 'minus' income, he lives well, appears to deny himself little in the way of comfort. He is not extravagant, but I could not estimate his expenditure on himself at less than two thousand pounds per annum."

My masters found this report so unsatisfactory that I was summoned to an interview. The head of the department at that time, Dai Evans, was a tubby and mercurial Welshman, like Lloyd George without the moustache. He was on Christian-name terms with all his staff; but he wasn't a good man to cross.

"Are you asking me to believe in miracles, Michael?" he said. "How can a man have a wallet full of notes to spend on himself each week if he doesn't earn them from somewhere?"

"Perhaps he makes them," I suggested.

Dai elected to take this seriously. "A forger, you mean. I wouldn't have thought it likely."

"No," I said. "I didn't quite mean that." (I knew as well as anyone that the skill and organization, to say nothing of the supplies of special paper, necessary for bank-note forgery were far beyond the resources of an ordinary citizen.) "I thought he might have a hoard. Some people do, you know. There's nothing intrinsically illegal in it."

Dai grunted. "Why should he trouble to keep up an office? You say it costs him money. Why wouldn't he shift his hoard to a safe deposit? That way he'd save himself money and work. I don't like it, Michael. We're on to something here, boy. Don't let it go."

So I returned to Lombards Inn, and kept my eyes and ears open. And as the weeks passed the mystery grew more irritating and more insoluble.

I made a careful calculation during the month which ensued. In the course of it Mr. Portway acted in the purchase of one house for £5,000, and the sale of another at about the same price. He drafted a lease of an office in the City. And fixed up a mortgage for an old lady with a Building Society. The costs he received for these transactions totalled £171 5*s*. And that was around five pounds less than he paid out, to keep the office going for the same period.

One day, about three o'clock in the afternoon, I took some papers in to him. I found him sitting in the chair beside the fireplace, *The Times* (which he read every day from cover to cover) in one hand, and in the other a glass.

He said, "You find me indulging in my secret vice. I'm one of the old school, who thinks that claret should be drunk after lunch, and burgundy after dinner."

I am fond of French wines myself and he must have seen the quick glance I gave at the bottle.

"It's a Pontet Canet," he said. "Of 1943. Certainly the best of the war years, and almost the best Château of that year. You'll find a glass in the filing cabinet."

You can't drink wine standing up. Before I knew what I was doing, we were seated on either side of the fireplace with the bottle between us. After a second glass Mr. Portway fell into a mood of reminiscence. I kept my ears open, of course, for any useful information, but only half of me, at that moment, was playing the spy. The other half was enjoying an excellent claret, and the company of a philosopher.

It appeared that Mr. Portway had come late to the law. He had studied art under Bertolozzi, the great Florentine engraver, and had spent a couple of years in the workshops of Herr Groener, who specialized in intaglios and metal relief work. He took down from the mantel-shelf a beautiful little reproduction in copper of the Papal Colophon which he had made himself. Then the first world war, most of which he had spent in Egypt and Palestine, had disoriented him.

"I felt need," he said, "of something a little more tangible in my life than the art of metal relievo." He had tried, and failed, to become an architect. And had then chosen law, to oblige an uncle who had no son.

"There have been Portways," he said, "in Lombards Inn for two centuries. I fear I shall be the last."

Then the telephone broke up our talk, and I went back to my room.

As I thought about things that night, I came to the conclusion that Mr. Portway had presented me with the answer to one problem, in the act of setting me another. I was being driven, step by step, to the only logical conclusion. That he had found some method, some perfectly safe and private method, of manufacturing money.

But not forgery, as the word is usually understood. Despite his bland admission of an engraver's training, the difficulties were too great. Where could he get his paper? And such notes as I had seen did not look in the least like forgeries.

I had come to one other conclusion. The heart of the secret lay in the strong-room. This was the one room that no one but Mr. Portway ever visited; the room of which he alone had the key. Try as I would I had never even seen inside the door. If he wanted a deed out of it, Mr. Portway would wait until I was at lunch before he went in to fetch it. And he was always last away from the office when we closed.

The door of the strong-room was a heavy old-fashioned affair, and if you have time to study it, and are patient enough, you can get the measure of any lock in the end. I had twice glimpsed the actual key, too, and that is a great help. It wasn't long before I had equipped myself with keys which I was pretty sure would open the door. The next thing was to find an opportunity to use them.

In the end I hit on quite a simple plan.

At about three o'clock one afternoon I announced that I had an appointment with the local Inspector of Taxes. I thought it would take an hour or ninety minutes. Would it be all right if I went straight home? Mr. Portway agreed. He was in the middle of drafting a complicated conveyance, and looked safely anchored in his chair.

I went back to my room, picked up my hat, raincoat and brief-case, and tiptoed down to the basement. The secretarial staff was massacring a typewriter in the outer office.

Quietly I opened the door of one of the basement storage rooms; I had used my last few lunch breaks, when I was alone in the office, to construct myself a hideaway, by moving a rampart of deed boxes a couple of feet out from the wall, and building up the top with bundles of old papers. Now I shut the door behind me, and squeezed carefully into my lair. Apart from the fact that the fresh dust I had disturbed made me want to sneeze, it wasn't too bad. Soon the dust particles resettled themselves, and I fell into a state of somnolence.

It was five o'clock before I heard Mr. Portway moving. His footsteps came down the passage outside, and stopped. I heard him open the door of the other strong-room opposite. A pause. The door shut again. The next moment my door opened and the lights sprang on.

I held my breath. The lights went out and the door shut. I heard the click of the key in the lock. Then the footsteps moved away.

He was certainly thorough. I even heard him look into the lavatory. (My first plan had been to lock myself in it. I was glad now that I had not.) At last the steps moved away upstairs; more pottering about, the big outer door slammed shut, and silence came down like a blanket.

I let it wait for an hour or two. The trouble was the cleaner, an erratic lady called Gertie. She had a key of her own and sometimes she came in the evening and sometimes early in the morning. I had studied her movements for several weeks. The latest she had ever left the premises was a quarter to eight at night.

By half-past eight I felt it was safe for me to start moving.

The room door presented no difficulties. The lock was on my side, and I simply unscrewed it. The strong-room door was a different matter. I had got what is known in the trade as a set of 'approximates'; which are blank keys of the type and, roughly, the shape to open a given lock. My job was to find the one that worked best, and then file it down and fiddle it until it would open the lock. (You can't do this with a modern lock, which is tooled to a hundredth of an inch, but old locks, which rely on complicated convolutions and strong springs, though they look formidable, are actually much easier.)

By half-past ten I heard the sweet click which means success, and I swung the steel door open, turned on the light switch and stepped in.

It was a small vault with walls of whitewashed brick, with a run of wooden shelves round two of the sides, carrying a line of black deed boxes. I didn't waste much time on them. I guessed the sort of things they would contain.

On the left, behind the door, was a table. On the table stood a heavy, brass-bound, teak box; the sort of thing that might have been built to contain a microscope, only larger. It was locked, and this was a small, Bramah-type lock, which none of my implements were really designed to cope with.

I worked for some time at it, but without a lot of hope. The only solution seemed to be to lug the box away with me—it was very heavy, but just portable—and get someone to work on it. I reflected that I should look pretty silly if it did turn out to be a valuable microscope that one of old Portway's clients had left with him for safe keeping.

Then I had an idea. On the shelf inside the door was a small black tin box with 'E. Portway. Personal' painted on the front. It was the sort of thing a careful man might keep his War Savings Certificates and passport in. It too was locked, but with an ordinary deed-box lock, which one of the keys on my ring fitted. I opened it, and, sure enough, lying on top of the stacked papers in it, the first thing that caught my eye was a worn leather keyholder containing a single, brass Bramah key.

I suddenly felt a little breathless. Perhaps the ventilation in that underground room was not all that it should have been. Moving with deliberation I fitted the brass key into the tiny keyhole, pressed home, and twisted. Then I lifted the top of the box. And came face to face with Mr. Portway's secret.

At first sight it was disappointing. It looked like nothing more than a handpress. The sort of thing you use for impressing a company seal, only larger. I lifted it out, picked up a piece of clean white paper off the shelf, slid it in and pressed down the handle. Then I released it and extracted the paper.

Imprinted on it was a neat, orange Revenue stamp for £20. I went back to the box. Inside was a tray, and arranged in it stamps of various denominations, starting at 10*s*., £1, £2 and £5 and so on upwards. The largest was for £100.

I picked one out and held it up to the light. It was beautifully made. Mr. Portway had not wasted his time at Bertolozzi's Florentine atelier. There was even an arrangement of cogs behind each stamp by which the three figures of the date could be set; tiny, delicate wheels, each a masterpiece of the watchmaker's art.

I heard the footsteps crossing the courtyard, and Mr. Portway was through the door before I even had time to put down the seal I was holding.

"What are you doing here?" I said stupidly.

"When anyone turns on the strong-room light," he said, "it turns on the light in my office, too. I've got a private arrangement with the caretaker of the big block at the end who keeps an eye open for me. If she sees my light on, she telephones me."

"I see," I said. Once I had got over the actual shock of seeing him there I wasn't alarmed. I was half his age and twice his size. "I've been admiring your homework. Every man his own stamp office. A lovely piece of work."

"Is it not?" agreed Mr. Portway, blinking at me under the strong light. I could read in his Chelonian face neither fear nor anger. Rather a sardonic amusement at the turn of affairs. "Are you a private detective, by any chance?"

I told him who I was.

"You have been admiring my little machine?"

"My only real surprise is that no one has thought of it before."

"Yes," he said. "It's very useful. To a practising solicitor, of course. I used to find it a permanent source of irritation that my clients should pay more to the Government—who, after all, hadn't raised a finger to earn it—than they did to me. Do you realise that if I act for the purchase of a London house for £5,000, I get about £43, whilst the Government's share is £100?"

"Scandalous," I agreed. "And so you devised this little machine to adjust the balance. Such a simple and fool-proof form of forgery, when you come to think of it." The more I thought of it the more I liked it. "Just think of the effort you would have to expend—to say nothing of stocks of special paper—if you set out to forge a hundred one-pound notes. Whereas with this machine—a small die—a simple pressure."

"Oh, there's more to it than that," said Mr. Portway. "A man would be a fool to forge Treasury notes. They have to be passed into circulation, and each one is a potential danger to its maker. Here, when I have stamped a document, it goes into a deed box. It may not be looked at again for twenty years. Possibly never."

"As a professional accountant," I said, "I am not sure that that angle is not the one that appeals to me most. Let me see. Take that purchase you were talking about. Your client would give you two cheques, one for your costs, which goes through the books in the ordinary way, and a separate one for the stamp duty."

"Made out to cash."

"Made out to cash, of course. Which you would yourself cash at the bank. Then come back here——"

"I always took the trouble to walk through the Stamp Office in case anyone should be watching me."

"Very sound," I said. "Then you came back here, stamped the document yourself that evening, and put the money in your pocket. It never appeared in your books at all."

"That's right," said Mr. Portway. He seemed gratified at the speed with which I had perceived the finer points of his arrangements.

"There's only one thing I can't quite see," I said. "You're a bachelor, a man with simple tastes. Could you not—I don't want to sound pompous—by working a little harder, have made sufficient money legitimately for your reasonable needs?"

Mr. Portway looked at me for a moment, his smile broadening. "I see," he said, "that you have not had time to examine the rest of my strong-room. My tastes are far from simple, and owing to the scandalous and confiscatory nature of modern taxation—oh, I beg your pardon. I was forgetting for the moment——"

"Don't apologize," I said. "I have often thought the same thing myself. You were speaking of expensive tastes."

Mr. Portway stepped over to a large, drop-fronted deed box, labelled 'Lord Lampeter's Settled Estate', and unlocked it with a key from a chain. Inside was a rack, and in the rack I counted the dusty ends of two dozen bottles.

"Château Margaux. The 1934 vintage. I shouldn't say that even now it has reached its peak. Now here"—he unlocked 'The Dean of Melchester. Family Affairs'—"I have a real treasure. A Mouton Rothschild of 1924."

"1924!"

"In magnums. I know that you appreciate a good wine. Since this may perhaps be our last opportunity——"

"Well——"

Mr. Portway took a corkscrew, a decanter, and two glasses from a small cupboard labelled 'Estate Duty Forms. Miscellaneous', drew the cork of the Mouton Rothschild with care and skill, and decanted it with a steady hand. Then he poured two glasses. We both held it up to the single unshaded light to note the dark, rich, almost black colour, and took our first, ecstatic mouthful. It went down like oiled silk.

"What did you say you had in the other boxes?" I enquired reverently.

"My preference has been for the clarets," said Mr. Portway. "Of course, as I only really started buying in 1945 I have nothing that you could call a museum piece. But I picked up a small lot of 1927 Château Talbot which has to be tasted to be believed. And if a good burgundy was offered, I didn't say no to it." He gestured towards the Marchioness of Gravesend in the corner. "There's a 1937 Romanée Conti—but your glass is empty. . . ."

As we finished the Mouton Rothschild in companionable silence I looked at my watch. It was two o'clock in the morning.

"You will scarcely find any transport to get you home now," said Mr. Portway. "Might I suggest that the only thing to follow a fine claret is a noble burgundy."

"Well——" I said.

I was fully aware that I was compromising my official position, but it hardly seemed to matter. Actually I think my mind had long since been made up. As dawn was breaking, and the Romanée Conti was sinking in the bottle, we agreed provisional articles of partnership.

The name of the firm is Portway & Gilbert of 7 Lombards Inn.

If you are thinking, by any chance, of buying a house——

Agatha Christie

THE WITNESS FOR THE PROSECUTION

★

Mr. Mayherne adjusted his pince-nez and cleared his throat with a little dry-as-dust cough that was wholly typical of him. Then he looked again at the man opposite him, the man charged with wilful murder.

Mr. Mayherne was a small man, precise in manner, neatly, not to say foppishly dressed, with a pair of very shrewd and piercing grey eyes. By no means a fool. Indeed, as a solicitor, Mr. Mayherne's reputation stood very high. His voice, when he spoke to his client, was dry but not unsympathetic.

"I must impress upon you again that you are in very grave danger, and that the utmost frankness is necessary."

Leonard Vole, who had been staring in a dazed fashion at the blank wall in front of him, transferred his glance to the solicitor.

"I know," he said hopelessly. "You keep telling me so. But I can't seem to realize yet that I'm charged with murder—*murder*. And such a dastardly crime too."

Mr. Mayherne was practical, not emotional. He coughed again, took off his pince-nez, polished them carefully, and replaced them on his nose. Then he said, "Yes, yes, yes. Now, my dear Mr. Vole, we're going to make a determined effort to get you off—and we shall succeed—we shall succeed. But I must have all the facts. I must know just how damaging the case against you is likely to be. Then we can fix the best line of defence."

Still the young man looked at him in the same dazed, hopeless fashion. To Mr. Mayherne the case had seemed black enough, and the guilt of the prisoner assured. Now, for the first time, he felt a doubt.

"You think I'm guilty," said Leonard Vole, in a low voice. "But, by God, I swear I'm not! It looks pretty black against me, I know that. I'm like a man caught in a net—the meshes of it all round me, entangling me whichever way I turn. But I didn't do it, Mr. Mayherne, I didn't do it!"

In such a position a man was bound to protest his innocence. Mr. Mayherne knew that. Yet, in spite of himself, he was impressed. It might be, after all, that Leonard Vole was innocent.

"You are right, Mr. Vole," he said gravely. "The case does look very black against you. Nevertheless, I accept your assurance. Now, let us get to facts. I want you to tell me in your own words exactly how you came to make the acquaintance of Miss Emily French."

"It was one day in Oxford Street. I saw an elderly lady crossing the road. She was carrying a lot of parcels. In the middle of the street she dropped them, tried to recover them, found a bus was almost on top of her and just managed to reach the kerb safely, dazed and bewildered by people having shouted at her. I recovered her parcels, wiped the mud off them as best I could, retied the string of one, and returned them to her."

"There was no question of your having saved her life?"

"Oh dear me, no. All I did was to perform a common act of courtesy. She was extremely grateful, thanked me warmly, and said something about my manners not being those of most of the younger generation—I can't remember the exact words. Then I lifted my hat and went on. I never expected to see her again. But life is full of coincidences. That very evening I came across her at a party at a friend's house. She recognized me at once and asked that I should be introduced to her. I then found out that she was a Miss Emily French and that she lived at Cricklewood. I talked to her for some time. She was, I imagine, an old lady who took sudden and violent fancies to people. She took one to me on the strength of a perfectly simple action which anyone might have performed. On leaving, she shook me warmly by the hand, and asked me to come and see her. I replied, of course, that I should be very pleased to do so, and she then urged me to name a day. I did not want particularly to go, but it would have seemed churlish to refuse, so I fixed on the following Saturday. After she was gone, I learned something about her from my friends.

That she was rich, eccentric, lived alone with one maid and owned no less than eight cats."

"I see," said Mr. Mayherne. "The question of her being well off came up as early as that?"

"If you mean that I inquired——" began Leonard Vole hotly, but Mr. Mayherne stilled him with a gesture.

"I have to look at the case as it will be presented by the other side. An ordinary observer would not have supposed Miss French to be a lady of means. She lived poorly, almost humbly. Unless you had been told the contrary, you would in all probability have considered her to be in poor circumstances—at any rate to begin with. Who was it exactly who told you that she was well off?"

"My friend, George Harvey, at whose house the party took place."

"Is he likely to remember having done so?"

"I really don't know. Of course it is some time ago now."

"Quite so, Mr. Vole. You see, the first aim of the prosecution will be to establish that you were in low water financially—that is true, is it not?"

Leonard Vole flushed.

"Yes," he said, in a low voice. "I'd been having a run of infernal bad luck just then."

"Quite so," said Mr. Mayherne again. "That being, as I say, in low water financially, you met this rich old lady and cultivated her acquaintance assiduously. Now if we are in a position to say that you had no idea she was well off, and that you visited her out of pure kindness of heart——"

"Which is the case."

"I dare say. I am not disputing the point. I am looking at it from the outside point of view. A great deal depends on the memory of Mr. Harvey. Is he likely to remember that conversation or is he not? Could he be confused by counsel into believing that it took place later?"

Leonard Vole reflected for some minutes. Then he said steadily enough, but with a rather paler face, "I do not think that that line would be successful, Mr. Mayherne. Several of those present heard his remark, and one or two of them chaffed me about my conquest of a rich old lady."

The solicitor endeavoured to hide his disappointment with a wave of the hand.

"Unfortunate," he said. "But I congratulate you upon your plain speaking, Mr. Vole. It is to you I look to guide me. Your judgment is quite right. To persist in the line I spoke of would have been disastrous. We must leave that point. You made the acquaintance of Miss French, you called upon her, the acquaintanceship progressed. We want a clear reason for all this. Why did you, a young man of thirty-three, good-looking, fond of sport, popular with your friends, devote so much of your time to an elderly woman with whom you could hardly have anything in common?"

Leonard Vole flung out his hands in a nervous gesture.

"I can't tell you—I really can't tell you. After the first visit, she pressed me to come again, spoke of being lonely and unhappy. She made it difficult for me to refuse. She showed so plainly her fondness and affection for me that I was placed in an awkward position. You see, Mr. Mayherne, I've got a weak nature—I drift—I'm one of those people who can't say 'No'. And believe me or not, as you like, after the third or fourth visit I paid her I found myself getting genuinely fond of the old thing. My mother died when I was young, an aunt brought me up, and she too died before I was fifteen. If I told you that I genuinely enjoyed being mothered and pampered, I dare say you'd only laugh."

Mr. Mayherne did not laugh. Instead he took off his pince-nez again and polished them, a sign with him that he was thinking deeply.

"I accept your explanation, Mr. Vole," he said at last. "I believe it to be psychologically probable. Whether a jury would take that view of it is another matter. Please continue your narrative. When was it that Miss French first asked you to look into her business affairs?"

"After my third or fourth visit to her. She understood very little of money matters, and was worried about some investments."

Mr. Mayherne looked up sharply.

"Be careful, Mr. Vole. The maid, Janet Mackenzie, declares that her mistress was a good woman of business and transacted all her own affairs, and this is borne out by the testimony of her bankers."

"I can't help that," said Vole earnestly. "That's what she said to me."

Mr. Mayherne looked at him for a moment or two in silence. Though he had no intention of saying so, his belief in Leonard Vole's innocence was at that moment strengthened. He knew something of the mentality of elderly ladies. He saw Miss French, infatuated with the good-looking young man, hunting about for pretexts that should bring him to the house. What more likely than that she should plead ignorance of business, and beg him to help her with her money affairs? She was enough of a woman of the world to realise that any man is slightly flattered by such an admission of his superiority. Leonard Vole had been flattered. Perhaps, too, she had not been averse to letting this young man know that she was wealthy. Emily French had been a strong-willed old woman, willing to pay her price for what she wanted. All this passed rapidly through Mr. Mayherne's mind, but he gave no indication of it, and asked instead a further question.

"And you did handle her affairs for her at her request?"

"I did."

"Mr. Vole," said the solicitor, "I am going to ask you a very serious question, and one to which it is vital I should have a truthful answer. You were in low water financially. You had the handling of an old lady's affairs—an old lady who, according to her own statement, knew little or nothing of business. Did you at any time, or in any manner, convert to your own use the securities which you handled? Did you engage in any transaction for your own pecuniary advantage which will not bear the light of day?" He quelled the other's response. "Wait a minute before you answer. There are two courses open to us. Either we can make a feature of your probity and honesty in conducting her affairs whilst pointing out how unlikely it is that you would commit murder to obtain money which you might have obtained by such infinitely easier means. If, on the other hand, there is anything in your dealings which the prosecution will get hold of—if, to put it baldly, it can be proved that you swindled the old lady in any way, we must take the line that you had no motive for the murder, since she was already a profitable source of income to you. You perceive the distinction. Now, I beg of you, take your time before you reply."

But Leonard Vole took no time at all.

"My dealings with Miss French's affairs were all perfectly fair and above board. I acted for her interests to the very best of my ability, as any one will find who looks into the matter."

"Thank you," said Mr. Mayherne. "You relieve my mind very much. I pay you the compliment of believing that you are far too clever to lie to me over such an important matter."

"Surely," said Vole eagerly, "the strongest point in my favour is the lack of motive. Granted that I cultivated the acquaintanceship of a rich old lady in the hopes of getting money out of her—that, I gather, is the substance of what you have been saying—surely her death frustrates all my hopes?"

The solicitor looked at him steadily. Then, very deliberately, he repeated his unconscious trick with his pince-nez. It was not until they were firmly replaced on his nose that he spoke.

"Are you not aware, Mr. Vole, that Miss French left a will under which you are the principal beneficiary?"

"What?" The prisoner sprang to his feet. His dismay was obvious and unforced. "My God! What are you saying? She left her money to me?"

Mr. Mayherne nodded slowly. Vole sank down again, his head in his hands.

"You pretend you know nothing of this will?"

"Pretend? There's no pretence about it. I knew nothing about it."

"What would you say if I told you that the maid, Janet Mackenzie, swears that you *did* know? That her mistress told her distinctly that she had consulted you in the matter, and told you of her intentions?"

"Say? That she's lying! No, I go too fast. Janet is an elderly woman. She was a faithful watchdog to her mistress, and she didn't like me. She was jealous and suspicious. I should say that Miss French confided her intentions to Janet, and that Janet either mistook something she said, or else was convinced in her own mind that I had persuaded the old lady into doing it. I dare say that she believes herself now that Miss French actually told her so."

"You don't think she dislikes you enough to lie deliberately about the matter?"

Leonard Vole looked shocked and startled.

"No, indeed! Why should she?"

"I don't know," said Mr. Mayherne thoughtfully. "But she's very bitter against you."

The wretched young man groaned again.

"I'm beginning to see," he muttered. "It's frightful. I made up to her, that's what they'll say, I got her to make a will leaving her money to me, and then I go there that night, and there's nobody in the house—they find her the next day—oh! My God, it's awful!"

"You are wrong about there being nobody in the house," said Mr. Mayherne. "Janet, as you remember, was to go out for the evening. She went, but about half-past nine she returned to fetch the pattern of a blouse sleeve which she had promised to a friend. She let herself in by the back door, went upstairs and fetched it, and went out again. She heard voices in the sitting-room, though she could not distinguish what they said, but she will swear that one of them was Miss French's and one was a man's."

"At half-past nine," said Leonard Vole. "At half-past nine. . . ." He sprang to his feet. "But then I'm saved—saved——"

"What do you mean, saved?" cried Mr. Mayherne, astonished.

"*By half-past nine I was at home again!* My wife can prove that. I left Miss French about five minutes to nine. I arrived home about twenty-past nine. My wife was there waiting for me. Oh! Thank God—thank God! And bless Janet Mackenzie's sleeve pattern."

In his exuberance, he hardly noticed that the grave expression of the solicitor's face had not altered. But the latter's words brought him down to earth with a bump.

"Who, then, in your opinion, murdered Miss French?"

"Why, a burglar, of course, as was thought at first. The window was forced, you remember. She was killed with a heavy blow from a crowbar, and the crowbar was found lying on the floor beside the body. And several articles were missing. But for Janet's absurd suspicions and dislike of me, the police would never have swerved from the right track."

"That will hardly do, Mr. Vole," said the solicitor. "The things that were missing were mere trifles of no value, taken as a blind. And the marks on the window were not at all conclusive. Besides, think for yourself. You say you were no longer in the house by half-past nine. Who, then, was the man Janet heard talking to Miss French in the sitting-room? She would hardly be having an amicable conversation with a burglar?"

"No," said Vole. "No——" He looked puzzled and discouraged. "But anyway," he added with reviving spirit, "it lets me out. I've got an *alibi*. You must see Romaine—my wife—at once."

"Certainly," acquiesced the lawyer. "I should already have seen Mrs. Vole but for her being absent when you were arrested. I wired to Scotland at once, and I understand that she arrives back to-night. I am going to call upon her immediately I leave here."

Vole nodded, a great expression of satisfaction settling down over his face.

"Yes, Romaine will tell you. My God! It's a lucky chance, that."

"Excuse me, Mr. Vole, but are you very fond of your wife?"

"Of course."

"And she of you?"

"Romaine is devoted to me. She'd do anything in the world for me."

He spoke enthusiastically, but the solicitor's heart sank a little lower. The testimony of a devoted wife—would it gain credence?

"Was there anyone else who saw you return at nine-thirty? A maid, for instance?"

"We have no maid."

"Did you meet anyone in the street on the way back?"

"Nobody I knew. I rode part of the way on a bus. The conductor might remember."

Mr. Mayherne shook his head doubtfully.

"There is no one, then, who can confirm your wife's testimony?"

"No. But it isn't necessary, surely?"

"I dare say not. I dare say not," said Mr. Mayherne hastily. "Now there's just one thing more. Did Miss French know that you were a married man?"

"Oh, yes."

"Yet you never took your wife to see her. Why was that?"

For the first time, Leonard Vole's answer came halting and uncertain.

"Well—I don't know."

"Are you aware that Janet Mackenzie says her mistress believed you to be single, and contemplated marrying you in the future?"

Vole laughed.

"Absurd! There was forty years' difference in age between us."

"It has been done," said the solicitor drily. "The fact remains. Your wife never met Miss French?"

"No——" Again the constraint.

"You will permit me to say," said the lawyer, "that I hardly understand your attitude in the matter."

Vole flushed, hesitated, and then spoke.

"I'll make a clean breast of it. I was hard up, as you know. I hoped that Miss French might lend me some money. She was fond of me, but she wasn't at all interested in the struggles of a young couple. Early on, I found that she had taken it for granted that my wife and I didn't get on—were living apart. Mr. Mayherne, I wanted the money—for Romaine's sake. I said nothing, and allowed the old lady to think what she chose. She spoke of my being an adopted son to her. There was never any question of marriage—that must be just Janet's imagination."

"And that is all?"

"Yes—that is all."

Was there just a shade of hesitation in the words? The lawyer fancied so. He rose and held out his hand.

"Good-bye, Mr. Vole." He looked into the haggard young face and spoke with an unusual impulse. "I believe in your innocence in spite of the multitude of facts arrayed against you. I hope to prove it and vindicate you completely."

Vole smiled back at him.

"You'll find the alibi is all right," he said cheerfully.

Again he hardly noticed that the other did not respond.

"The whole thing hinges a good deal on the testimony of Janet Mackenzie," said Mr. Mayherne. "She hates you. That much is clear."

"She can hardly hate me," protested the young man.

The solicitor shook his head as he went out.

"Now for Mrs. Vole," he said to himself.

He was seriously disturbed by the way the thing was shaping.

The Voles lived in a small shabby house near Paddington Green. It was to this house that Mr. Mayherne went.

In answer to his ring, a big slatternly woman, obviously a charwoman, answered the door.

"Mrs. Vole? Has she returned yet?"

"Got back an hour ago. But I dunno if you can see her."

"If you will take my card to her," said Mr. Mayherne quietly, "I am quite sure that she will do so."

The woman looked at him doubtfully, wiped her hand on her apron and took the card. Then she closed the door in his face and left him on the step outside.

In a few minutes, however, she returned with a slightly altered manner.

"Come inside, please."

She ushered him into a tiny drawing-room. Mr. Mayherne, examining a drawing on the wall, started up suddenly to face a tall pale woman who had entered so quietly that he had not heard her.

"Mr. Mayherne? You are my husband's solicitor, are you not? You have come from him? Will you please sit down?"

Until she spoke he had not realized that she was not English. Now, observing her more closely, he noticed the high cheekbones, the dense blue-black of the hair, and an occasional very slight movement of the hands that was distinctly foreign. A strange woman, very quiet. So quiet as to make one uneasy. From the very first Mr. Mayherne was conscious that he was up against something that he did not understand.

"Now, my dear Mrs. Vole," he began, "you must not give way——"

He stopped. It was so very obvious that Romaine Vole had not the slightest intention of giving way. She was perfectly calm and composed.

"Will you please tell me all about it?" she said. "I must know everything. Do not think to spare me. I want to know the worst." She hesitated, then repeated in a lower tone with a curious emphasis which the lawyer did not understand, "I want to know the worst."

Mr. Mayherne went over his interview with Leonard Vole. She listened attentively, nodding her head now and then.

"I see," she said, when he had finished. "He wants me to say that he came in at twenty minutes past nine that night?"

"He did come in at that time?" said Mr. Mayherne sharply.

"That is not the point," she said coldly. "Will my saying so acquit him? Will they believe me?"

Mr. Mayherne was taken aback. She had gone so quickly to the core of the matter.

"That is what I want to know," she said. "Will it be enough? Is there anyone else who can support my evidence?"

There was a suppressed eagerness in her manner that made him vaguely uneasy.

"So far there is no one else," he said reluctantly.

"I see," said Romaine Vole.

She sat for a minute or two perfectly still. A little smile played over her lips.

The lawyer's feeling of alarm grew stronger and stronger.

"Mrs. Vole," he began, "I know what you must feel——"

"Do you?" she said. "I wonder."

"In the circumstances——"

"In the circumstances—I intend to play a lone hand."

He looked at her in dismay.

"But, my dear Mrs. Vole—you are overwrought. Being so devoted to your husband——"

"I beg your pardon?"

The sharpness of her voice made him start. He repeated in a hesitating manner, "Being so devoted to your husband——"

Romaine Vole nodded slowly, the same strange smile on her lips.

"Did he tell you that I was devoted to him?" she asked softly. "Ah! Yes, I can see he did. How stupid men are! Stupid—stupid—stupid——"

She rose suddenly to her feet. All the intense emotion that the lawyer had been conscious of in the atmosphere was now concentrated in her tone.

"I hate him, I tell you! I hate him. I hate him. I hate him! I would like to see him hanged by the neck till he is dead."

The lawyer recoiled before her and the smouldering passion in her eyes.

She advanced a step nearer, and continued vehemently, "Perhaps I *shall* see it. Supposing I tell you that he did not come in that night at twenty-past nine, but at twenty-past *ten*? You say that he tells you he knew nothing about the money coming to him. Supposing I tell you he knew all about it, and counted on it, and committed murder to get it? Supposing I tell you that he admitted to me that night when he came in what he had done? That there was blood on his coat? What then? Supposing that I stand up in court and say all these things?"

Her eyes seemed to challenge him. With an effort, he concealed his growing dismay, and endeavoured to speak in a rational tone.

"You cannot be asked to give evidence against your husband——"

"He is not my husband!"

The words came out so quickly that he fancied he had misunderstood her.

"I beg your pardon? I——"

"He is not my husband."

The silence was so intense that you could have heard a pin drop. "I was an actress in Vienna. My husband is alive but in a madhouse. So we could not marry. I am glad now."

She nodded defiantly.

"I should like you to tell me one thing," said Mr. Mayherne. He contrived to appear as cool and unemotional as ever. "Why are you so bitter against Leonard Vole?"

She shook her head, smiling a little.

"Yes, you would like to know. But I shall not tell you. I will keep my secret. . . ."

Mr. Mayherne gave his dry little cough and rose.

"There seems no point in prolonging the interview," he remarked. "You will hear from me again after I have communicated with my client."

She came closer to him, looking into his eyes with her own wonderful dark ones.

"Tell me," she said, "did you believe—honestly—that he was innocent when you came here to-day?"

"I did," said Mr. Mayherne.

"You poor little man." She laughed.

"And I believe so still," finished the lawyer. "Good evening, madam."

He went out of the room, taking with him the memory of her startled face.

"This is going to be the devil of a business," said Mr. Mayherne to himself as he strode along the street.

Extraordinary, the whole thing. An extraordinary woman. A very dangerous woman. Women were the devil when they got their knife into you.

What was to be done? That wretched young man hadn't a leg to stand upon. Of course, possibly he did commit the crime. . . .

"No," said Mr. Mayherne to himself. "No—there's almost too much evidence against him. I don't believe this woman. She was trumping up the whole story. But she'll never bring it into court."

He wished he felt more conviction on the point.

The police court proceedings were brief and dramatic. The principal witnesses for the prosecution were Janet Mackenzie, maid to the dead woman, and Romaine Heilger, Austrian subject, the mistress of the prisoner.

Mr. Mayherne sat in court and listened to the damning story that the latter told. It was on the lines she had indicated to him in their interview.

The prisoner reserved his defence and was committed for trial.

Mr. Mayherne was at his wits' end. The case against Leonard Vole was black beyond words. Even the famous K.C. who was engaged for the defence held out little hope.

"If we can shake that Austrian woman's testimony, we might do something," he said dubiously. "But it's a bad business."

Mr. Mayherne had concentrated his energies on one single point. Assuming Leonard Vole to be speaking the truth, and to have left the murdered woman's house at nine o'clock, who was the man Janet had heard talking to Miss French at half-past nine?

The only ray of light was in the shape of a scapegrace nephew who had in bygone days cajoled and threatened his aunt out of various sums of money. Janet Mackenzie, the solicitor learned, had always been attached to this young man, and had never ceased urging his claims upon her mistress. It certainly seemed possible that it was this nephew who had been with Miss French after Leonard Vole left, especially as he was not to be found in any of his old haunts.

In all other directions, the lawyer's researches had been negative in their result. No one had seen Leonard Vole entering his own house, or leaving that of Miss French. No one had seen any other man enter or leave the house in Cricklewood. All inquiries drew blanks.

It was the eve of the trial when Mr. Mayherne received the letter which was to lead his thoughts in an entirely new direction.

It came by the six o'clock post. An illiterate scrawl, written on common paper and enclosed in a dirty envelope with the stamp stuck on crooked.

Mr. Mayherne read it through once or twice before he grasped its meaning.

"Dear Mister:

"Youre the lawyer chap wot acks for the young feller. If you want that painted foreign hussy showd up for wot she is an her pack of lies you come to 16 Shaw's Rents Stepney to-night It ull cawst you 2 hundred quid Arsk for Missis Mogson."

The solicitor read and re-read this strange epistle. It might, of course, be a hoax, but when he thought it over, he became increasingly convinced that it was genuine, and also convinced that it was the one hope for the prisoner. The evidence of Romaine Heilger damned him completely, and the line the defence meant to pursue, the line that the evidence of a woman who had admittedly lived an immoral life was not to be trusted, was at best a weak one.

Mr. Mayherne's mind was made up. It was his duty to save his client at all costs. He must go to Shaw's Rents.

He had some difficulty in finding the place, a ramshackle building in an evil-smelling slum, but at last he did so, and on inquiry for Mrs. Mogson was sent up to a room on the third floor. On this door he knocked, and getting no answer, knocked again.

At this second knock, he heard a shuffling sound inside, and presently the door was opened cautiously half an inch and a bent figure peered out.

Suddenly the woman, for it was a woman, gave a chuckle and opened the door wider.

"So it's you, dearie," she said, in a wheezy voice. "Nobody with you, is there? No playing tricks? That's right. You can come in—you can come in."

With some reluctance the lawyer stepped across the threshold into the small dirty room, with its flickering gas jet. There was an untidy unmade bed in a corner, a plain deal table and two rickety chairs. For the first time Mr. Mayherne had a full view of the tenant of this unsavoury apartment. She was a woman of middle age, bent in figure, with a mass of untidy grey hair and a scarf wound tightly round her face. She saw him looking at this and laughed again, the same curious toneless chuckle.

"Wondering why I hide my beauty, dear? He, he, he. Afraid it may tempt you, eh? But you shall see—you shall see."

She drew aside the scarf and the lawyer recoiled involuntarily before the almost formless blur of scarlet. She replaced the scarf again.

"So you're not wanting to kiss me, dearie? He, he, I don't wonder. And yet I was a pretty girl once—not so long ago as you'd think, either. Vitriol, dearie, vitriol—that's what did that. Ah! But I'll be even with 'em——"

She burst into a hideous torrent of profanity which Mr. Mayherne tried vainly to quell. She fell silent at last, her hands clenching and unclenching themselves nervously.

"Enough of that," said the lawyer sternly. "I've come here because I have reason to believe you can give me information which will clear my client, Leonard Vole. Is that the case?"

Her eyes leered at him cunningly.

"What about the money, dearie?" she wheezed. "Two hundred quid, you remember."

"It is your duty to give evidence and you can be called upon to do so."

"That won't do, dearie. I'm an old woman, and I know nothing. But you give me two hundred quid, and perhaps I can give you a hint or two. See?"

"What kind of hint?"

"What should you say to a letter? A letter from *her*. Never mind how I got hold of it. That's my business. It'll do the trick. But I want my two hundred quid."

Mr. Mayherne looked at her coldly, and made up his mind.

"I'll give you ten pounds, nothing more. And only that if this letter is what you say it is."

"Ten pounds?" She screamed and raved at him.

"Twenty," said Mr. Mayherne, "and that's my last word."

He rose as if to go. Then, watching her closely, he drew out a pocketbook, and counted out twenty one-pound notes.

"You see," he said. "That is all I have with me. You can take it or leave it."

But already he knew that the sight of the money was too much for her. She cursed and raved impotently, but at last she gave in. Going over to the bed she drew something out from beneath the tattered mattress.

"Here you are, damn you!" she snarled. "It's the top one you want."

It was a bundle of letters that she threw to him, and Mr. Mayherne untied them and scanned them in his usual cool, methodical manner. The woman, watching him eagerly, could gain no clue from his impassive face.

He read each letter through, then returned again to the top one and read it a second time. Then he tied the whole bundle up again carefully.

They were love letters, written by Romaine Heilger, and the man they were written to was not Leonard Vole. The top letter was dated the day of the latter's arrest.

"I spoke true, dearie, didn't I?" whined the woman. "It'll do for her, that letter?"

Mr. Mayherne put the letters in his pocket, then he asked a question.

"How did you get hold of this correspondence?"

"That's telling," she said with a leer. "But I know something more. I heard in court what that hussy said. Find out where *she* was at twenty-past ten, the time she says she was at home. Ask at the Lion Road Cinema. They'll remember—a fine upstanding girl like that—curse her!"

"Who is the man?" asked Mr. Mayherne. "There's only a Christian name here."

The other's voice grew thick and hoarse, her hands clenched and unclenched. Finally she lifted one to her face.

"He's the man that did this to me. Many years ago now. She took him away from me—a chit of a girl she was then. And when I went after him—and went for him too—he threw the cursed stuff at me! And she laughed—damn her! I've had it in for her for years. Followed her, I have, spied upon her. And now I've got her! She'll suffer for this, won't she, Mr. Lawyer? She'll suffer?"

"She will probably be sentenced to a term of imprisonment for perjury," said Mr. Mayherne quietly.

"Shut away—that's what I want. You're going, are you? Where's my money? Where's that good money?"

Without a word Mr. Mayherne put down the notes on the table. Then, drawing a deep breath, he turned and left the squalid room. Looking back, he saw the old woman crooning over the money.

He wasted no time. He found the cinema in Lion Road easily enough, and, shown a photograph of Romaine Heilger, the commissionaire recognized her at once. She had arrived at the cinema with a man some time after ten o'clock on the evening in question. He had not noticed her escort particularly, but he remembered the lady who had spoken to him about the picture that was showing. They stayed until the end, about an hour later.

Mr. Mayherne was satisfied. Romaine Heilger's evidence was a tissue of lies from beginning to end. She had evolved it out of her passionate hatred. The lawyer wondered whether he would ever know what lay behind that hatred. What had Leonard Vole done to her? He had seemed dumbfounded when the solicitor had reported her attitude to him. He had declared earnestly that such a thing was incredible—yet it had seemed to Mr. Mayherne that after the first astonishment his protests had lacked sincerity.

He *did* know. Mr. Mayherne was convinced of it. He knew, but he had no intention of revealing the fact. The secret between those two remained a secret. Mr. Mayherne wondered if some day he should come to learn what it was.

The solicitor glanced at his watch. It was late, but time was everything. He hailed a taxi and gave an address.

"Sir Charles must know of this at once," he murmured to himself as he got in.

The trial of Leonard Vole for the murder of Emily French aroused widespread interest. In the first place the prisoner was young and good-looking, then he was accused of a particularly dastardly crime, and there was the further interest of Romaine Heilger, the principal witness for the prosecution. There had been pictures of her in many papers, and several fictitious stories as to her origin and history.

The proceedings opened quietly enough. Various technical evidence came first. Then Janet Mackenzie was called. She told substantially the same story as before. In cross-examination counsel for the defence succeeded in getting her to contradict herself once or twice over her account of Vole's association with Miss French; he emphasized the fact that though she had heard a man's voice in the sitting-room that night, there was nothing to show that it was Vole who was there, and he managed to drive home a feeling that jealousy and dislike of the prisoner were at the bottom of a good deal of her evidence.

Then the next witness was called.

"Your name is Romaine Heilger?"

"Yes."

"You are an Austrian subject?"

"Yes."

"For the last three years you have lived with the prisoner and passed yourself off as his wife?"

Just for a moment Romaine Heilger's eyes met those of the man in the dock. Her expression held something curious and unfathomable.

"Yes."

The questions went on. Word by word the damning facts came out. On the night in question the prisoner had taken out a crowbar with him. He had returned at twenty minutes past ten, and had confessed to having killed the old lady. His cuffs had been stained with blood, and he had burned them in the kitchen stove. He had terrorized her into silence by means of threats.

As the story proceeded, the feeling of the court, which had, to begin with, been slightly favourable to the prisoner, now set dead against him. He himself sat with downcast head and moody air, as though he knew he were doomed.

Yet it might have been noted that her own counsel sought to restrain Romaine's animosity. He would have preferred her to be more unbiased.

Formidable and ponderous, counsel for the defence arose.

He put it to her that her story was a malicious fabrication from start to finish, that she had not even been in her own house at the time in question, that she was in love with another man and was deliberately seeking to send Vole to his death for a crime he did not commit.

Romaine denied these allegations with superb insolence.

Then came the surprising dénouement, the production of the letter. It was read aloud in court in the midst of a breathless stillness.

"*Max, beloved, the Fates have delivered him into our hands! He has been arrested for murder—but, yes, the murder of an old lady! Leonard who would not hurt a fly! At last I shall have my revenge. The poor chicken! I shall say that he came in that night with blood upon him—that he confessed to me. I shall hang him, Max—and when he hangs he will know and realize that it was Romaine who sent him to his death. And then—happiness, beloved! Happiness at last!*"

There were experts present ready to swear that the handwriting was that of Romaine Heilger, but they were not needed. Confronted with the letter, Romaine broke down utterly and confessed everything. Leonard Vole had returned to the house at the time he said, twenty past nine. She had invented the whole story to ruin him.

With the collapse of Romaine Heilger, the case for the Crown collapsed also. Sir Charles called his few witnesses, the prisoner himself went into the box and told his story in a manly straightforward manner, unshaken by cross-examination.

The prosecution endeavoured to rally, but without great success. The judge's summing up was not wholly favourable to the prisoner, but a reaction had set in and the jury needed little time to consider their verdict.

"We find the prisoner not guilty."

Leonard Vole was free!

Little Mr. Mayherne hurried from his seat. He must congratulate his client.

He found himself polishing his pince-nez vigorously, and checked himself. His wife had told him only the night before that he was getting a habit of it. Curious things, habits. People themselves never knew they had them.

An interesting case—a very interesting case. That woman, now, Romaine Heilger.

The case was dominated for him still by the exotic figure of Romaine Heilger. She had seemed a pale, quiet woman in the house at Paddington, but in court she had flamed out against the sober background, flaunting herself like a tropical flower.

If he closed his eyes he could see her now, tall and vehement, her exquisite body bent forward a little, her right hand clenching and unclenching itself unconsciously all the time.

Curious things, habits. That gesture of hers with the hand was her habit, he supposed. Yet he had seen someone else do it quite lately. Who was it now? Quite lately——

He drew in his breath with a gasp as it came back to him. *The woman in Shaw's Rents. . . .*

He stood still, his head whirling. It was impossible—impossible—— Yet, Romaine Heilger was an actress.

The K.C. came up behind him and clapped him on the shoulder.

"Congratulated our man yet? He's had a narrow shave, you know. Come along and see him."

But the little lawyer shook off the other's hand.

He wanted one thing only—to see Romaine Heilger face to face.

He did not see her until some time later, and the place of their meeting is not relevant.

"So you guessed," she said, when he had told her all that was in his mind. "The face? Oh, that was easy enough, and the light of that gas jet was too bad for you to see the make-up."

"But why—why——"

"Why did I play a lone hand?" She smiled a little, remembering the last time she had used the words.

"Such an elaborate comedy!"

"My friend—I had to save him. The evidence of a woman devoted to him would not have been enough—you hinted as much yourself. But I know something of the psychology of crowds. Let my evidence be wrung from me, as an admission, damning me in the eyes of the law, and a reaction in favour of the prisoner would immediately set in."

"And the bundle of letters?"

"One alone, the vital one, might have seemed like a—what do you call it?—put-up job."

"Then the man called Max?"

"Never existed, my friend."

"I still think," said little Mr. Mayherne, in an aggrieved manner, "that we could have got him off by the—er—normal procedure."

"I dared not risk it. You see you *thought* he was innocent——"

"And you *knew* it? I see," said little Mr. Mayherne.

"My dear Mr. Mayherne," said Romaine, "you do not see at all. I knew—he was guilty!"

W. Somerset Maugham

THE HAPPY COUPLE

★

I don't know that I very much liked Landon. He was a member of a club I belonged to, and I had often sat next to him at lunch. He was a judge at Old Bailey, and it was through him I was able to get a privileged seat in court when there was an interesting trial that I wanted to attend. He was an imposing figure on the bench in his great full-bottomed wig, his red robes and his ermine tippet; and with his long, white face, thin lips and pale blue eyes, a somewhat terrifying one. He was just, but harsh; and sometimes it made me uncomfortable to hear the bitter scolding he gave a convicted prisoner whom he was about to sentence to a long term of imprisonment. But his acid humour at the lunch-table and his willingness to discuss the cases he had tried made him sufficiently good company for me to disregard the slight malaise I felt in his presence. I asked him once whether he did not feel a certain uneasiness of mind after he had sent a man to the gallows. He smiled as he sipped his glass of port.

"Not at all. The man's had a fair trial; I've summed up as fairly as I could, and the jury has found him guilty. When I condemn him to death, I sentence him to a punishment he richly deserves; and when the court rises, I put the case out of my head. Nobody but a sentimental fool would do anything else."

I knew he liked to talk to me, but I never thought he looked upon me as anything but a club acquaintance, so I was not a little surprised when one day I received a telegram from him saying that he was spending his vacation on the Riviera, and would like to stay with me for two or three days on his way to Italy. I wired that I should be glad to see him. But it was with a certain trepidation that I met him at the station.

On the day of his arrival, to help me out I asked Miss Gray, a neighbour and an old friend of mine, to dinner. She was of mature age, but charming, and she had a flow of lively conversation which I knew nothing could discourage. I gave them a very good dinner, and though I had no port to offer the judge, I was able to provide him with a good bottle of Montrachet and an even better bottle of Mouton Rothschild. He enjoyed them both; and I was glad of that, because when I had offered him a cocktail, he had refused with indignation.

"I have never understood," he said, "how people presumably civilized can indulge in a habit that is not only barbarous but disgusting."

I may state that this did not deter Miss Gray and me from having a couple of dry Martinis, though it was with impatience and distaste that he watched us drink them.

But the dinner was a success. The good wine and Miss Gray's sprightly chatter combined to give Landon a geniality I had never before seen in him. It was plain to me that notwithstanding his austere appearance he liked feminine society; and Miss Gray in a becoming dress, with her neat head only just touched with grey and her delicate features, her sparkling eyes, was still alluring. After dinner the judge, with some old brandy still further to mellow him, let himself go, and for a couple of hours held us entranced while he told us of celebrated trials in which he had been concerned. I was not surprised therefore that when Miss Gray asked us to lunch with her next day, Landon, even before I could answer, accepted with alacrity.

"A very nice woman," he said when she had left us. "And a head on her shoulders. She must have been very pretty as a girl. She's not bad now. Why isn't she married?"

"She always says nobody asked her."

"Stuff and nonsense! Women ought to marry. Too many of these women about who want their independence. I have no patience with them."

Miss Gray lived in a little house facing the sea at St. Jean, which is a couple of miles from my own house at Cap Ferrat. We drove down next day at one and were shown into her sitting-room.

"I have a surprise for you," she said to me, as we shook hands. "The Craigs are coming."

"You've got to know them at last."

"Well, I thought it was too absurd that we should live next door to one another, and bathe from the same beach every day and not speak. So I forced myself on them, and they've promised to come to lunch today. I wanted you to meet them, to see what you make of them." She turned to Landon. "I hope you don't mind."

But he was on his best behaviour.

"I'm sure I shall be delighted to meet any friends of yours, Miss Gray," he said.

"But they're not friends of mine. I've seen a lot of them, but I never spoke to them till yesterday. It'll be a treat for them to meet an author and a celebrated judge."

I had heard a good deal of the Craigs from Miss Gray during the previous three weeks. They had taken the cottage next to hers, and first she feared they would be a nuisance. She liked her own company and did not want to be bothered with the trivialities of social intercourse. But she very quickly discovered that the Craigs were as plainly disinclined to strike up an acquaintance with her as she with them. Though in that little place they could not but meet two or three times a day, the Craigs never by so much as a glance gave an indication that they had ever seen her before. Miss Gray told me she thought it very tactful of them to make no attempt to intrude upon her privacy, but I had an idea that she was not affronted, a little puzzled rather, that they apparently wanted to know her as little as she wanted to know them. I had guessed some time before that she would not be able to resist making the first advance. On one occasion, while we were walking, we passed them, and I was able to have a good look at them. Craig was a handsome man, with a red, honest face, a grey moustache and thick strong grey hair. He held himself well, and there was a bluff heartiness of manner about him that suggested a broker who had retired on a handsome fortune. His wife was a woman hard of visage, tall and of masculine appearance, with dull, fair hair too elaborately dressed, a large nose, a large mouth and a weather-beaten skin. She was not only plain but grim. Her clothes, pretty, flimsy and graceful, sat oddly upon her, for they would better have suited a girl of eighteen, and Mrs. Craig was certainly forty. Miss Gray told me they were well cut and expensive. I thought he looked commonplace and she looked disagreeable, and I told Miss Gray she was lucky that they were obviously disposed to keep themselves to themselves.

"There's something rather sweet about them," she answered.

"What?"

"They love one another. And they adore the baby."

For they had a child that was not more than a year old; and from this Miss Gray had concluded that they had not long been married. She liked to watch them with their baby. A nurse took it out every morning in a pram, but before this, father and mother spent an ecstatic quarter of an hour teaching it to walk. They stood a few yards apart and urged the child to flounder from one to the other; and each time it tumbled into the parental arms, it was lifted up and rapturously embraced. And when finally it was tucked up in the smart pram, they hung over it with charming baby talk and watched it out of sight as though they couldn't bear to let it go.

Miss Gray used often to see them walking up and down the lawn of their garden arm in arm; they did not talk, as though they were so happy to be together that conversation was unnecessary; and it warmed her heart to observe the affection which that dour, unsympathetic woman so obviously felt for her tall, handsome husband. It was a pretty sight to see Mrs. Craig brush an invisible speck of dust off his coat, and Miss Gray was convinced that she purposely made holes in his socks in order to have the pleasure of darning them. And it looked as though he loved her as much as she loved him. Every now and then he would give her a glance, and she would look up at him and smile, and he gave her cheek a little pat. Because they were no longer young, their mutual devotion was peculiarly touching.

I never knew why Miss Gray had never married; I felt as certain as the judge that she had had plenty of chances; and I asked myself, when she talked to me about the Craigs, whether the sight of this matrimonial felicity didn't give her a slight pang. I suppose complete happiness is very rare in this world, but these two people seemed to enjoy it, and it may be that Miss Gray was so strangely interested in them only because she could not quite suppress the feeling in her heart that by remaining single she had missed something.

Because she didn't know what their first names were, she called them Edwin and Angelina. She made up a story about them. She told it to me one day; and when I ridiculed it, she was quite short with me. This, as far as I can remember, is how it went: They had fallen in love with one another years before—perhaps twenty years—when Angelina, a young girl then, had the fresh grace of her teens and Edwin was a brave youth setting out joyously on the journey of life. And since the gods, who are said to look upon young love with kindliness, nevertheless do not bother their heads with practical matters, neither Edwin nor Angelina had a penny. It was impossible for them to marry, but they had courage, hope and confidence. Edwin made up his mind to go out to South America or Malaya or where you like, make his fortune and return to marry the girl who had patiently waited for him. It couldn't take more than two or three years, five at the utmost; and what is that, when you're twenty and the whole of life is before you? Meanwhile of course Angelina would live with her widowed mother.

But things didn't pan out according to schedule. Edwin found it more difficult than he had expected to make a fortune; in fact, he found it hard to earn enough money to keep body and soul together, and only Angelina's love and her tender letters gave him the heart to continue the struggle. At the end of five years he was not much better off than when he started. Angelina would willingly have joined him and shared his poverty, but it was impossible for her to leave her mother, bedridden as she was, poor thing, and there was nothing for them to do but have patience. And so the years passed slowly, and Edwin's hair grew grey, and Angelina became grim and haggard. Hers was the harder lot, for she could do nothing but wait. The cruel glass showed such charms as she had possessed slipping away from her one by one; and at last she discovered that youth, with a mocking laugh and a pirouette, had left her for good. Her sweetness turned sour from long tending of a querulous invalid; her mind was narrowed by the society of the small town in which she lived. Her friends married and had children, but she remained a prisoner to duty.

She wondered if Edwin still loved her. She wondered if he would ever come back. She often despaired. Ten years went by, and fifteen, and twenty. Then Edwin wrote to say that his affairs were settled, he had made enough money for them to live upon in comfort, and if she were still willing to marry him, he would return at once. By a merciful interposition of providence, Angelina's mother chose that very moment to abandon a world in which she had made herself a thorough nuisance. But when after so long a separation they met, Angelina saw with dismay that Edwin was as young as ever. It's true his hair was grey, but it infinitely became him. He had always been good-looking, but now he was a very handsome man in the flower of his age. She felt as old as the hills. She was conscious of her narrowness, her terrible provincialism, compared with the breadth he had acquired by his long sojourn in foreign countries. He was gay and breezy as of old, but her spirit was crushed. The bitterness of life had warped her soul. It seemed monstrous to bind that alert and active man to her by a promise twenty years old, and she offered him his release. He went deathly pale.

"Don't you care for me any more?" he cried brokenly.

And she realized on a sudden—oh, the rapture, oh, the relief!—that to him too she was just the same as she had ever been. He had thought of her always as she was; her portrait had been, as it were, stamped on his heart, so that now, when the real woman stood before him, she was, to him, still eighteen.

So they were married.

"I don't believe a word of it," I said when Miss Gray had brought her story to its happy ending.

"I insist on your believing it," she said. "I'm convinced it's true, and I haven't the smallest doubt that they'll live happily together to a ripe old age." Then she made a remark that I thought rather shrewd. "Their love is founded on an illusion, perhaps; but since it has to them all the appearance of reality, what does it matter?"

While I have told you this idyllic story of Miss Gray's invention, the three of us, our hostess, Landon and myself, waited for the Craigs to come.

"Have you ever noticed that if people live next door to you, they're invariably late?" Miss Gray asked the judge.

"No, I haven't," he answered acidly. "I'm always punctual myself, and I expect other people to be punctual."

"I suppose it's no good offering you a cocktail?"

"None whatever, madam."

"But I have some sherry that they tell me isn't bad."

The judge took the bottle out of her hands and looked at the label. A faint smile broke on his thin lips.

"This is a civilized drink, Miss Gray. With your permission I will help myself. I never knew a woman yet who knew how to pour out a glass of wine. One should hold a woman by the waist, but a bottle by the neck."

While he was sipping the old sherry with every sign of satisfaction, Miss Gray glanced out of the window.

"Oh, that's why the Craigs are late. They were waiting for the baby to come back."

I followed her eyes and saw that the nurse had just pushed the pram past Miss Gray's house on her way home. Craig took the baby out of the pram and lifted it high in the air. The baby, trying to tug at his moustache, crowed gleefully. Mrs. Craig stood by watching, and the smile on her face made her harsh features almost pleasant. The window was open, and we heard her speak.

"Come along, darling," she said, "we're late."

He put the baby back in the pram, and they came up to the door of Miss Gray's house and rang the bell. The maid showed them in. They shook hands with Miss Gray, and because I was standing near, she introduced me to them. Then she turned to the judge.

"And this is Sir Edward Landon—Mr. and Mrs. Craig."

One would have expected the judge to move forward with an outstretched hand, but he remained stock-still. He put his eyeglass up to his eye, that eyeglass I had on more than one occasion seen him use with devastating effect in court, and stared at the newcomers.

"Gosh, what a dirty customer," I said to myself.

He let the glass drop from his eye.

"How do you do," he said. "Am I mistaken in thinking that we've met before?"

The question turned my eyes to the Craigs. They stood side by side close to one another, as though they had drawn together for mutual protection. They did not speak. Mrs. Craig looked terrified. Craig's red face was darkened by a purple flush, and his eyes appeared almost to start out of his head. But that only lasted a second.

"I don't think so," he said in a rich, deep voice. "Of course I've heard of you, Sir Edward."

"More people know Tom Fool than Tom Fool knows," said he.

Miss Gray meanwhile had been giving the cocktail-shaker a shake, and now she handed cocktails to her two guests. She had noticed nothing. I didn't know what it all meant; in fact, I wasn't sure it meant anything. The incident, if incident there was, passed so quickly that I was half inclined to think that I had read into the strangers' momentary embarrassment on being introduced to a celebrated man something for which there was no foundation. I set about making myself pleasant. I asked them how they liked the Riviera and if they were comfortable in their house. Miss Gray joined in, and we chatted, as one does with strangers, of commonplace things. They talked easily and pleasantly. Mrs. Craig said how much they enjoyed the bathing and complained of the difficulty of getting fish at the seaside. I was aware that the judge did not join in the conversation, but looked down at his feet as though he were unconscious of the company.

Lunch was announced. We went into the dining-room. We were only five, and it was a small round table, so the conversation could not be anything but general. I must confess that it was carried on chiefly by Miss Gray and myself. The judge was silent, but he often was, for he was a moody creature, and I paid no attention. I noticed that he ate the omelette with good appetite, and when it was passed round again took a second helping. The Craigs struck me as a little shy, but that didn't surprise me, and as the second course was produced they began to talk more freely. It didn't strike me that they were very amusing people; they didn't seem interested in very much besides their baby, the vagaries of the two Italian maids they had, and an occasional flutter at Monte Carlo; and I couldn't help thinking that Miss Gray had erred in making their acquaintance. Then suddenly something happened: Craig rose abruptly from his chair and fell headlong to the floor. We jumped up. Mrs. Craig threw herself down, over her husband, and took his head in her hands.

"It's all right, George," she cried in an agonized tone. "It's all right!"

"Put his head down," I said. "He's only fainted."

I felt his pulse and could feel nothing. I said he had fainted, but I wasn't sure it wasn't a stroke. He was the sort of heavy, plethoric man who might easily have one. Miss Gray dipped her napkin into water and dabbed his forehead. Mrs. Craig seemed distraught. Then I noticed that Landon had remained quietly sitting in his chair.

"If he's fainted, you're not helping him to recover by crowding round him," he said acidly.

Mrs. Craig turned her head and gave him a look of bitter hatred.

"I'll ring up the doctor," said Miss Gray.

"No, I don't think that's necessary," I said. "He's coming to."

I could feel his pulse growing stronger, and in a minute or two he opened his eyes. He gasped when he realized what had happened, and tried to struggle to his feet.

"Don't move," I said. "Lie still a little longer."

I got him to drink a glass of brandy, and the colour came back to his face.

"I feel all right now," he said.

"We'll get you into the next room, and you can lie on the sofa for a bit."

"No, I'd sooner go home. It's only a step."

He got up from the floor.

"Yes, let's go back," said Mrs. Craig. She turned to Miss Gray. "I'm so sorry; he's never done anything like this before."

They were determined to go, and I thought myself it was the best thing for them to do.

"Put him to bed and keep him there, and he'll be as right as rain tomorrow."

Mrs. Craig took one of his arms and I took the other; Miss Gray opened the door, and though still a bit shaky, he was able to walk. When we arrived at the Craigs' home, I offered to go in and help undress him; but they would neither of them hear of it. I went back to Miss Gray's and found them at dessert.

"I wonder why he fainted," Miss Gray was saying. "All the windows are open, and it's not particularly hot today."

"I wonder," said the judge.

I noticed that his thin pale face bore an expression of some complacency. We had our coffee; and then, since the judge and I were going to play golf, we got into the car and drove up the hill to my house.

"How did Miss Gray get to know those people?" Landon asked me. "They struck me as rather second-rate. I shouldn't have thought they were very much her mark."

"You know women. She likes her privacy, and when they settled in next door, she was quite decided that she wouldn't have anything to do with them; but when she discovered that they didn't want to have anything to do with her, she couldn't rest till she'd made their acquaintance."

I told him the story she had invented about her neighbours. He listened with an expressionless face.

"I'm afraid your friend Miss Gray is a sentimental donkey, my dear fellow," he said when I had come to an end. "I tell you, women ought to marry. She'd soon have had all that nonsense knocked out of her if she'd had half a dozen brats."

"What do you know about the Craigs?" I asked.

He gave me a frigid glance.

"I? Why should I know anything about them? I thought they were very ordinary people."

I wish I knew how to describe the strong impression he gave me, both by the glacial austerity of his look and by the rasping finality of his tone, that he was not prepared to say anything more. We finished the drive in silence.

Landon was well on in his sixties, and he was the kind of golfer who never hits a long ball but is never off the straight, and he was a deadly putter, so, though he gave me strokes, he beat me handsomely. After dinner I took him in to Monte Carlo, where he finished the evening by winning a couple of thousand francs at the roulette table. These successive events put him into a remarkably good humour.

"A very pleasant day," he said when we parted for the night. "I've thoroughly enjoyed it."

I spent the next morning at work, and we did not meet till lunch. We were just finishing when I was called to the telephone.

When I came back my guest was drinking a second cup of coffee.

"That was Miss Gray," I said.

"Oh? What had she to say?"

"The Craigs have done a bolt. They disappeared last night. The maids live in the village; and when they came this morning, they found the house empty. They'd skipped—the Craigs, the nurse and the baby—and taken their luggage with them. They left money on the table for the maids' wages, the rent to the end of their tenancy and the tradesmen's bills."

The judge said nothing. He took a cigar from the box, examined it carefully and then lit it with deliberation.

"What have you got to say about that?" I asked.

"My dear fellow, are you obliged to use these American phrases? Isn't English good enough for you?"

"Is that an American phrase? It expresses exactly what I mean. You can't imagine I'm such a fool as not to have noticed that you and the Craigs had met before; and if they've vanished into thin air like figments of the imagination, it's a fairly reasonable conclusion that the circumstances under which you met were not altogether pleasant."

The judge gave a little chuckle, and there was a twinkle in his cold blue eyes.

"That was a very good brandy you gave me last night," he said. "It's against my principles to drink liqueurs after lunch, but it's a very dull man who allows his principles to enslave him, and for once I think I should enjoy one."

I sent for the brandy and watched the judge while he poured himself out a generous measure. He took a sip with obvious satisfaction.

"Do you remember the Wingford murder?" he asked me.

"No."

"Perhaps you weren't in England at the time. Pity—you might have come to the trial. You'd have enjoyed it. It caused a lot of excitement; the papers were full of it.

"Miss Wingford was a rich spinster of mature age who lived in the country with a companion. She was a healthy woman for her age;

and when she died rather suddenly her friends were surprised. Her physician, a fellow called Brandon, signed the certificate and she was duly buried. The will was read, and it appeared that she had left everything she had, something between sixty and seventy thousand pounds, to her companion. The relations were very sore, but there was nothing they could do about it. The will had been drawn up by her lawyer and witnessed by his clerk and Dr. Brandon.

"But Miss Wingford had a maid who had been with her for thirty years and had always understood that she would be remembered in the will; she claimed that Miss Wingford had promised to leave her well provided for, and when she found that she wasn't even mentioned, she flew into a passion. She told the nephew and the two nieces who had come down for the funeral that she was sure Miss Wingford had been poisoned, and she said that if they didn't go to the police, she'd go herself. Well, they didn't do that, but they went to see Dr. Brandon. He laughed. He said that Miss Wingford had had a weak heart and he'd been treating her for years. She died just as he had always expected her to die, peacefully in her sleep; and he advised them not to pay any attention to what the maid said. She had always hated the companion, a Miss Starling, and been jealous of her. Dr. Brandon was highly respected; he had been Miss Wingford's doctor for a long time, and the two nieces, who'd stayed with her often, knew him well. He was not profiting by the will, and there seemed no reason to doubt his word, so the family thought there was nothing to do but make the best of a bad job and went back to London.

"But the maid went on talking; she talked so much that at last the police, much against their will, I must admit, were obliged to take notice, and an order to exhume the body was made. There was an inquest, and it was found that Miss Wingford had died from an overdose of veronal. The coroner's jury found that it had been administered by Miss Starling, and she was arrested. A detective was sent down from Scotland Yard, and he got together some unexpected evidence. It appeared that there'd been a good deal of gossip about Miss Starling and Dr. Brandon. They'd been seen a lot together in places in which there was no reason for them to be except that they wanted to be together, and the general impression in the village was that they were only waiting for Miss Wingford to die to get married. That put a very different complexion on the case. To make a long story short, the police got enough evidence in their opinion to justify them in arresting the doctor and charging him and Miss Starling with the murder of the old lady."

The judge took another sip of brandy.

"The case came up for trial before me. The case for the prosecution was that the accused were madly in love with one another and had done the poor old lady to death so that they could marry on the fortune Miss Starling had wheedled her employer into leaving her. Miss Wingford always had a cup of cocoa when she went to bed, which Miss Starling prepared for her; and the counsel for the prosecution claimed that it was in this that Miss Starling had dissolved the tablets that caused Miss Wingford's death. The accused elected to give evidence on their own behalf, and made a miserable showing in the witness-box. They lied their heads off. Though witnesses testified they had seen them walking together at night with their arms round one another's waists, though Brandon's maid testified she had seen them kissing one another in the doctor's house, they swore they were no more than friends. And oddly enough, medical evidence proved that Miss Starling was *virgo intacta*.

"Brandon admitted that he had given Miss Wingford a bottle of veronal tablets because she complained of sleeplessness, but declared he had warned her never to take more than one, and then only when absolutely necessary. The defence sought to prove that she had taken the tablets either by accident or because she wanted to commit suicide. That didn't hold water for a moment. Miss Wingford was a jolly, normal old lady who thoroughly enjoyed life; and her death occurred two days before the expected arrival of an old friend for a week's visit. She hadn't complained to the maid of sleeping badly—in fact, her maid had always thought her a very good sleeper. It was impossible to believe that she had accidentally taken a sufficient number of tablets to kill herself. Personally, I had no doubt that it was a put-up job between the doctor and the companion. The motive was obvious and sufficient. I summed up and I hope summed up fairly; but it was my duty to put the facts before the jury, and to my mind the facts were damning. The jury filed out. I don't suppose you know that when you are sitting on the bench, you somehow get the feeling of the court. You have to be on your guard against it, to be sure it doesn't influence you. I never had it more strongly than on that day that there wasn't a soul in court who wasn't convinced that those two people had committed the crime with which they were charged. I hadn't the shadow of a doubt that the jury would bring in a verdict of guilty. Juries are incalculable. They were out for three hours, and when they came back I knew at once that I was mistaken. In a murder case, when the jury is going to bring in a verdict of guilty they won't look at the prisoner; they look away. I noticed that three or four of the jurymen glanced at the two prisoners in the dock. They brought in a verdict of not guilty. The real names of Mr. and Mrs. Craig are Dr. and Mrs. Brandon. I'm just as certain as I am that I'm sitting here that they committed between them a cruel and heartless murder and richly deserved to be hanged."

"What do you think made the jury find them not guilty?"

"I've asked myself that; and do you know the only explanation I can give? The fact that it was conclusively proved that they had never been lovers. And if you come to think of it, that's one of the most curious features of the whole case. That woman was prepared to commit murder to get the man she loved, but she wasn't prepared to have an illicit love-affair with him."

"Human nature is very odd, isn't it?"

"Very," said Landon, helping himself to another glass of brandy.

Frank O'Connor

LEGAL AID

★

Delia Carty came of a very respectable family. It was going as maid to the O'Gradys of Pouladuff that ruined her. That whole family was slightly touched. The old man, a national teacher, was hardly ever at home, and the daughters weren't much better. When they weren't away visiting, they had people visiting them, and it was nothing to Delia to come in late at night and find one of them plastered round some young fellow on the sofa.

That sort of thing isn't good for any young girl. Like mistress like maid; inside six months she was smoking, and within a year she was carrying on with one Tom Flynn, a farmer's son. Her father, a respectable, hard-working man, knew nothing about it, for he would have realized that she was no match for one of the Flynns, and even if Tom's father, Ned, had known he would never have thought it possible that any labourer's daughter could imagine herself a match for Tom.

Not, God knows, that Tom was any great catch. He was a big uncouth galoot who was certain that lovemaking, like drink, was one of the simple pleasures his father tried to deprive him of, out of spite. He used to call at the house while the O'Gradys were away, and there would be Delia in one of Eileen O'Grady's frocks and with Eileen O'Grady's lipstick and powder on, doing the lady over the tea things in the parlour. Throwing a glance over his shoulder in case anyone might spot him, Tom would heave himself onto the sofa with his boots over the end.

"Begod, I love sofas," he would say with simple pleasure.

"Put a cushion behind you," Delia would say.

"Oh, begod," Tom would say, making himself comfortable, "if ever I have a house of my own 'tis unknown what sofas and cushions I'll have. Them teachers must get great money. What the hell do they go away at all for?"

Delia loved making the tea and handing it out like a real lady, but you couldn't catch Tom out like that.

"Ah, what do I want tay for?" he would say with a doubtful glance at the cup. "Haven't you any whisky? Ould O'Grady must have gallons of it. . . . Leave it there on the table. Why the hell don't they have proper mugs with handles a man could get a grip on? Is that taypot silver? Pity I'm not a teacher!"

It was only natural for Delia to show him the bedrooms and the dressing-tables with the three mirrors, the way you could see yourself from all sides, but Tom, his hands under his head, threw himself with incredulous delight on the low double bed and cried: "Springs! Begod, 'tis like a car!"

What the springs gave rise to was entirely the O'Gradys' fault since no one but themselves would have left a house in a lonesome part to a girl of nineteen to mind. The only surprising thing was that it lasted two years without Delia showing any signs of it. It probably took Tom that time to find the right way.

But when he did he got into a terrible state. It was hardly in him to believe that a harmless poor devil like himself whom no one ever bothered his head about could achieve such unprecedented results on one girl, but when he understood it he knew only too well what the result of it would be. His father would first beat hell out of him and then throw him out and leave the farm to his nephews. There being no hope of conciliating his father, Tom turned his attention to God, who, though supposed to share Ned Flynn's views about fellows and girls, had some nature in Him. Tom stopped seeing Delia, to persuade God that he was reforming and to show that anyway it wasn't his fault. Left alone he could be a decent, good-living young fellow, but the Carty girl was a forward, deceitful hussy who had led him on instead of putting him off the way any well-bred girl would do. Between lipsticks, sofas, and tay in the parlour, Tom put it up to God that it was a great wonder she hadn't got him into worse trouble.

Delia had to tell her mother, and Mrs. Carty went to Father Corcoran to see could he induce Tom to marry her. Father Corcoran was a tall, testy old man who, even at the age of sixty-five, couldn't make out for the life of him what young fellows saw in girls, but if he didn't know much about lovers he knew a lot about farmers.

"Wisha, Mrs. Carty," he said crankily, "how could I get him to marry her? Wouldn't you have a bit of sense? Some little financial arrangement, maybe, so that she could leave the parish and not be a cause of scandal—I might be able to do that."

He interviewed Ned Flynn, who by this time had got Tom's version of the story and knew financial arrangements were going to be the order of the day unless he could put a stop to them. Ned was a man of over six foot with a bald brow and a smooth unlined face as though he never had a care except his general concern for the welfare of humanity which made him look so abnormally thoughtful. Even Tom's conduct hadn't brought a wrinkle to his brow.

"I don't know, father," he said, stroking his bald brow with a die-away air, "I don't know what you could do at all."

"Wisha, Mr. Flynn," said the priest who, when it came to the pinch, had more nature than twenty Flynns, "wouldn't you do the handsome thing and let him marry her before it goes any farther?"

"I don't see how much farther it could go, father," said Ned.

"It could become a scandal."

"I'm afraid 'tis that already, father."

"And after all," said Father Corcoran, forcing himself to put in a good word for one of the unfortunate sex whose very existence was a mystery to him, "is she any worse than the rest of the girls that are going? Bad is the best of them, from what I see, and Delia is a great deal better than most."

"That's not my information at all, father," said Ned, looking like "The Heart Bowed Down".

"That's a very serious statement, Mr. Flynn," said Father Corcoran, giving him a challenging look.

"It can be proved, father," said Ned gloomily. "Of course I'm not denying the boy was foolish but the cleverest can be caught."

"You astonish me, Mr. Flynn," said Father Corcoran, who was

beginning to realize that he wasn't even going to get a subscription. "Of course I can't contradict you, but 'twill cause a terrible scandal."

"I'm as sorry for that as you are, father," said Ned, "but I have my son's future to think of."

Then, of course, the fun began. Foolish to the last, the O'Gradys wanted to keep Delia on till it was pointed out to them that Mr. O'Grady would be bound to get the blame. After this, her father had to be told. Dick Carty knew exactly what became a devoted father, and he beat Delia till he had to be hauled off her by the neighbours. He was a man who loved to sit in his garden reading his paper; now he felt he owed it to himself not to be seen enjoying himself, so instead he sat over the fire and brooded. The more he brooded the angrier he became. But seeing that, with the best will in the world, he could not beat Delia every time he got angry, he turned his attention to the Flynns. Ned Flynn, that contemptible bosthoon, had slighted one of the Cartys in a parish where they had lived for hundreds of years with unblemished reputations; the Flynns, as everyone knew, being mere upstarts and outsiders without a date on their gravestones before 1850—nobodies!

He brought Delia to see Jackie Canty, the solicitor in town. Jackie was a little jenny-ass of a man with thin lips, a pointed nose, and a pince-nez that wouldn't stop in place, and he listened with grave enjoyment to the story of Delia's misconduct. "And what happened then, please?" he asked in his shrill singsong, looking at the floor and trying hard not to burst out into a giggle of delight. "The devils!" he thought. "The devils!" It was as close as Jackie was ever likely to get to the facts of life, an opportunity not to be missed.

"Anything in writing?" he sang, looking at her over the pince-nez. "Any letters? Any documents?"

"Only a couple of notes I burned," said Delia, who thought him a very queer man, and no wonder.

"Pity!" Jackie said with an admiring smile. "A smart man! Oh, a very smart man!"

"Ah, 'tisn't that at all," said Delia uncomfortably, "only he had no occasion for writing."

"Ah, Miss Carty," cried Jackie in great indignation, looking at her challengingly through the specs while his voice took on a steely ring, "a gentleman in love always finds plenty of occasion for writing. He's a smart man; your father might succeed in an action for seduction, but if 'tis defended 'twill be a dirty case."

"Mr. Canty," said her father solemnly, "I don't mind how dirty it is so long as I get justice." He stood up, a powerful man of six feet, and held up his clenched first. "Justice is what I want," he said dramatically. "That's the sort I am. I keep myself to myself and mind my own business, but give me a cut, and I'll fight in a bag, tied up."

"Don't forget that Ned Flynn has the money, Dick," wailed Jackie.

"Mr. Canty," said Dick with a dignity verging on pathos, "you know me?"

"I do, Dick, I do."

"I'm living in this neighbourhood, man and boy, fifty years, and I owe nobody a ha'penny. If it took me ten years, breaking stones by the road, I'd pay it back, every penny."

"I know, Dick, I know," moaned Jackie. "But there's other things as well. There's your daughter's reputation. Do you know what they'll do? They'll go into court and swear someone else was the father."

"Tom could never say that," Delia cried despairingly. "The tongue would rot in his mouth."

Jackie had no patience at all with this chit of a girl, telling him his business. He sat back with a weary air, his arm over the back of his chair.

"That statement has no foundation," he said icily. "There is no record of any such thing happening a witness. If there was, the inhabitants of Ireland would have considerably less to say for themselves. You would be surprised the things respectable people will say in the witness box. Rot in their mouths indeed! Ah, dear me, no. With documents, of course, it would be different, but it is only our word against theirs. Can it be proved that you weren't knocking round with any other man at this time, Miss Carty?"

"Indeed, I was doing nothing of the sort," Delia said indignantly.

"I swear to God I wasn't, Mr. Canty. I hardly spoke to a fellow the whole time, only when Tom and myself might have a row and I'd go out with Timmy Martin."

"Timmy Martin!" Canty cried dramatically, pointing an accusing finger at her. "There is their man!"

"But Tom did the same with Betty Daly," cried Delia on the point of tears, "and he only did it to spite me. I swear there was nothing else in it, Mr. Canty, nor he never accused me of it."

"Mark my words," chanted Jackie with a mournful smile, "he'll make up for lost time now."

In this he showed considerably more foresight than Delia gave him credit for. After the baby was born and the action begun, Tom and his father went to town to see their solicitor, Peter Humphreys. Peter, who knew all he wanted to know about the facts of life, liked the case much less than Jackie. A cross-eyed, full-blooded man who had made his money when law was about land, not love, he thought it a terrible comedown. Besides, he didn't think it nice to be listening to such things.

"And so, according to you, Timmy Martin is the father?" he asked Tom.

"Oh, I'm not swearing he is," said Tom earnestly, giving himself a heave in his chair and crossing his legs. "How the hell could I? All I am saying is that I wasn't the only one, and what's more she boasted about it. Boasted about it, begod!" he added with a look of astonishment at such female depravity.

"Before witnesses?" asked Peter, his eyes doing a double cross with hopelessness.

"As to that," replied Tom with great solemnity, looking over his shoulder for an open window he could spit through, "I couldn't swear."

"But you understood her to mean Timmy Martin?"

"I'm not accusing Timmy Martin at all," said Tom in great alarm, seeing how the processes of law were tending to involve him in a row with the Martins, who were a turbulent family with ways of getting their own back unknown to any law. "Timmy Martin is one man she used to be round with. It might be Timmy Martin or it might be someone else, or what's more," he added with the look of a man who has had a sudden revelation, "it might be more than one." He looked from Peter to his father and back again to see what effect the revelation was having, but like other revelations it didn't seem to be going down too well. "Begod," he said, giving himself another heave, "it might be any God's number. . . . But, as to that," he added cautiously, "I wouldn't like to swear."

"Nor indeed, Tom," said his solicitor with a great effort at politeness, "no one would advise you. You'll want a good counsel."

"Begod, I suppose I will," said Tom with astonished resignation before the idea that there might be people in the world bad enough to doubt his word.

There was great excitement in the village when it became known that the Flynns were having the Roarer Cooper as counsel. Even as a first-class variety turn Cooper could always command attention, and everyone knew that the rights and wrongs of the case would be relegated to their proper position while the little matter of Eileen O'Grady's best frock received the attention it deserved.

On the day of the hearing the court was crowded. Tom and his father were sitting at the back with Peter Humphreys, waiting for Cooper, while Delia and her father were talking to Jackie Canty and their own counsel, Ivers. He was a well-built young man with a high brow, black hair and half-closed, red-tinged sleepy eyes. He talked in a bland drawl.

"You're not worrying, are you?" he asked Delia kindly. "Don't be a bit afraid. . . . I suppose there's no chance of them settling, Jackie?"

"Musha, what chance would there be?" Canty asked scoldingly. "Don't you know yourself what sort they are?"

"I'll have a word with Cooper myself," said Ivers. "Dan isn't as bad as he looks." He went to talk to a coarse-looking man in wig and gown who had just come in. To say he wasn't as bad as he looked was no great compliment. He had a face that was almost a square, with a big jaw and blue eyes in wicked little slits that made deep dents across his cheekbones.

"What about settling this case of ours, Dan?" Ivers asked gently.

Cooper didn't even return his look; apparently he was not responsive to charm.

"Did you ever know me to settle when I could fight?" he growled.

"Not when you could fight your match," Ivers said, without taking offence. "You don't consider that poor girl your match?"

"We'll soon see what sort of girl she is," replied Cooper complacently as his eyes fell on the Flynns. "Tell me," he whispered, "what did she see in my client?"

"What you saw yourself when you were her age, I suppose," said Ivers. "You don't mean there wasn't a girl in a tobacconist's shop that you thought came down from heaven with the purpose of consoling you?"

"She had nothing in writing," Cooper replied gravely. "And, unlike your client, I never saw double."

"You don't believe that yarn, do you?"

"That's one of the things I'm going to inquire into."

"I can save you the trouble. She was too fond of him."

"Hah!" snorted Cooper as though this were a good joke. "And I suppose that's why she wants the cash."

"That girl doesn't care if she never got a penny. Don't you know yourself what's behind it? A respectable father. Two respectable fathers! The trouble about marriage in this country, Dan Cooper, is that the fathers always insist on doing the coorting."

"Hah!" grunted Cooper, rather more uncertain of himself. "Show me this paragon of the female sex, Ivers."

"There in the brown hat beside Canty," said Ivers without looking round. "Come on, you old devil, and stop trying to pretend you're Buffalo Bill. It's enough going through what she had to go through. I don't want her to go through any more."

"And why in God's name do you come to me?" Cooper asked in sudden indignation. "What the hell do you take me for? A Society for Protecting Fallen Women? Why didn't the priest make him marry her?"

"When the Catholic Church can make a farmer marry a labourer's daughter the Kingdom of God will be at hand," said Ivers. "I'm surprised at you, Dan Cooper, not knowing better at your age."

"And what are the neighbours doing here if she has nothing to hide?"

"Who said she had nothing to hide?" Ivers asked lightly, throwing in his hand. "Haven't you daughters of your own? You know she played the fine lady in the O'Gradys' frocks. If 'tis any information to you she wore their jewellery as well."

"Ivers, you're a young man of great plausibility," said Cooper, "but you can spare your charm on me. I have my client's interests to consider. Did she sleep with the other fellow?"

"She did not."

"Do you believe that?"

"As I believe in my own mother."

"The faith that moves mountains," Cooper said despondently. "How much are ye asking?"

"Two hundred and fifty," replied Ivers, shaky for the first time.

"Merciful God Almighty!" moaned Cooper, turning his eyes to the ceiling. "As if any responsible Irish court would put that price on a girl's virtue. Still, it might be as well. I'll see what I can do."

He moved ponderously across the court and with two big arms outstretched like wings shepherded out the Flynns.

"Two hundred and fifty pounds?" gasped Ned, going white. "Where in God's name would I get that money?"

"My dear Mr. Flynn," Cooper said with coarse amiability, "that's only half the yearly allowance his Lordship makes the young lady that obliges him, and she's not a patch on that girl in court. After a lifetime of experience I can assure you that for two years' fornication with a fine girl like that you won't pay a penny less than five hundred."

Peter Humphreys' eyes almost grew straight with the shock of such reckless slander on a blameless judge. He didn't know what had come over the Roarer. But that wasn't the worst. When the settlement was announced and the Flynns were leaving he went up to them again.

"You can believe me when I say you did the right thing, Mr. Flynn," he said. "I never like cases involving good-looking girls. Gentlemen of his Lordship's age are terribly susceptible. But tell me, why wouldn't your son marry her now as he's about it?"

"Marry her?" echoed Ned, who hadn't yet got over the shock of having to pay two hundred and fifty pounds and costs for a little matter he could have compounded for with Father Corcoran for fifty. "A thing like that!"

"With two hundred and fifty pounds, man?" snarled Cooper. "'Tisn't every day you'll pick up a daughter-in-law with that. . . . What do you say to the girl yourself?" he asked Tom.

"Oh, begod, the girl is all right," said Tom.

Tom looked different. It was partly relief that he wouldn't have to perjure himself, partly astonishment at seeing his father so swiftly overthrown. His face said: "The world is wide."

"Ah, Mr. Flynn, Mr. Flynn," whispered Cooper scornfully, "sure you're not such a fool as to let all that good money out of the family?"

Leaving Ned gasping, he went on to where Dick Carty, aglow with pride and malice, was receiving congratulations. There were no congratulations for Delia who was standing near him. She felt a big paw on her arm and looked up to see the Roarer.

"Are you still fond of that boy?" he whispered.

"I have reason to be, haven't I?" she retorted bitterly.

"You have," he replied with no great sympathy. "The best. I got you that money so that you could marry him if you wanted to. Do you want to?"

Her eyes filled with tears as she thought of the poor broken china of an idol that was being offered her now.

"Once a fool, always a fool," she said sullenly.

"You're no fool at all, girl," he said, giving her arm an encouraging squeeze. "You might make a man of him yet. I don't know what the law in this country is coming to. Get him away to hell out of this till I find Michael Ivers and get him to talk to your father."

The two lawyers made the match themselves at Johnny Desmond's pub, and Johnny said it was like nothing in the world so much as a mission, with the Roarer roaring and threatening hellfire on all concerned, and Michael Ivers piping away about the joys of heaven. Johnny said it was the most instructive evening he ever had. Ivers was always recognized as a weak man so the marriage did him no great harm, but of course it was a terrible comedown for a true Roarer, and Cooper's reputation has never been the same since then.

Henry Cecil

PAINSWICK v. GLOSTER

★

Martin Painswick wrote a letter to America and, after he had had a reply, he walked into the offices of one of the best-known firms of solicitors in the City, Messrs. Broadacre, Barley and Merryweather.

"I would like to see one of the partners," he told a clerk in the outer office. "My name is Martin Painswick. I am a son of Mr. Justice Painswick and I want to consult your firm about an action I wish to bring."

Normally a firm of this standing would only deal with a new client upon a suitable introduction. However, the son of a High Court judge is a different matter. At that time nothing was known publicly against him, and accordingly he was soon shown into the office of Mr. Merryweather. They shook hands.

"I understand you are a son of Mr. Justice Painswick."

"That's right," said Martin. "I expect you know my father."

"Not personally, but our firm have often had cases tried before him."

"I hope you were satisfied."

"If I may respectfully say so, your father is a very great judge."

"Thank you very much. I've always heard so."

"Now what is it we can do for you? I understand you want to bring an action against someone."

"That's right," said Martin. "I'll tell you about it."

He then proceeded to explain to Mr. Merryweather the nature of the action he wanted to bring. The more he said, the less Mr. Merryweather liked it, but a High Court judge is a very important person from any solicitor's point of view, however reputable and distinguished the solicitor, and Mr. Merryweather decided to go on listening. However, after about half an hour he came to a definite decision in the matter.

"I'm afraid," he said, "that this really isn't the sort of case we do."

"Oh dear," said Martin, "I thought you did a lot of litigation."

"That's quite true, but your case isn't quite in our line."

Mr. Merryweather thought for a moment.

"I tell you what I can do, though. There's an extremely able young man I know who's in practice on his own. I can thoroughly recommend him, and, if you like, I'll telephone and ask if he can see you."

"That will be very kind," said Martin, "though, of course, I should have preferred to have your firm."

Mr. Merryweather thereupon telephoned to Mr. Gordon Huntley, and arranged an appointment for Martin for the same day. As soon as Martin had gone, however, he telephoned Mr. Huntley again.

"Look here," he said, "I don't want to say too much, and I may be quite wrong, but I don't care for this thing very much. Don't take it on if you don't want it, but look out if you do."

Mr. Huntley thanked Mr. Merryweather and said he would suspend judgment until he had seen Martin.

The interview with Mr. Huntley did not last very long. He was a young and able solicitor and an extremely scrupulous one. He wanted new clients and, on the face of it, the son of a High Court judge would be an admirable client; but, even if he had not been warned by Mr. Merryweather, he would have refused to take on the case. He did not wish to turn Martin away without doing something for him, however, and he in turn telephoned to Messrs. Braggs, Golightly and Sharpe. That firm did not, in fact, contain a Braggs, a Golightly or a Sharpe; and although its notepaper stated that it incorporated Hugg, Neadham and Charlesmith, its sole proprietor was a Mr. Harold Spratt. Mr. Huntley knew Mr. Spratt to be a moderately able and industrious solicitor, anxious to get as much business as possible, and fairly considered in the profession to be sharp. That was not to say that he did anything that was likely to be discovered as dishonest or unprofessional. He was too clever for that. Those who were against him, however, had to look out for themselves, or they were likely to be outsmarted. He was not too particular what kind of work he took on, provided he was sure of his money. That was indispensable, but, given that, there was hardly a case he would refuse. If it looked a little disreputable on arriving at his office, he dressed it up nicely before it went into Court, washed its hands, combed its hair, and, if necessary, gave it an almost entirely new suit. Mr. Huntley rightly thought that Mr. Martin Painswick and Mr. Spratt were admirably suited to each other as client and solicitor. And client and solicitor they duly became.

"Come in, Mr. Painswick," said Mr. Spratt at their first interview. "I hope I shall be able to be of service to you. I know your father well, only as a judge, of course. A fine judge, should go to the Court of Appeal. You're not in the law, I gather?"

"No. I did start to read for the Bar, but I gave it up and became an accountant."

"Well, now what's the trouble?"

"I've got a claim against Frank Gloster, the M.P., you know."

"What for?"

"Commission on a deal. Introduced him to someone who introduced him to someone who introduced him to someone at the Ministry of Supply. Surplus goods, you know. Going very cheap. He made the hell of a profit, and now he won't pay."

"What was the agreement?"

"Well, he said he'd see me all right if it went through."

"How d'you know it did go through?"

"Well, I happened to meet a chap who bought some of the goods from Gloster's people."

"Gloster didn't buy them himself then?"

"Oh, no, it was one of his companies."

"D'you know the name?"

"He's got about half a dozen. We can easily find out which it was."

"Does he own all the shares in these companies?"

"A majority, but not in his own name of course. He has nominees all over the place."

"It looks as though you may have some difficulty in proving your case."

"I don't think so, but he won't fight it when he sees we mean business."

"That's what everyone says."

"Maybe, but he can't fight this case."

"Why not?"

"He's a Member of Parliament, and supposed to be respectable."

"Well, what of it?"

"I happen to know something about Mr. Gloster which the public doesn't—yet."

"Oh?"

"He once served a sentence of a year's imprisonment for fraud in the U.S.A."

"How d'you know?"

"I've checked up on it. Look at this." Martin handed Mr. Spratt the letter he had received from America.

"Yes, that looks all right. Quite useful. Of course, it doesn't prove our claim, but it's quite a useful little weapon. What rate of commission d'you claim?"

"Twenty per cent."

"What on—the profit?"

"Yes."

"How much was it?"

"No idea, but it must have run into five or six figures, at least."

"Well, let me have the details, and we'll write to Mr. Gloster and see what he says."

A few days later Mr. Gloster received the following letter:

Braggs, Golightly and Sharpe,
Solicitors
(incorporating Hugg, Neadham and Charlesmith)

12 *Bunthorne Street,*
Strand, W.C.2

Harold Spratt, LL.B.

1st *July,* 19—

Dear Sir,

We have been consulted by our client, Mr. Martin Painswick, in regard to a claim for commission against you, which our client informs us you are refusing to meet. Our client instructs us that on an occasion last year you asked him if he knew where you could obtain a large quantity of parachute silk and, on the terms that you would pay our client a reasonable commission on the deal, our client introduced you to a Mr. Scroope. As a result of that introduction you made a very large purchase of parachute silk from the Ministry of Supply and our client requires payment of his commission on the profit you have made. Our client says that 25 per cent is the proper commission but he is prepared to accept 20 per cent if his claim is now met without delay. We shall be glad to hear that you are prepared to let us know the total profit made by you and to accord to our client his share, or alternatively we desire to have the name and address of solicitors who will accept service of a writ on your behalf. We should add that the reason for the delay in putting forward our client's claim is that he has been extremely busy with other matters, some of them involving correspondence with the U.S.A.

Yours faithfully,

BRAGGS, GOLIGHTLY AND SHARPE.

A few days later they received a reply from Mr. Gloster's solicitors.

Our client is amazed at the effrontery of your client's claim. Our client has only once met your client when a discussion took place about a possible sale to your client, by a company in which our client was interested, of some ladies' underwear. The business fell through as your client could not provide satisfactory references or pay cash. It is quite true that Mr. Scroope did effect an introduction which resulted in the purchase to which you presumably refer. It is also true that our client made a substantial profit on the transaction. It is, however, quite untrue, as your client well knows, that your client ever introduced Mr. Scroope to our client. Unfortunately (as your client presumably knows) Mr. Scroope is dead, but our client is not going to let this fact deter him from contesting a bogus claim. In this connection we should like to know the meaning of the last sentence in your letter.

Almost by return of post Mr. Gloster's solicitors received a reply from Messrs. Braggs, Golightly and Sharpe. It ran:

It does not surprise us, in view of information which we have about your client, that your client should repudiate his obligations and instruct you to write a libellous letter to us. It does, however, surprise us that a firm of solicitors of your standing, or, indeed, any firm of solicitors, should make such allegations without first enquiring into the facts. The expression 'bogus claim' is gravely defamatory of our client and unless we have an immediate withdrawal and apology from you and an offer to compensate our client in damages (a moderate sum will suffice at the present time) proceedings for libel will be taken against your firm personally. Our regret at having to take action against brother solicitors is modified by our feeling that people who write letters of that kind should be taught a lesson. We should add for your assistance that on the occasion when our client introduced your client to the late Mr. Scroope (our client regrets very much to learn of his death as he would certainly have confirmed our client's statement) a witness was present who is still alive and well. You do not state that you will accept service on behalf of your client and accordingly we have arranged for the writ to be served on him personally.

A writ for libel will be issued against your firm personally in default of the conditions referred to above being complied with in seven days.

With regard to the last sentence in your letter, the last sentence in our previous letter meant exactly what it said, i.e.: (1) our client had been busy, and (2) he had been corresponding with the U.S.A.

The reply from Mr. Gloster's solicitors came within a very few days:

We have not the slightest intention of apologising to your client, and we shall be obliged if you will refrain from referring to us as 'brother solicitors'. Your letter under reply imputes that we have been guilty of unprofessional conduct and, unless we receive an unqualified withdrawal and apology (we do not at the moment require damages), we shall take proceedings against your firm personally for libel. May we add that we shall have no regret whatever in taking such proceedings, which may perhaps lead you to be more careful in the future, in criticising the conduct of the solicitors on the other side just because their instructions do not coincide with yours. Our statement that your client was making a bogus claim was made by us in good faith and without malice towards your client (of whom we had never heard before) upon our client's instructions, and upon those instructions we repeat it. Our client would be very interested to know the name of the witness to an interview which did not take place. If we do not receive your apology within seven days a writ will be issued. Will you accept service yourselves?

With regard to the last sentence of your letter, we should like to know the relevance of your client's correspondence with the U.S.A. If irrelevant, as it appears to be, it has a menacing flavour.

The reply (which was delivered by hand) was as follows:

The bearer will serve you with the writ which we warned you would be served against your firm personally. As the matters in dispute between us are going to be litigated there seems little point in continuing this correspondence, but we must deal with certain points.

We have nothing to apologise for in any of our letters. We said we were surprised at your behaviour. We were, but we shall not be in the future. We will accept service of your threatened proceedings which we can only assume are a counterblast to our client's genuine claims against you and your client.

The last sentence in your letter is extremely libellous. The plain suggestion is that this is a blackmailing claim by our client. Further proceedings will be taken in respect of this libel unless an immediate apology with substantial compensation is offered. We daresay your client would like to know the name of the witness to the interview at which your client was introduced to Mr. Scroope by our client. May we respectfully suggest that you and your client should do your fishing elsewhere, though you are not likely to catch much if you bluster and make as much noise as you do in your letters.

The reply:

Having regard to your other conduct we are not surprised at your discourtesy in serving the writ upon us personally. Your letter under reply is a further libel upon us, and, in view of the previous libel and the tone of your letters, we do not propose to correspond further in the matter. The Court will be left to judge of your behaviour.

We do not propose to follow your discourteous example and accordingly we enclose two original and copy writs against your firm for acceptance of service. Please endorse the originals and return them.

We need only add that never in the course of our professional experience (and we have had to deal at times with some extremely unpleasant firms) have we been treated with such unwarranted and deliberate rudeness and discourtesy.

To which the answer (also sent by hand) was:

We accept service of the writs issued by you and enclose original writs duly endorsed. You never informed us that you would accept service on your own behalf nor do you even now. We have accordingly not been guilty of the least discourtesy towards you. On the contrary your failure to offer to accept service (which was obviously deliberate and implied that we do not really intend to take proceedings) was most discourteous to us. As you still do not offer to accept service the bearer will serve you with a further writ and your client will again be served personally, and we should add that the same course will be taken in regard to the service of any future proceedings which your conduct may render necessary unless and until you extend to us the normal courtesies of the profession and tell us that you will accept service in the normal way.

The matter then passed out of the realm of correspondence into that of litigation, but it must not be thought that there was not ample opportunity during the course of the litigation for the respective solicitors to fire letters at each other, always, of course, at the clients' expense. Ample opportunity there was, too, for the representatives of the two firms to meet and say rude things to and about each other, again at their clients' expense. The first step to be taken after a writ has been served is for the defendant (or, if he is represented, his solicitor on his behalf) to enter an appearance to the writ. This is a purely formal proceeding. You simply go to the offices at the Law

Courts or to a district registry (if the writ has been issued in the country) and fill in a form saying that an appearance has been entered and give notice of such appearance to the other side. There is, however, a limited time for taking this step—namely, eight days from the day on which the writ is served. If no appearance is entered within the required period, it is open for the plaintiff or his solicitor to take judgment in default of appearance. In that event, if his claim is for a specific sum of money he gets judgment for that amount; if it is for damages, he gets judgment for damages to be assessed. At any time, however, before he has taken judgment it is open to the defendant, however much out of time he may be, to enter an appearance. In the present case Mr. Gloster's solicitors, Messrs. Toothcombe and Witley, by an unfortunate oversight, miscounted the days. Messrs. Braggs, Golightly and Sharpe, wild with glee, rushed off to the Law Courts and signed judgment in default in respect of three writs, two of them for libel against Messrs. Toothcombe and Witley and their client (who as principal could be held responsible for his agents' letters), and one against Mr. Gloster for Martin's commission. As the clerk (a Mr. Bole) was coming out from taking judgment, he ran into the clerk from Toothcombe and Witley (a Mr. Drive), who was about to enter an appearance in all three actions. They knew each other by sight.

"Just signed judgment against you," said Bole.

"What are you talking about?" asked Drive. "Today's my last day."

"Have another think," said Bole.

It was a nasty shock for Mr. Drive, whose responsibility it had been to enter an appearance on the last day. He knew that Bole would not have been able to sign judgment in the normal way, unless he was right. He went suddenly white, Bole *was* right. He could imagine what Mr. Toothcombe would say to him.

"Look here, old boy," he said, as coaxingly as possible, "I must have miscounted. Let's go to the master and have it set aside by consent. I'll pay your costs. Much better than making a song and dance about it."

"I bet you think so," said Bole.

The position was this. If a plaintiff signs judgment in default of appearance, it is always open for the defendant to apply to the Court to have the judgment set aside and, provided he applies soon enough, can show that he has some sort of defence and will pay the costs thrown away, his application will be granted almost automatically. The application is made by a summons which is heard by a kind of minor judge called a master. By consent it would have been possible for both clerks to go to one of the masters there and then and have this done, but only by consent.

"Look here, old boy, you know it was only a slip. I'd do the same for you any day."

"You won't have to, old man. I can count."

"Oh, you never make mistakes, I suppose."

"Not this time, old boy. So long."

With a heavy heart Mr. Drive went to the department just to make certain that he hadn't been bluffed. But he didn't expect any luck, and he didn't have any. Judgment had been duly signed. He went back to his office to report to his principal—Mr. Toothcombe. Mr. Toothcombe danced up and down like a scalded cat. Letting Braggs and Co. have the laugh on him almost before the action had begun. The anger with which he had written the letters to that firm was nothing to the display he provided for the benefit of Mr. Drive. When he had finished he told Mr. Drive to issue a summons to have the judgment set aside.

On being served with the summons, Mr. Spratt decided to take a small risk—solely for the purpose of annoying Messrs. Toothcombe and Witley. It need hardly be added that the risk was entirely at the expense of Martin. He decided to brief counsel to oppose the application to set aside the judgment. He knew that the application would be granted, but it was in the master's discretion to allow the fee for counsel attending or not as he thought fit. If he allowed it and ordered the defendant to pay the costs, the amount he would have to pay would be very much higher, and whether or not Toothcombe and Witley paid it themselves (they were certainly liable to do so, as it was entirely their fault—but he knew what he would have done) they would be extremely annoyed. A summons attended by counsel will ordinarily cost altogether not less than about £10. So Mr. Spratt went down to the Temple to have a conference with Mr. Kendall

Grimes, a junior of long standing whom he briefed regularly. When he arrived for his appointment he found the clerk was out. "He'll be back in a minute," said the junior clerk—knowing quite well that it was most unlikely that he would be back in a minute, unless they didn't have a third round. His senior was making what he used to term 'a routine call'. It certainly was part of his normal routine. He was at the Feathers. The reason why Mr. Spratt so much wanted to see the clerk was to impress on him the necessity for Mr. Grimes attending the summons in person. One might have thought that, if Mr. Grimes accepted a brief to appear on a particular matter, he would be there. But it doesn't necessarily follow. He may be engaged somewhere else and send a deputy. That is the way to give experience to younger barristers and to annoy solicitors. It cannot always be avoided, and though it is good experience for the deputy, it is sometimes rather nerve-shattering for him, if he is young and has not been long in practice. For example:

"Go on," says a hoarse voice in his ear, that of the solicitor's managing clerk, "ask him if he's ever been bankrupt."

"But," whispers counsel, "are you sure——"

"Go on," says the voice, "ask him."

"Have you ever been bankrupt?"

"Certainly not! What a monstrous suggestion."

"Mr. Green," says the judge, "I suppose you asked that question on instructions?"

"Yes, your Honour," says counsel, rather unhappily.

"It is a very serious allegation to make. The matter can be proved beyond doubt, and I cannot believe that the witness would dare to deny it if it were true."

During this speech counsel is endeavouring to turn round and ask the managing clerk what to say.

"Mr. Green," goes on the judge, "I wish you would listen to me instead of trying to take instructions from what I suspect is a very ill-informed source."

"I'm sorry, your Honour."

"Now, do you accept the witness's denial or do you wish for an adjournment to enable you to put the date and place of the receiving order in bankruptcy to him?"

"I accept the denial, your Honour."

"You accept it very readily, Mr. Green. I cannot believe that counsel—on the propriety of whose questions I normally rely with complete confidence—I cannot believe that counsel would put such a question without there being some justification for it. You do definitely accept it, do you?"

"Well, your Honour, perhaps I had better ask for an adjournment."

"Well, which is it? First you ask a very grave question of the witness, then you say you accept his answer, then you say you want an adjournment; really, Mr. Green, there must be some limit to all this. If you don't know what you want, I don't see how I can."

"Will your Honour let me take instructions?"

"Well, Mr. Green, if you think they can be of any assistance to you or to me, by all means do so. But, if I were you, I should think a little before you act on them."

"Your Honour," says the now miserable Mr. Green, "I think I ought to explain that I'm only doing this case for Mr. Brown. I only saw the papers this morning."

"Is that a reason for asking improper questions?"

"No, your Honour."

"Then I do not see the point of the observation."

Mr. Green then turns round to the managing clerk and asks him whether to apply for an adjournment.

"You're doing this case, not me," says the managing clerk, "and a nice mess you're making of it. I don't care what you do. You can jump out of the window if you like."

Mr. Green starts to turn round to face the judge again, feeling very much like a small boy at school who is homesick. "And take the judge with you," adds the managing clerk as Mr. Green turns away from him.

"Well, Mr. Green, have you your instructions now? You know, I've other cases to try. It doesn't matter to me in the least how much time you waste, but I'm thinking of those concerned in the cases which come after you."

Mr. Green now devoutly wishes that he had never come to the Bar.

"Your Honour," he begins shakily, having very little idea of what he is going to say. He pauses so long that the judge says:

"Yes, Mr. Green?" in an unpleasantly encouraging tone.

"Your Honour," begins Mr. Green again.

"Yes, you said that before," says the judge. "It doesn't carry me very far."

If only I'd gone into the Canadian Mounted Police, thinks Mr. Green, or become a commercial traveller or anything rather than this. I don't know what to say to him. Whatever I say will be wrong. I should like to drop my papers and run away. At that moment the managing clerk puts in a word:

"Go on, say something."

Something moves inside Mr. Green. He turns round to the managing clerk: "Shut up!" he says. In those two words he has made an enemy for life. The managing clerk is outraged at a twopennyhalf-penny whipper-snapper talking to him like that. He makes a mental note never in any circumstances to brief Mr. Green. However, Mr. Green isn't at the moment worrying about his future; he's only concerned (and very much concerned) with his present. Eventually he manages to find something to say, and after a five-minute lecture by the judge and a further ten minutes of agony while he loses the case, he retires to the robing-room, very red and very hot.

The managing clerk simply says: "I'll take the papers," and goes away.

Mr. Green goes sorrowfully back to chambers, trying, not very successfully, to convince himself that there was nothing else he could have done in the circumstances. He meets Mr. Brown as he gets into chambers.

"Win that all right?" says Mr. Brown.

On being told the result: "Oh, well, it can't be helped. Thanks very much. I expect you did everything possible." By this Mr. Brown means that it could have been helped.

Subsequently they have a post-mortem and Mr. Green has to endure things like this:

"What did he say when you asked him about the cheque?"

"As a matter of fact, I don't think I did ask him about it."

"Not ask him about the cheque? Oh—well, never mind. Anyway, how did the judge get over *Abbot* and *Crankshaft*?"

"Well—I didn't actually read it to him——"

"Not read it to him?"

"He said he knew all about it."

"And you left it at that?"

"I'm afraid so."

"Oh—well, never mind. I expect you put up a jolly good show really."

Well, Mr. Green could have learned a great deal from his experience. His future partly depends on how much he really did learn. Most practitioners (however brilliant their later career) have been a Mr. Green in their time. It isn't, therefore, so bad for them, but the litigants who provide them with the experience don't fare quite so well. That was the sort of thing which Mr. Spratt wished to avoid.

Before the clerk had returned, he went into Mr. Grimes' room. It was traditionally dirty, Mr. Grimes having been in practice too long to be infected with the new-fangled idea, which is slowly spreading in the Temple, that there is no real objection to a clean, orderly, well-furnished set of chambers with a decent lavatory.

"How are you, my dear fellow?" said Mr. Grimes cordially. He was always very cordial to his clients. "Very glad to see you. Now, what can I do for Mr. Spratt? Take a chair, my dear fellow. That's right, that's right, that's right."

He had a little habit of repeating his last words two or three times.

"It's only a small thing really, Mr. Grimes, but I feel rather strongly about it."

He then explained what the position was.

"I'd like you to see the correspondence, Mr. Grimes."

It is an extraordinary thing that solicitors are always most proud of the letters of which they should be most ashamed.

"They're dreadful people, Toothcombe and Witley," he added.

Mr. Grimes read the correspondence. To himself he said what any intelligent person would have said and, for all his mannerisms, Mr. Grimes was quite intelligent. To Mr. Spratt he said:

"Well, we'll do the best we can for you, my dear fellow, but the masters are very difficult about these things. They were only a day late, and you didn't actually give them any warning."

"Why should we," said Mr. Spratt indignantly, "after the way they behaved?"

"Quite, my dear fellow, but the masters are so difficult, so difficult, so difficult."

"Well, Mr. Grimes, if you don't think there's any point in my briefing you——" began Mr. Spratt.

"It's a toss-up, my dear fellow. You never know, we can have a try. That's the way."

"All right, Mr. Grimes, if you think there's a fair chance of getting the costs and certificate for counsel, I'll put it in counsel's list."

"There's a chance, my dear fellow, but I can't say more than that —can't say more than that."

"All right, we'll chance it. Thank you very much, Mr. Grimes. You will be there yourself, won't you? I haven't yet been able to see your clerk."

"Oh, yes, I'll be there, my dear fellow, I'll be there. What would Mr. Spratt think of me if I wasn't there? Good-bye, my dear fellow, good-bye, bye, bye, bye."

Mr. Spratt felt he could still hear Mr. Grimes saying 'bye, bye, bye' as he reached the Strand. There he met Mr. Grimes' clerk on his cheerful way back to chambers.

"How are you, Mr. Spratt? Just been to see us, have you?"

"Yes, a summons for Monday. You can be there, can't you?"

"Sir, sir, sir; have we ever let you down before?"

"Well, not often," conceded Mr. Spratt.

"When, sir, never sir, we shall be there, sir," and happily, uncertainly, but (in his own mind) efficiently, Mr. Grimes' clerk rolled away.

Summonses are heard in private in a room in which the master sits behind a counter, and counsel or solicitor or solicitor's clerks or litigants in person, as the case may be, address him from in front of the counter. Large numbers of summonses are issued, and many of them are quite unnecessary. A summons has to be issued whenever one side wants something which the other side will not give. This may apply to many things during the course of one action. A summons may relate to particulars which the plaintiff wants of the defendant's defence, to a document which the plaintiff refuses to let the defendant see, to inspection of the defendant's factory, or to a host of other things. In many cases either the person asking has no right to the thing for which he is asking, or the person asked ought to have conceded the point without a summons being issued. Some people seem to think that the reason why the leading barristers win nearly all their summonses is because of the weight which their experience, reputation and ability has with the masters. This is so only to a very limited extent indeed. The real reason why they win is because in the normal way they never let their clients oppose a request which ought to be granted, or press a request which ought not to be granted. There are, of course, from time to time some extremely difficult matters which have to be fought out on a summons and may affect seriously the whole litigation. Sometimes, too, the result of a summons is vital to one party or the other. But these cases are the exception. There are also some routine summonses which have to be taken out in any event. The amount of money wasted, however, owing to the ignorance and obstinacy of some counsel and solicitors is substantial. Some of them seem to think that a sufficient reason for refusing a request by the other side is the fact that it has been made. In the present case, for example, in the first place Messrs. Braggs and Co. should not have signed judgment without writing a letter warning the defendant's solicitors that, if they did not enter an appearance at once, judgment would be signed. They knew quite well that a mistake must have been made and that the defendants did not intend to let the actions go by default. Secondly, having signed judgment, Mr. Bole should have agreed to Mr. Drive's request to have the judgments set aside at once. The cost would have been negligible. As it was, an expenditure of about £10 was about to be incurred on a matter which could only end in one way. It can be said to the credit of solicitors and counsel that it is only in a very small percentage of cases that summonses are issued or opposed with a view to increasing the costs (though such cases do undoubtedly occur from time to time); the usual reason is obstinacy, ignorance or stupidity. These three qualities add considerably to the cost of litigation. It may be said that there has been some marked improvement during the last twenty-five years, but there is room for a good deal more. It will be appreciated that the five actions which were now pending, one as a result of Martin's claim for commission and four as a result of the acrimonious correspondence between the solicitors, gave ample scope to both sides to incur unnecessary costs, particularly as each side would now be watching the other, waiting for some mistake.

In due course the summons to set aside the judgments came on for hearing. It was last in Master Peabody's list. This meant that both counsel had to wait some time to be heard. It was open to them to agree to go before another master, if one happened to be free, but this could only be done by consent. On the day in question, when the two counsel met outside the room where the summons was to be heard, Mr. Grimes said to his opponent, Mr. Larkins:

"My dear fellow, would you go before another master? We'll have to wait here quite a long time."

"It depends which," said Mr. Larkins. "I won't go before Trotter in any circumstances. I don't mind any of the others."

Mr. Larkins' judgment of Master Trotter was the generally accepted one. The masters, like the judges, vary in ability. Master Trotter came well at the bottom of the class. He was pleasant enough, except when he lost his temper—which on an average was not more than three times a day—but his mind was so small and so heavily fortified on the outside that it was almost impossible to penetrate it. In consequence, the only people who willingly went before him were those who had a bad case. You never knew what might happen.

Before Mr. Grimes could reply, Mr. Larkins went on:

"But won't you agree to an order? There's nothing in this. The judgment's bound to be set aside. It's only a haggle over costs. I'll agree to costs in cause." This would have meant that the costs would follow the eventual result of the action.

"I daresay you would, my dear fellow. I daresay you would. Is there anything else you would like as well, my dear fellow?"

"All right. We'll have to fight, but it was a bit sharp of your people, and I'm going to ask for the costs."

"We shall see, my dear fellow, we shall see. Seems a bit novel that a defendant who's out of time should ask for the costs of putting himself right, but we shall see, my dear fellow, we shall see."

Meanwhile, Mr. Spratt had arrived a little out of breath.

"Ah! I'm glad you haven't gone in yet," he said.

"How are you, my dear fellow, how are you? We'd always wait for Mr. Spratt, wouldn't we?"

"I shouldn't have wanted you to wait, but I'd like to be there."

"You'll be there, Mr. Spratt, you'll be there. We may all be here some time. The amount of time we waste standing about here is dreadful. I don't mind telling you, my dear fellow, I think it's a scandal. Always have thought so. A scandal, that's what it is, my dear fellow, a scandal."

No other available master could be found, but at last Master Peabody had finished the other cases in his list, and Mr. Grimes and Mr. Larkins, followed by their respective solicitors, walked in. As Master Peabody saw Mr. Grimes, an acute observer might have detected him give the suspicion of a sigh. Mr. Grimes was what was known as a fighter. However bad his case, however clear the judge or master may have made it that he was going to decide against him, Mr. Grimes argued and argued, repeating himself time and again; practically no one could stop him. If the tribunal said nothing, he just went on and on and on. If the tribunal interrupted, it merely added fuel to the flames of his eloquence and gave him something extra to say. Master Peabody, having finished all his cases but one, was looking forward to leaving early when he saw Mr. Grimes. However, he quickly controlled his automatic reaction and sat back in his chair to await the onslaught. He was one of the best masters. In face he resembled Mr. Pickwick, and he was quite as friendly. At the same time he had a judicial mind and manner, an excellent knowledge of the practice, a quiet and occasionally mischievous sense of fun, and a great fund of patience. Perhaps that was his only fault. Too much patience on these occasions is inclined to prolong the hearing, particularly in the case of advocates like Mr. Grimes. The master was relieved that Mr. Grimes' opponent was Mr. Larkins, and not, say, 'Foaming Billy', as Mr. William Chance was commonly called. This nickname was partly due to the fact that Mr. Chance was as eloquent and persistent as Mr. Grimes, and partly due to the fact that his floods of oratory were literally floods—or perhaps spray is a more appropriate word. They tell a story (no doubt quite untrue) of an occasion when counsel opposed to 'Foaming Billy' on a summons before a master, held his brief up between him and 'Foaming Billy' while the latter was speaking.

"Why are you holding your brief like that?" asked the master.

"Please, Master, he's splashing me."

"Splashing you? Splashing you? Why—good gracious, he's been splashing me too. I couldn't make out why my glasses were getting blurred."

Mr. Larkins began to address the master.

"Master," he said, "this is an application to set aside judgment in default of appearance. I don't know why my learned friend Mr. Grimes is here to oppose it."

"My learned friend is here," put in Mr. Grimes.

"You put it in counsel's list," replied Mr. Larkins.

"I think I'll hear Mr. Larkins first, Mr. Grimes," put in the master gently.

"If you please, Master, if you please," said Mr. Grimes.

"My clients were one day out. They miscounted the day. The clerk who signed judgment actually met my client's clerk who was going to enter an appearance. He offered to pay the costs if the plaintiff would agree to the judgment being set aside at once, but they wouldn't hear of it."

"That was without prejudice, Master, I believe," put in Mr. Grimes. "I object to my friend mentioning it."

"It wasn't without prejudice," retorted Mr. Larkins, "and I wish my friend would not keep interrupting."

"But, Master, Master," said Mr. Grimes, "my friend oughtn't to mention it if it's without prejudice."

"Really," said Mr. Larkins, "this is too bad. Am I going to be allowed to open this summons or not?"

"Mr. Grimes," said the master, "are your instructions quite definite that the conversation was without prejudice?"

"Will you excuse me a moment, Master?"

There was a whispered conversation between Mr. Spratt and Mr. Grimes in which Mr. Spratt could just be heard to say:

"It might have been, I'm not sure."

"I won't take the point, Master," said Mr. Grimes. "My client isn't quite sure."

"Very well," said the master.

"Really," said Mr. Larkins, "I'm amazed. I hope that *now* my learned friend will keep quiet while I address you. I really cannot stand these persistent and unwarranted interruptions."

"They've stopped now," said the master.

"For the moment," said Mr. Larkins.

"Now, don't provoke Mr. Grimes, Mr. Larkins."

"There are three actions, Master, and there's an affidavit of merits showing that there is a defence in each of them. There was no warning of any kind. It's about as bad an instance of a snapped judgment as I've ever known. I hope you will bring it home to these people that the Court does not encourage conduct of this kind, and I ask you to make the plaintiffs pay the costs of this application which is entirely due to their precipitate haste."

"Well, your clients *were* out of time," said the master.

Mr. Spratt nodded his head vigorously in agreement. What a good master you are, he was trying to convey; you hit the nail on the end at once; good master, clever master, knock him for six, Master.

"But, of course," the master added, "it was only one day. Normally some kind of warning is given in a case where a defence is expected."

Mr. Spratt stopped nodding, and Mr. Toothcombe took it up instead.

"Exactly, Master," said Mr. Larkins. "Quite outrageous."

Mr. Toothcombe beamed.

"I wouldn't put it like that," said the master, "but a trifle quick on the draw, shall we say. . . . I expect there's a little feeling in the case. Would you care for me to look at the correspondence?"

Both solicitors nodded vigorously.

"It's exhibited to the affidavit, Master," said Mr. Larkins.

The master picked up the bundle and began to read. As he read he could not repress a faint smile.

"Dear, dear," he said. "Quite a bit of feeling, really."

He wanted to add—"Reminds me of when I was a boy," but managed to check himself.

Having finished reading the letters, the master turned to Mr. Grimes with, "Yes, Mr. Grimes?"

Mr. Grimes, once unleashed, set off like a greyhound. It would be impossible to repeat here the whole of his speech without inconvenience, because it took nearly an hour. But, among other things, he said this:

"Master, the first thing the defendant has to satisfy you about is that he has a defence to the action; he must show merits, Master, merits."

"Quite so, Mr. Grimes, but what about the affidavit?" said the master.

"I'm coming to that, Master, I'm coming to that. I'm going to submit to you, Master, that in two of the actions, at any rate, he shows no merits at all, none whatever."

"Which two actions?"

"The two libel actions, Master. Now, Master, if you look at the letters in question, they're obviously defamatory—'bogus claim', 'menacing flavour' . . . quite obviously defamatory, Master."

"Isn't that a matter for the judge or jury at the trial, Mr. Grimes?"

"Oh, yes, Master, if the action goes to trial; but my submission is that it shouldn't. If a defendant in a libel action doesn't enter an appearance——"

"One day out," breathed Mr. Larkins softly, but so that it could be heard.

"Really, Master, I would ask you to tell my friend not to make these offensive observations."

"I expect I'm a little deaf, Mr. Grimes. I didn't hear anything. Do continue with your argument. I'm most interested."

"That's very kind of you, Master. I was about to say that, if the document is plainly defamatory, the defendant must show some sort of defence. He doesn't say he didn't write it, he doesn't say it's true —what defence is there?"

"If you ask me——" began the master.

"Oh, I can't ask you questions, Master."

"I'm delighted to answer them, Mr. Grimes. What do you say to privilege as a defence?"

"Malice, Master, malice. Have you ever seen letters so full of malice?"

"On whose part, Mr. Grimes?"

"On the defendants', Master, on the defendants'. I don't want to read all the letters to you again, Master——"

This meant that he was about to do so unless some immediate avoiding action were taken.

"I think I have them well in mind, Mr. Grimes."

"Thank you so much, Master, I'm sure you have, Master. In the light of those letters, Master, I submit that the only question to be decided is the amount of damages, and on that issue, of course, my friend can be heard."

"Isn't malice a question for the judge or jury, Mr. Grimes?"

"In the normal way, yes, Master, but if a defendant has a regular judgment against him he must show that he has some defence. In the present case he must show that he might win on the issue of malice."

"Well, Mr. Grimes, I'm sure you think he won't and your client probably thinks so even more definitely, but can I say that he has no chance whatever?"

"Well, Master, if he only has a very faint chance he ought to have entered an appearance in time."

"Only one day late, Mr. Grimes."

"Yes, Master, but one day *late*."

"Yes, Mr. Grimes, but only *one* day. I don't think, Mr. Grimes, I ought to turn him away from the judgment seat at this stage. After all, a good deal of heat does seem to have been engendered in the correspondence. I gather there are two actions against your clients by the defendants."

"Yes, Master."

"I suppose you have entered an appearance in time?" said the master with a twinkle.

"Oh, yes, Master."

"Well, I think that if the parties want to have their quarrels decided in public, they'd better all be decided. I shall set aside the judgment in the libel actions. What about the other action?"

"Oh, Master, the affidavit does say that there was no agreement to pay commission, and, if you set aside the judgment in the two actions, I think I shall have to concede that that should be done in the third, but, Master—I do submit that——"

And Mr. Grimes was about to start all over again about the libel actions. He would even have read the correspondence again if given the chance. But an hour of all this was enough even for the patience of Master Peabody.

"No, Mr. Grimes," he said pleasantly but firmly, "you must appeal to the judge if you don't like my decision."

"If you please, Master," said Mr. Grimes resignedly, "if you please."

"Now, what about terms?" said the master.

This was the real question the parties had come to fight about. Everybody, including Mr. Grimes, knew quite well that the judgments would be set aside, but Mr. Grimes argued so strenuously against this being done for two reasons: first, he hoped that by doing so he might in some way improve his case on the issue of terms; secondly, it was against his nature not to argue a point, however forlorn, and many of his clients came to him because of this.

"I ask for the usual terms, Master," said Mr. Grimes.

"What do you say they are?" said the master.

"All costs thrown away to be taxed and paid by the defendants as a condition of the judgments being set aside, Master. Would you say to be taxed as between solicitor and client, Master?"

"I haven't said anything yet, Mr. Grimes," replied the master. "What do you say, Mr. Larkins?"

"Master, I submit that my clients should have the costs. We've been here an hour fighting about nothing really, but my learned friend has opposed this application and lost. He ought to pay us for having to listen to him so long."

"If my friend is going to be offensive——" began Mr. Grimes.

"I am sure you wouldn't follow suit, Mr. Grimes," interrupted the master.

"In any event," went on Mr. Larkins, "all this waste of time is because the plaintiffs snapped a judgment."

"I think on the whole," said the master, "that justice will be done if costs follow the result of the trial. Costs in cause."

"But, Master," put in Mr. Grimes, "I haven't finished my submission on costs. I thought you were going to put the defendants on terms."

"Costs in cause, Mr. Grimes," said the master.

"But, Master, Master," said Mr. Grimes, his voice rising as though in agony, "I want to address you further on the matter——"

"I'm afraid you'll have to keep it for the judge, Mr. Grimes," said the master pleasantly.

"If you please, Master, if you please."

Although Mr. Grimes took a lot of stopping, once he was really stopped he deflated like a pricked balloon—though, of course, he was ready to go on on any other subject if the occasion offered.

"Will you certify for counsel, Master?" asked Mr. Larkins.

"Well," said the master, "you have, of course, been of the greatest assistance to me, but, on the whole, I think it was a case which your solicitors could have dealt with quite competently; certainly, judging from the correspondence, there would have been no lack of advocacy. No, I'm afraid not, Mr. Larkins."

"But I was brought here, Master. The other side put it in counsel's list."

"Very pleased to see you, Mr. Larkins, but in this particular case I think the order I have made is about right. I thank you very much, both of you."

"Too bad, my dear fellow," said Mr. Grimes, when they were outside the master's room, in an effort to comfort Mr. Spratt, "but they will do these things, you know, they will do these things."

The net result of all this was that, whatever happened in the case, both Martin Painswick and his opponent would be about £5 out of pocket, and neither had anything to show for the money. There should be some simple means of making solicitors themselves pay for frolics of this kind, but in practice there is not.

Martin's action (together with the satellite actions of the solicitors themselves) went ahead quite quickly. His was a very simple case. Too simple, really, though it was safer than 'kite flying', and had a fair chance of success. The recipe runs something like this.

You find a wealthy business man with a moderately unsavoury past. That is not terribly difficult. If he happens to be a Member of Parliament or a Mayor or filling some other public position, so much the better. You wait until he has brought off some perfectly legitimate deal. There is no trouble about that. You then say that you introduced the deal to him directly or indirectly on the terms that you would be paid commission. There are various ways of proving your introduction, but the one which is most satisfactory can be used if a man, who really was a link in the chain of introduction, is dead. You then claim that you introduced the wealthy businessman to the dead man. Only your opponent can dispute that you did, but you have available as a witness your partner in crime, although he professes to have no interest whatever in your claim. Now what is the position? Here are you, a person against whom (at the moment) nothing discreditable is known, and your partner, a person in a similar position, both swearing that a certain interview has taken place and there is only the defendant to deny it. But when he does deny it, you are able to discredit his evidence somewhat by bringing up his unsavoury past. In the case of Mr. Gloster, it was the conviction for fraud in America. You may think that most people would have known about such a conviction, but this is by no means always the case. Even the police did not know it. Both Mr. Merryweather and Mr. Huntley had felt instinctively that there was something wrong with the claim and hence they would have nothing to do with it. On the face of it, there was nothing wrong whatsoever. It was just a little too simple, and, although likely to succeed, liable to be destroyed by something equally simple. When you try to prove that something has happened which has never happened at all, it is astounding how often the nakedness of the land suddenly appears. The mistake that most people make is failing to clothe their dummy with the clothes it would have been likely to be wearing had it been genuine. When a real interview of this kind takes place, all sorts of things are said, but it is surprising how often it is that, when the interview is a pure fake, the only thing which the perjurer can remember about it is the one sentence which suits his purpose. In consequence, there is no life to his story, and, fortunately, it is often (and indeed usually) disbelieved. It is not easy to invent interviews with success. The only thing of that kind which is more difficult is forgery. That is an extremely difficult task and very rarely succeeds. There are so many pitfalls that it is most probable that the forger will fall into one of them at some stage of the proceedings. In the present case Martin took no such chances. He did not suggest that there was anything in writing. His case was that he trusted Mr. Gloster who, after all, was a Member of Parliament. Not infrequently commission agreements of the kind may be made by word of mouth, and, by carelessness, each side may forget or not bother to confirm in writing. Martin also had in mind that, from Mr. Gloster's point of view, there was not only the possibility of his losing the action but there was the possibility that his conviction in the U.S.A. would be made public. Although Mr. Gloster did not tell his solicitors immediately what the reference to the U.S.A. in the first letter must certainly have been, he realised that he was being blackmailed. It was a very serious matter for him. It was the most deadly form of blackmail because it could not be stigmatised as such in its initial stages.

There could be no 'Mr. X' for Mr. Gloster.

"Make sure you tell him," said Martin to Mr. Spratt, "that I've been in correspondence with the U.S.A."

Mr. Spratt was prepared to do what he was asked to do, though a more reputable solicitor would, of course, have refused.

Martin prepared his case very thoroughly. He worked out the interview carefully with Mr. Fuller, giving it real flesh and blood, and ensuring that his story and Mr. Fuller's should not be exactly the same except on essential matters. Although, however, his claim against Mr. Gloster was contained in formal legal documents and made through the Courts, had the truth of the matter been proved he could have been convicted of blackmail just as if his demand had been barefaced and by letter signed 'The Black Hand'. It is as well that people, who bring proceedings for which they know there is no foundation, should realise this. Blackmail is a dreadful crime, and Martin had only two excuses for committing it—first, he needed the money; secondly, Mr. Gloster was, in effect, an impostor and ought not to have been allowed to remain a Member of Parliament. He was quite as crooked as Martin. But, of course, that is the sort of person whom it is easy to blackmail. It is next to the impossible to obtain anything by threats from a person who has nothing to fear. Martin was certainly reverting to type. Although old Uriah Painswick settled down to an otherwise respectable life after retiring from 'the road' to become an innkeeper, he could not resist supplementing his income by extracting levies from highwaymen in return for his silence. If they paid, however, he did not inform against them thereafter, unless it was absolutely necessary for his own preservation. Strange that none of Uriah's vices were to be found in Mr. Justice Painswick, and yet most of them in his son. This was certainly not due to the judge's late wife, who was herself a person of the highest character and who came from a long line of virtuous parents.

A civil action normally proceeds at only a moderate pace and may be a long time before it is heard. This would not have suited Martin, who was staving off his creditors with some of the money furnished by his father and with promises of the fruits of this action against Mr. Gloster. Accordingly, he instructed Mr. Spratt to set a fast pace. In the course of an action, each side has to deliver a number of documents to the other, and there is a time limit for such delivery. If a party cannot deliver the document within the time limited, he applies to his opponent for an extension of time. This is usually, though not always, granted in the first instance, but if it is refused or if a later request is refused, a summons for an extension of time has to be issued. Solicitors sometimes get quite angry with their opponents on the subject of extension of time, and allegations of trying to delay the action are frequent in their correspondence on this matter. One such dispute resulted in what must be the shortest letter on record. It is an old story, but it has the merit of truth, and as it has never been told in writing before, here it is. It consists of two letters, the first from solicitor A. to solicitor B., and the second from B. to A.

Dear Sirs,

We have received your letter of the 20th ult. We think we had better set the facts on record. On the 1st May your defence became due and you asked for an extension of fourteen days, which we granted. On the 15th May, after we warned you on the telephone that, as no defence has been delivered, we should sign judgment in default, you asked us for a further ten days, and this was granted. On the day before the defence was due, you asked for a further extension of seven days. When we refused, you issued a summons and were granted a further seven days. The defence not being delivered within that time, we again telephoned you out of courtesy to warn you, and you asked for a further three days, promising that the defence would be duly delivered within that time. We acceded to your request. Are we now to understand that you are asking us to give you yet a further seven days' extension?

Yours faithfully,
A.

Back came the reply:

Dear Sirs,
Yes.
Yours faithfully,
B.

In *Painswick v. Gloster and Others,* no extensions of time were granted by either side, and so, whenever extra time was wanted, a summons was issued and the application for time bitterly opposed. In addition to such summonses, several others were issued in the course of the litigation. Among them was one issued by the defendant to ascertain certain particulars of Martin's Statement of Claim. A Statement of Claim is a document which sets out in detail the demands of the plaintiff. The most important item from Mr. Gloster's point of view was the place and date of the interview when the alleged agreement was supposed to have been made. This had been left fairly vague in the Statement of Claim. As the result of an order for particulars, however, Martin was pinned down to a 'date in May which the plaintiff cannot more particularly specify at the Cleveland Palace Hotel at about 12.30 p.m.'. The defendant had sought unsuccessfully to obtain the name of the alleged witness. A party is not entitled to be told the names of the other side's witnesses, but he may learn them incidentally if he can show that mention of the names is necessary to a clear presentation of the other party's case. That was the ground on which this information was asked for in Martin's case.

"The plaintiff has not said on which date the interview was, but only that it was in May. How can the defendant identify it on that information?"

The master pointed out that the defendant said there was no interview with the plaintiff at all at that time. How could it legitimately help him to be told the name of the witness?

"No order," said the master.

Another dispute, however, assumed much larger proportions and actually went to the Court of Appeal. The beginning of Martin's Statement of Claim was as follows:

"The Defendant Gloster is and was at all material times a Member of Parliament. The Defendant firm acts and at all material times acted as his solicitors and in particular wrote the letters complained of in paragraph 5 hereof on the instructions of and on behalf of the Defendant Gloster."

The document then went on to allege the agreement to pay commission and the failure to pay it and then to complain of the allegedly libellous letters.

The defendants applied to have the first sentence of the first paragraph of the Statement of Claim struck out as being scandalous or unnecessary or as an abuse of the process of the Court or likely to prejudice the fair trial of the action.

Master Trotter struck out the allegation.

The plaintiff appealed to the Judge in Chambers, who restored it, and the defendant obtained leave from the judge (who had only recently been appointed) to appeal to the Court of Appeal.

(The total costs involved in summonses and appeals of this kind may approach £100, and no one is normally any better off (apart from the counsel and solicitors involved) except that, if one side obtains all the costs against the other, the payment of such a bill before an action comes on for trial can act as a discouragement to the party who has to pay. Sometimes, therefore, such applications are indulged in by counsel solely for this purpose.)

The defendants argued that the fact that Mr. Gloster was a Member of Parliament was wholly irrelevant to the proceedings and had only been inserted as an implied threat to Mr. Gloster, the threat being that of publicity. The plaintiff disclaimed any such object.

"If," said Mr. Grimes, "the action had only been for commission, the allegations would certainly have been irrelevant and would not have been made. There are, however, claims for libel as well. The character of the libeller must be relevant. A libel by a notorious criminal carries little weight. One by a Church dignitary or a Member of Parliament is of far greater importance and may add to the damages."

To this Mr. Spelthorne, K.C. (leading Mr. Larkins), replied that, if the libel had been in a newspaper or book or in a letter to a stranger, that might have been the case. In fact, however, the publication of the libel was a pure technicality, being only to the typists or clerks or partners in the two firms of solicitors. He repeated that the only object of the sentence was to try to frighten Mr. Gloster.

"Well," put in Lord Justice Mew, after Mr. Spelthorne had gone on in reply for some time, "you are responsible for the publicity so far. No one would have known anything about it if you hadn't appealed from the Judge in Chambers."

"That may be, my Lord, but——"

"Surely," said Lord Justice Rowe, "this was a matter for the discretion of the learned Judge in Chambers? How can we interfere with his discretion?"

"My Lord, I respectfully submit that——"

"Really, Mr. Spelthorne," said Lord Justice Mew, "I cannot think how your client is in the least prejudiced. Granted that the allegation may not affect the damages very acutely, what harm does it do?"

"I respectfully suggest, my Lord——"

"You haven't yet answered the criticism that it is you who are causing all the publicity at the moment," added Lord Justice Torr.

"My Lord, that criticism——"

"I notice," said Lord Justice Rowe, "that the name of the plaintiff is a very distinguished legal name. That hasn't by any chance anything to do with the publicity now being accorded to the case?"

"My Lord, I am sorry to think——"

"Really, Mr. Spelthorne," said Lord Justice Mew, "can you carry the matter any further? We've already heard you at some length."

"I would like to say this," said Mr. Spelthorne, "the publicity in your Lordships' Court——"

"But that has really nothing to do with the matter," put in Lord Justice Torr. "It was only mentioned in passing by my brother when you were complaining of threats. I think you've said everything that can possibly be said, Mr. Spelthorne."

"Rather more," whispered Lord Justice Mew, in an aside to Lord Justice Rowe.

So Mr. Spelthorne sat down, the appeal was dismissed with costs, and Mr. Spratt walked out of the Court, his face wreathed in smiles.

"Better luck next time," he said, with an exasperating grin, to Mr. Toothcombe.

Mr. Toothcombe made no reply, but turned his back on him and spoke to Mr. Spelthorne.

"One can't always be up against gentlemen," he said.

"Did you say something?" asked Mr. Spratt angrily.

"Yes," said Mr. Toothcombe, "to Mr. Spelthorne."

"Well, I should be a little careful if I were you," said Mr. Spratt.

Mr. Toothcombe again turned his back on Mr. Spratt and addressed Mr. Spelthorne. "Listeners," he said, "seldom hear any good of themselves."

It is extraordinary how many grown-up people behave at times as though they were still in the Lower Fourth. This is by no means confined to solicitors.

Eventually the time arrived for what is called discovery of documents. Each party has to disclose in an affidavit all the documents which are, or ever have been, in his possession, custody or power. The affidavit is prepared by the solicitor and sworn by the client. Such affidavits are notoriously incomplete. This is sometimes due to a client not making sufficient disclosure to his solicitor, sometimes to a solicitor not asking sufficient questions of his client, and, more often than not, to the affidavit being carelessly prepared in the solicitor's office. The arrival of the time for discovery presented an acute problem to Mr. Toothcombe. If he had been a solicitor of integrity, it would have presented no problem at all. He was not a man who would have dreamed of converting his clients' money, or doing anything of that nature. But, when it came to discovery of documents, he was quite prepared to stretch a point (as he called drawing up a false affidavit). He was particularly prepared to do so in the present case where he was determined to hit the plaintiff, and his solicitors, as hard as possible. He was, in fact, in a very strong position to do this. It has already been pointed out that a simple case, based on faked evidence, may sometimes be destroyed very simply. The document about which Mr. Toothcombe could not make up his mind was Mr. Gloster's passport, which showed that he was out of England from April 3rd to July 1st. If that document were to be disclosed in his client's affidavit (as, of course, it should have been) it might have one of two results. The plaintiff might surrender at once. This would be too soon for Mr. Toothcombe's liking—insufficient costs would have been incurred and it would be much more effective and pleasant to see the discomfiture of Mr. Spratt in open court. The other possible result would be that the plaintiff would amend his Statement of Claim, and allege that the agreement took place in a different month. He would, of course, have to make some excuse for the mistake and this would not be easy. It would not, however, be impossible, and it might be that the plaintiff would have sufficient ingenuity to invent a plausible tale. If, however, the passport were suddenly produced in Court after the plaintiff had in cross-examination been compelled to pledge himself to the month of May, and no other month, it would then be too late. Mr. Toothcombe could imagine the cross-examination:

MR. SPELTHORNE, K.C.: Are you sure this interview took place?

THE PLAINTIFF: Of course I am.

MR. SPELTHORNE, K.C.: And that it took place at the Cleveland Palace Hotel?

THE PLAINTIFF: Certainly.

MR. SPELTHORNE, K.C.: And in May?

THE PLAINTIFF: Yes.

MR. SPELTHORNE, K.C.: Why so sure it was at the Cleveland Palace Hotel?

THE PLAINTIFF: Because I remember being there. We were in the lounge. We'd just had or were about to have a drink. We certainly had one with Mr. Gloster. I had a sherry—Tio Pepe; that's easy to remember because I always have one. I can't honestly remember what Mr. Gloster had. It may have been a dry Martini. I'm not sure.

MR. SPELTHORNE, K.C.: What did Mr. Fuller have?

THE PLAINTIFF: I really can't remember at this distance of time. All I do know is that we had drinks, and mine was Tio Pepe.

MR. SPELTHORNE, K.C.: Are you quite sure it was in May?

THE PLAINTIFF: Positive.

MR. SPELTHORNE, K.C.: Why so sure?

THE PLAINTIFF: Because, as a matter of fact, we went to the theatre that night and I remember the play, *Bitter Almonds*.

MR. SPELTHORNE, K.C.: But that play was on in April, June and July, was it not?

THE PLAINTIFF: As a matter of fact, it was not. It wasn't on at one of the West End theatres, but at one of the small repertory theatres. It only ran for a month, May.

MR. SPELTHORNE, K.C.: Quite sure of that? How do you know?

THE PLAINTIFF: I've looked it up.

MR. SPELTHORNE, K.C.: No possibility of mistake, I suppose?

THE PLAINTIFF: None whatever.

MR. SPELTHORNE, K.C.: And so you swear beyond any question of doubt or mistake that on some date in May you met Mr. Gloster in the Cleveland Palace Hotel?

THE PLAINTIFF: I've already done so.

MR. SPELTHORNE, K.C.: And you don't want to go back on it?

THE PLAINTIFF: Certainly not.

At this stage in his imagination Mr. Toothcombe positively oozed with excitement. The plaintiff had been tied up completely. There was no hope of retreat and the ripe plum, all ready for plucking, was about to be plucked. A lovely moment. There would, of course, be a bit of a song and dance about the non-disclosure of the passport, but that would be lost in the complete overthrow of the plaintiff. This is how it would go:

MR. SPELTHORNE, K.C.: Well, Mr. Painswick, would you mind having a look at this?

MR. GRIMES: What document are you handing to the witness?

MR. SPELTHORNE, K.C.: You'll see.

MR. GRIMES: It looks like a passport, and no passport has been disclosed.

MR. SPELTHORNE, K.C.: It *is* a passport, Mr. Gloster's passport. Will you look at it, please, Mr. Painswick?

MR. GRIMES: My Lord, I object to this. I don't know what the effect of it is——

MR. SPELTHORNE, K.C.: I'm sure you don't.

MR. GRIMES: Will my learned friend kindly not interrupt. This passport, if relevant, ought to have been disclosed.

THE JUDGE: What do you want me to do about it? Exclude it from being given in evidence?

MR. GRIMES: Well, my Lord——

THE JUDGE: You know I can't do that. Of course, if it is relevant, it ought to have been disclosed, and we shall have to see what the explanation is, but I can't keep it out. Perhaps I'd better look at it first. (*After a pause.*) Yes, this does seem to show that Mr. Gloster wasn't in England between April and July, but I'm not quite sure what Mr. Painswick can say about it. He says he was. Perhaps he'd better look at it. D'you see that, Mr. Painswick?

THE PLAINTIFF: Which page does your Lordship mean? I only see the names of countries on this page.

THE JUDGE: Now you've lost the place. Give it back to me, usher.

MR. SPELTHORNE, K.C.: Perhaps you'd rather not see it, Mr. Painswick. Still sure you saw Mr. Gloster in May?

THE PLAINTIFF: Well—I suppose I could have made a mistake.

THE JUDGE: Now look at it again. Keep the place for him, usher. It does look as though Mr. Gloster couldn't have been at the Cleveland Palace Hotel in May, doesn't it? Unless, of course, this is a forgery.

THE PLAINTIFF: Yes, it does look as though he couldn't have been there. I must have been wrong.

MR. SPELTHORNE, K.C.: What about *Bitter Almonds*? You checked that.

THE PLAINTIFF: I must have mixed it up with another play. That's where the misunderstanding must have been, but I was sure it was *Bitter Almonds*. I can't understand it.

MR. SPELTHORNE, K.C.: Of course, if the interview never took place at all, as my client says, that explains everything, doesn't it, Mr. Painswick?

THE PLAINTIFF: It did take place.

MR. SPELTHORNE, K.C.: Let me have the passport back, please. Well, as you've made a mistake—to what would you like to amend it? You'll forgive me if I ask you for an answer before you examine the passport any more? You see, you might hit on another date when Mr. Gloster was abroad. What month do you now suggest?

(*No answer.*)

What year?

(*No answer.*)

What, can't you suggest one? Are you wondering, by any chance, what other alibi Mr. Gloster might prove?

(*No answer.*)

Do you think it might be awkward if you made another mistake?

(*No answer.*)

You do realise you are giving evidence on oath, don't you?

(*No answer.*)

I'm only asking you one question at a time, and I'm only going on because you don't answer any of them.

THE PLAINTIFF: My Lord, I don't feel very well——

Mr. Toothcombe visualised it all. It would be just perfect. Spratt would be there, kicking himself for not having thought of it before. But if he disclosed the passport before the trial, the plaintiff could alter his story and would be prepared for the obvious cross-examination. Unfortunately Mr. Gloster had no other perfect alibis that year. So the plaintiff could say March, April or July, instead of May. It was a nasty decision to have to make. He wasn't worried about the morality of it, but the possible consequences of non-disclosure. Normally such things get by with, at worst, a rap over the knuckles in Court. But Spratt would be vindictive and press the matter as hard as he could. Well, Gloster and he could invent a story about his having forgotten he was abroad then, and only thinking of the matter and getting hold of his passport just before the plaintiff was cross-examined. Of course, even then it ought to have been disclosed at once. If he gave it to Spelthorne too soon, he'd tell the other side. He must wait until the plaintiff was being cross-examined and take the consequences for not telling his counsel before. If, however, he were pressed on that he would have to concede that he held it back so as to take the plaintiff by surprise. Well, the proof of the pudding would have to be in the eating, but some judges could be very unpleasant about it. The matter might be reported to the Law Society. After much careful thought, Mr. Toothcombe eventually decided most regretfully that he mustn't take the risk. It wasn't a very large one, but it was too definite to be taken. So, into the affidavit of documents went the passport. He tried it first in the privileged documents (that is, documents which, although disclosable in the affidavit, need not be shown to the other side), but the plaintiff issued a summons, the master ordered him to produce it and an appeal to the judge failed. He didn't feel like going to the Court of Appeal again, particularly as his claim to privilege could not possibly be justified. So the plaintiff and his solicitors saw the passport—and Martin had to think again. But, as Mr. Toothcombe realised sadly, it was much more pleasant for him to have to think again well before the trial, in a solicitor's office, than to have to do so in the witness-box. "It's a shame," he said to himself. "The rules about discovery are ridiculous."

The disclosure of the passport was a very nasty blow for Mr. Spratt. He sent for Martin at once and told him.

"Oh dear," said Martin, "that's awkward. I must have made a mistake."

"And your friend Mr. Fuller as well?"

"Yes, he too. We often do make mistakes, you know."

"Mr. Painswick, this is a serious matter. If the interview definitely did take place, it can't have been in May."

"No, nor June for that matter, and there's only April 1st and 2nd, and I don't much care for the sound of the 1st, and anyway, I ought to have remembered it if it had been on that day. What about March? That begins with an 'Ma' too. Perhaps it was your mistake, and not mine, and you wrote down May instead of March. Solicitors do make mistakes like that, I suppose, sometimes."

"Mr. Painswick, we did not make a mistake. You know quite well that, when the defendants asked for particulars, I pressed you for the date and you said the best you could say was May. I asked you if it might have been April or June, and you said 'No'."

"March isn't April or June. I didn't say it couldn't be March."

"Mr. Painswick, if I didn't know you to be a respectable son of a distinguished father, I should have grave doubts of the honesty of your claim."

"Oh, don't bring my father into it. He's got nothing to do with it. Come to think of it, it was March. I remember now. Of course. But I suppose Mr. Gloster wasn't abroad in March as well. You had a look for that too?"

"No, as I told you, he was away that year only from April 3rd to July 1st."

"Good. Well, that's all right, then. It was March. I'm glad that's fixed. Anything else you want? When will the trial be?"

"Mr. Painswick, you don't seem to appreciate the gravity of the situation at all. It's quite true we can get leave to amend our particulars by changing from May to March, but the comment which will be made by counsel for the defence will be very strong."

"Of course it will. That's what he's paid for."

"And in my view very effective. I think we'd better go and see Mr. Grimes and get his opinion as to whether it's worth going on with the action."

"Worth going on? What a fuss you make about a small alteration like that. Substitute 'rch' for 'y'. You lawyers are particular. Anyway, why can't you say it was your mistake—a silly typist or something?"

"Mr. Painswick, you may or may not know that, when you gave me instructions, I wrote them down. If we wanted to prove that it was my mistake, I should have to give evidence and produce my notes."

"Well, that's simple enough. Scrap the old notes and write some more. Surely I don't have to teach you your job."

Mr. Spratt was quite used to dealing with dishonest clients, he was even quite used to stories being changed and a nod or wink passing between him and his client during the process, but this barefaced suggestion of fraud, and the open manner in which Martin wanted him to forge his notes, was a novelty to him and quite shocking. It was against all the rules of the game.

"I can only assume you are joking, Mr. Painswick, and, if I may say so, not in very good taste."

"You're a funny fellow," said Martin. "I thought you were on my side. I make a perfectly sensible suggestion, and instead of thanking me for it, you go off the deep end. I thought one employed a solicitor to help, not to hinder. First of all, you or your typist, or both of you, make a most important mistake, and then, when, instead of being angry, I suggest that you should do the obvious thing and put it right, you start telling me I'm acting in bad taste. It's beyond me."

"We did not make a mistake, and you know it."

"Just let me think. I know—we'll ask my friend Fuller; I fancy he'll confirm that both of us told you March."

"Mr. Painswick, I regret to have to say this to a client—particularly a client with such a distinguished father——"

"I asked you before. Please leave my father out of it. He wasn't at the interview, either in March or May."

"Nor, in my opinion, Mr. Painswick, was anyone else. I regret to have to say that, in my view, you are the most unprincipled scoundrel with whom I have had the misfortune to deal."

"And what, may I ask, is your experience in that line? How many have you met? If it's only one or two, your sweeping statement counts for nothing."

"I am not prepared to continue this conversation. I assume you would like to consult another solicitor."

"Certainly not. I've hired you for the journey. Never change horses in mid-stream, I say—or mules," he added.

"Mr. Painswick, I was giving you the chance of withdrawing your instructions yourself, but I must tell you quite plainly that I should not dream of continuing to act for you either in this or any other matter. I will send you my firm's bill for the work done to date, and that is the last thing I have to say. I don't propose to let even a judge's son stay here and insult me. Good morning, sir."

"Well, well, well," said Martin. "I've a lot to learn yet, I see. Now what do I do?"

"Leave this office, sir, if you please."

"Very well, Mr. Spratt. Good-bye, and please remember me to Mr. Braggs, Mr. Golightly and Mr. Sharpe, and don't forget to incorporate Mr. Hugg, Mr. Neadham and Mr. Charlesmith when you do so."

As soon as he had gone, Mr. Spratt picked up the telephone and asked to speak to Mr. Toothcombe.

"Old boy," he said, to Mr. Toothcombe's surprise, "*Painswick* v. *Gloster and Others*. I'm not acting for the plaintiff any more. I thought I'd let you know at once."

"That's very kind of you," said Mr. Toothcombe, adopting an equally friendly tone. "Anything the matter?"

"Plenty. I've just slung him out of my office. I won't say more, but you may want to subpœna me to be present so that I shall be available to give evidence of the instructions given to me, if the plaintiff wants to go into all that."

"That's very civil of you, old boy."

"Well, I thought it was the only decent thing. We've always got on very well with you in the past."

"Of course we have, old man. I'm glad you rang up. About those libel actions—shall we call it a day as far as our firms are concerned?"

"I was just going to say the same thing. We'll write each other a friendly note and discontinue all of them, shall we?"

"I'll do it today. That still leaves over Painswick's claim for libel against us."

"I shouldn't worry about that very much. Are you doing anything for lunch?"

"Wait a moment. No, I'm free."

"Good; come and have lunch with me at the Law Society."

"Delighted, old boy. One o'clock?"

"O.K. So long. Tell you some more then."

Mr. Toothcombe was now very pleased that he had disclosed the passport. All his anger against Mr. Spratt had disappeared and he had no feelings at all about the plaintiff, who would either discontinue the action or bring it to trial. In either case he would be bound to lose, now that Mr. Spratt had clearly indicated what the position was. The four stupid libel actions, which were taking up time and space in the office, were out of the way, and while he enjoyed acrimonious correspondence, he equally enjoyed restoring friendly relations with his opposite numbers. He went off to meet Mr. Spratt in high spirits. They had a somewhat convivial lunch in the course of which, in the strictest confidence, they told each other a number of things about their own clients which they had learned from their respective clients also in the strictest confidence.

Meanwhile Martin had to make up his mind whether he would give in, instruct another solicitor, or conduct the case in person. As he had no other plan for making enough money to satisfy his creditors and there was no time to make one, he ruled out the first course. If he fought and lost the action, he wouldn't be worse off than if he gave it up now, and there was always the chance that he would win. He realised, however, that everything would depend upon how he and Fuller could stand cross-examination on the change of month. Having regard to his experience with Mr. Spratt, he decided not to employ any other solicitors in case he should wish to change his story again and they also were too squeamish to be parties to it. So he went on with the action in person. First of all, he applied for and obtained leave to amend his particulars by changing May to 'in or about March'. The defendants also amended by justifying the statement that it was a bogus claim. Until the production of the passport and its consequences, they had not thought it wise to do so, but now they felt confident. Accordingly, they put as the main defence to the claim for libel that it was true. In due course the case came up for hearing before Mr. Justice Pantin.

Martin gave his evidence extremely well in the first instance. He was careful to draw the judge's attention to the amendment and to say what a shock it was to him when he saw the passport. He had been quite sure it was in May. Now he realised it could not have been. It could not have been after May for various reasons which he gave and which seemed adequate. It must have been before, in March or, at the earliest, the end of February. He gave full details of the interview, making it look as though it really had taken place. Eventually Mr. Spelthorne rose to cross-examine.

"Have you a good memory?" was his first question.

MARTIN: For some things, not for dates.

SPELTHORNE, K.C.: You seem to have details of the interview at your finger-tips.

MARTIN: Is that a question or a comment to his Lordship?

SPELTHORNE, K.C.: Yes, it was a question. I'm sorry you did not catch the note of interrogation. I will add 'haven't you?'

MARTIN: Yes, I have. I've thought a lot about it.

SPELTHORNE, K.C.: Since when?

MARTIN: Ever since Mr. Gloster refused to honour his promise.

SPELTHORNE, K.C.: And how long ago was that?

MARTIN: About nine months or so.

SPELTHORNE, K.C.: So for the last nine months you have had in mind the details of this interview?

MARTIN: Yes.

SPELTHORNE, K.C.: Including the place?

MARTIN: Yes.

SPELTHORNE, K.C.: And month?

MARTIN: I made a mistake about the month. I've already said so.

SPELTHORNE, K.C.: At the time you made the mistake the interview was under a year old.

MARTIN: Quite right. A lot can happen in a year.

SPELTHORNE, K.C.: You must have known, say in January, what your movements were in the preceding February, March, April and May.

MARTIN: Generally, yes, but it's very easy to confuse a month. I had a good number of interviews with a good number of people at the time.

SPELTHORNE, K.C.: On what subjects?

MARTIN: On all sorts.

SPELTHORNE, K.C.: Such as?

MARTIN: Buying goods, selling goods.

SPELTHORNE, K.C.: Anything else?

MARTIN: Oh, all manner of things: arranging things here, settling up something there, meeting friends, discussing business deals and so on, etcetera.

SPELTHORNE, K.C.: Any commission agreements apart from this one?

MARTIN: Very likely.

SPELTHORNE, K.C.: Can you mention a single one? Please bear in mind that I shall ask for details of each transaction and request you to produce the documents.

MARTIN: A lot of my work is done without documents.

SPELTHORNE, K.C.: Come, Mr. Painswick, are you saying that you normally enter into legitimate commission agreements and have nothing in writing—not even a cheque?

MARTIN: Possibly.

SPELTHORNE, K.C.: Can you mention a single one with or without documents?

MARTIN: Not at the moment. I'm not prepared for a cross-examination of all my business transactions over a year. I shall have to look it up.

SPELTHORNE, K.C.: Then there are documents?

MARTIN: Or think about it.

SPELTHORNE, K.C.: Are you prepared to swear that there was a single commission agreement except the one you allege with Mr. Gloster?

MARTIN: I can't be sure.

SPELTHORNE, K.C.: Then there can't have been many or you would swear there was at least one?

MARTIN: Possibly not.

THE JUDGE: It does not sound as though there can have been many.

MARTIN: No, my Lord, but I do want to explain that I don't attach much importance to the nature of a business deal; buy goods, sell goods, sell on commission, commission agreement and so on, etcetera, I lump them all together.

SPELTHORNE, K.C.: I'll ask you a little about your buying and selling goods in a moment, but first of all I do want to know if you can give any explanation of how you came to make the mistake.

MARTIN: None at all, except that it isn't the first I've made or the last. The same applies to everyone, I suppose.

SPELTHORNE, K.C.: The witness you say you're going to call, for instance. Funny he should have made the same mistake.

MARTIN: He didn't, as a matter of fact. He always thought it was March, but I persuaded him out of it. I was sure it was May, and I eventually got him to agree.

SPELTHORNE, K.C.: Perhaps he didn't think there was an interview at all, and you eventually got him to agree that there was.

MARTIN: Did I catch a note of interrogation in that sentence?

THE JUDGE: Mr. Painswick, kindly behave yourself. If you genuinely don't understand a question say so, but don't try to be funny. It will not do you any good.

MARTIN: My Lord, it seems rather hard that I should have to guess whether I am being asked a question. Counsel loves to put in a comment during cross-examination if he gets the chance. Why should I have to sort out the question from the comment? I mean no disrespect, but counsel is quite capable of looking after himself and I'm having to conduct the case myself.

The Judge: I am here to see that you are treated fairly and also that you behave. I hope I shall discharge both duties. Now, don't let's have any more nonsense. Repeat your question, Mr. Spelthorne.

Spelthorne, K.C.: Was your witness reluctant to agree that there was an interview until you persuaded him?

Martin: Not at all. It was he who reminded me that he was there at all. I'd forgotten.

Spelthorne, K.C.: I thought that the details stood out so well in your memory.

Martin: So they have—in the last nine months. Mr. Fuller told me a year ago.

Spelthorne, K.C.: Mr. Fuller is your witness then?

Martin: That's right.

Spelthorne, K.C.: He also happens to be your partner in a firm called Treetop Traders?

Martin: Yes.

Spelthorne, K.C.: Not doing very well at the moment, are they?

Martin: Unfortunately not. We owe a lot of money.

Spelthorne, K.C.: Any chance of paying it?

Martin: I hope so.

Spelthorne, K.C.: If you win this case, I suppose?

Martin: Certainly, if I win this case.

Spelthorne, K.C.: That would be a help to your partner, then?

Martin: Yes, I suppose, looking at it in that way, it would.

Spelthorne, K.C.: So he can hardly be termed independent.

Martin: Isn't that for his Lordship to say? I can only tell you his relationship to me.

Spelthorne, K.C.: Coming back to this interview, can you say on what day of the week it was?

Martin: I'm not sure. Could have been a Monday or a Tuesday.

Spelthorne, K.C.: It could have been any day, but I suppose you won't pledge yourself to any day or even any two days?

Martin: No, I won't. I'm here to tell the truth.

Spelthorne, K.C.: Yes, that's what you're here for, but are you?

Martin: To the best of my ability.

Spelthorne, K.C.: I suggest that the reason you won't pledge yourself to anything but some day in late February or March is that you were so shocked by the passport that you're frightened that, if you commit yourself to the slightest extent, your story will again be upset.

MARTIN: Naturally you put that construction on it, but that is not the case. I don't mind admitting that I was very much shaken by production of the passport. I was sure the interview was in May.

SPELTHORNE, K.C.: Why are you now sure it was in February or March?

MARTIN: Only because you've proved it wasn't in May, and I know it wasn't later than May or earlier than late February. To be quite frank, I still think it was May, although I know it wasn't, if you follow me.

SPELTHORNE, K.C.: Now another matter. Yours is a genuine claim according to you, I gather?

MARTIN: Of course. You don't imagine I'd go to this expense and trouble if it wasn't.

SPELTHORNE, K.C.: It is quite a plain straightforward case?

MARTIN: Absolutely. But, of course, I had nothing in writing.

SPELTHORNE, K.C.: Is that why you thought it necessary to threaten the defendant?

MARTIN: Threaten? When and in what way? I've demanded my legal rights, that's all.

SPELTHORNE, K.C.: Just look at the first letter your solicitors wrote when they made the claim on your behalf. What does the last sentence mean?

MARTIN: That I've been corresponding with the U.S.A.?

SPELTHORNE, K.C.: You seem to know what I'm going to ask you. Yes, that's right. What was that about?

MARTIN: I'd rather not say.

SPELTHORNE, K.C.: But, subject to his Lordship's direction, you must say.

MARTIN: I will if I must, but I don't want to.

THE JUDGE: You will answer the question.

MARTIN: Oh—very well. I was satisfied that Mr. Gloster had cheated me out of my commission. It wasn't the first time he'd cheated anybody. I wanted to remind him of what happened to cheats. I'd hoped he'd learned by experience. Do you want any more?

SPELTHORNE, K.C.: Well?

MARTIN: Do you want any more? I'm not in the least anxious to raise these matters in public. I told you I didn't want to answer your questions about it, but if you want the whole story I'll give it you. Otherwise I won't say another word about it unless your client swears there was no agreement.

THE JUDGE: Well, Mr. Spelthorne, do you wish the witness to go on? He is entitled to, you know, but says he would rather not do so. Do you want him to finish?

SPELTHORNE, K.C.: I'll put the question another way. Were you not by that sentence threatening the defendant with some kind of exposure if he didn't meet your claim?

MARTIN: It wasn't a threat any more than if I'd said, "You've done previous people out of their commission and I'm not going to let you do me. Let me remind you in particular of the expense you were put to in trying to evade paying on a previous occasion." That's all I did, and, if that's wrong, I did wrong. All I can say is that unless his Lordship tells me not to do so, I shall do it again in similar circumstances. A person who bilks his creditors must expect to be shot at. The remedy is to pay them, as he can well afford to do.

THE JUDGE: Don't make speeches, Mr. Painswick.

MARTIN: I'm sorry, my Lord, but being called a blackmailer is very unpleasant.

THE JUDGE: Mr. Spelthorne didn't actually use that expression, though I must agree it was implied.

MARTIN: They talk of 'menacing flavour' in their letters, my Lord.

THE JUDGE: Show me. Oh, yes, I see. Yes, Mr. Spelthorne, do you wish to ask any more questions about this matter?

SPELTHORNE, K.C.: I think not, my Lord.

Mr. Spratt, who would have been delighted at the way the plaintiff was coming through the witness-box if he had still been acting for him, was now as anxious about the case as Mr. Toothcombe. Martin, realising what would happen if he threw the slightest blame on his solicitor, had been careful to accept full responsibility himself. In consequence, Mr. Spratt could not be of the least use to the defendants. No one would have thought a month or so previously that

Mr. Spratt and Mr. Toothcombe would have lunched together on the first day of the trial and tried to think of some method of breaking Martin down. Mr. Spratt would willingly have given in evidence his last conversation with Martin, but such evidence would not have been admissible. It was nothing like so pleasant a lunch as the one they had on the previous occasion.

"He's very clever," said Mr. Spratt.

"Look at his father," said Mr. Toothcombe. "You'd expect him to be."

"You see how well he's paved the way for Fuller. I wish I'd had a proof from him. You would have been able to use that somehow. He's only got to go into the witness-box and say, 'Oh, yes, it was in March, I've always thought it was March, but Mr. Painswick was so sure, I thought I must be wrong.' How can Spelthorne break that down? I'm afraid you're going to lose this case. It's a fishy story, no date at first, then a wrong month and no documents, but unless one or other of them is broken down, it's a bit difficult for the judge to say there was no interview at all. Then your client can be cross-examined as to credit. I don't like it at all. Do you?"

"I can't say I do, old boy. I wonder if we ought to settle. I'll see what Spelthorne says. But Gloster won't want to and I don't blame him. You and I know he's right. I don't know what I'd do in his place. How much d'you think Painswick would take?"

"Not less than £10,000. I know that's the least that's any use to him."

"It's the devil of a lot to pay if you don't owe anything."

Before the resumed hearing the defendant and Mr. Toothcombe had a consultation with Mr. Spelthorne and Mr. Larkins. Mr. Spelthorne forecast a victory for the plaintiff. "It isn't a certainty," he said, "and, of course, if I could break Fuller down all would be well. But his part is too easy, and I doubt if I shall. It's up to you, Mr. Gloster. I wouldn't pay voluntarily myself if I weren't liable and I believe you when you say you're not, but you're the man who's got to foot the bill and it'll cost you less to settle than to go on and lose."

Mr. Gloster decided to fight. The plaintiff's evidence was accordingly completed and then Fuller gave evidence. He was not such a good witness as Martin, but he had learned his part well and it had certainly been made easy for him. He left the box unshaken. Then Mr. Gloster gave evidence. All he could do was to deny the interview, but he had to admit that it was physically possible for him to have been there in February or March.

When Martin rose to cross-examine he said:

"I think there's only one question I want to ask you. I'm not the first person you've cheated, am I?"

THE WITNESS: I haven't cheated you. You're trying to cheat me.

MARTIN: Oh—well, I'll have to ask more than one question then. Now, just assume for the purposes of argument that you have cheated me. I wouldn't have been the first, would I?

THE WITNESS: I will not assume any such thing.

MARTIN: I shall have to ask more than two questions. Substitute 'this dispute' for 'cheating me'. Now it will run—you have cheated people before before this dispute, haven't you?

THE WITNESS: It depends on what you mean by cheating.

MARTIN: Oh, dear, you are difficult. For the moment I will assume that we both mean the same thing by cheating. Well?

THE WITNESS: Well what?

THE JUDGE: Have you ever cheated anyone before this litigation started?

THE WITNESS: I have been accused of it.

MARTIN: Did you dispute it?

THE WITNESS: I was told that if I pleaded guilty to what was little more than a technical offence, I should only be fined.

MARTIN: So you admitted the technical offence?

THE WITNESS: Yes.

MARTIN: And how much were you fined?

THE WITNESS: I wasn't fined.

MARTIN: Let off altogether?

THE WITNESS: I got twelve months.

MARTIN: Twelve months' imprisonment for the technical offence?

THE WITNESS: Yes.

MARTIN: The technical offence had something to do with cheating, had it not?

THE WITNESS: I don't remember what they called it.

MARTIN: It was worth twelve months, anyway—or perhaps I

couldn't expect you to agree to that. That is all I wish to ask, my Lord.

Mr. Spelthorne's prophecy came true and, after he had addressed the judge as long as he properly could, judgment was given in favour of the plaintiff. Altogether, including the damages for libel, Martin eventually received just over £15,000. In the course of making his £15,000 he had committed at least four crimes—perjury, subornation of perjury, conspiracy and blackmail, a list which must have made his ancestor Uriah look upon him with approbation and consider overlooking the disgrace of having a High Court judge in the family.

EDITOR'S NOTE

Mr. Cecil desires me to say that the above was published in 1951. If any legal reader notices any slight changes in law and procedure which have taken place since then, this fact is self-explanatory. It does not in any way reduce its value as a most amusing and accurate account of the course of an action.

J.W.

Cyril Hare

MURDERER'S LUCK

★

Everybody who knows London knows the Progress Club. It is one of the most impressive buildings in Pall Mall, and every line of its architecture proclaims that for the best people Progress stopped in 1850 or thereabouts. I am not a member, but my friend Prothero is, and I was his guest there at dinner one evening recently. Prothero likes to call himself a "criminologist". Murder is his hobby, and I have long since lost count of the famous crimes which he has "written up". I was not surprised, therefore, that among the friends of his who joined us in the smoking-room after dinner was a rather exalted official at Scotland Yard by the name of Wrestall.

Over our coffee and liqueurs Wrestall happened to ask me whether I had been in the club before.

"Yes," I told him, "but not for several years. I remember that the last time I was here the member who entertained me was Sylvester Kemball."

It was not a very tactful remark, seeing that Kemball had quite recently been hanged for murdering his wife. But my companions took it in good part.

"I have always thought," said Prothero, rather pontifically, "that the Kemball case was one of the most successful examples of modern detective methods. It was a great triumph for our police organisation —and for you personally, Wrestall," he added.

"If you say so," said Wrestall modestly. "But, as a matter of fact, it was only by the merest stroke of luck that we obtained the evidence to bring it home to him."

"Luck!" said Prothero. "When you come to think of it, it is astonishing how often the most astute and careful criminal is defeated by some quite unforeseen accident—often by an extravagantly unlikely event which he could not possibly have guarded against. Take the Abertillery murder, for example. . . ."

But we never took the Abertillery murder. A man in the far corner of our group interrupted him without ceremony. "The unluckiest murderer within my recollection," he said, "was Anthony Edward Fitzpatrick Pugh."

Everybody turned to look at him. He was not much to look at—a small, insignificant fellow with a disagreeably complacent expression. I recollected that his name was Hobson and that like myself he was present as the guest of a member.

"Pugh?" repeated Prothero, and he contrived to make the name sound almost insulting. "Anthony Pugh, did you say?"

"Anthony Edward Fitzpatrick Pugh."

"You surprise me very much. I think I am tolerably well acquainted with every crime of any significance during the last century and a half, and I have never come across the name before. Wrestall, are you familiar with the case of the homicidal Mr. Pugh?"

Wrestall shook his head.

"You see, Mr. Hobson," Prothero went on, "you appear to be the possessor of knowledge quite unknown even to Scotland Yard. I hesitate to make the suggestion, but are you quite sure of your facts?"

"Perfectly. Would you care to hear them?"

"We are all ears." Prothero settled himself back in his chair with an indulgent smile.

"It's a very simple story, really," said Hobson, "and I only mentioned it because whenever the subject of bad luck comes up it always brings Pugh to my mind. Mind you, he deserved his luck, as people generally do. He was a disagreeable type, selfish and greedy as they make them. His bad luck began when he entrusted practically the whole of the fortune he had inherited from his parents to a get-rich-quick schemer in the City. He should have known better, of course, but there it was. He lost the lot. Then he brought an action at law to recover his money. He secured a judgment quite easily.

Ten thousand pounds and costs. It must have sounded most impressive. But it's one thing to get a decision from the courts and quite another to make it effective, as Pugh found out. His lawyers went through the usual motions, of course, which added quite a tidy figure to the bill of costs which Pugh had to foot. It was no good. Their man went gracefully and artistically bankrupt. Pugh could whistle for his money—it simply wasn't there. What made things still more aggravating for him, destitution didn't seem to make the slightest difference to the debtor's style of living. He remained in residence on his comfortable estate in Sussex. He continued to travel up to London every day with a reserved seat in a first-class smoker, and the porters touched their caps to him. Poor Pugh lived in the same neighbourhood and caught the same train, travelled third-class non-smoker, because he grudged the cost of a packet of cigarettes, thinking about his ten thousand pounds every mile of the way.

"The secret of the happy bankrupt's prosperity, of course, was that he personally had never owned anything. Every stick and stone of the Sussex mansion, the pedigree Jerseys in the park, the race-horses in the stables, the money that paid the servants' wages and the butcher's bills and the first-class fares to London—the whole boiling, in fact—was the sole, separate property of his wife—who was, incidentally, a very attractive, good-natured woman, and much too good for her scamp of a husband, who treated her extremely badly.

"That daily encounter on the railway station platform made Pugh feel positively murderous. One could hardly have blamed him if one fine morning he had slaughtered the man out of hand. But Pugh wasn't that sort. Money was what he cared about, not revenge, and killing his debtor wouldn't have got his ten thousand back. What he wanted was to find some means of putting money into his debtor's pocket, where his lawyers could get at it. He thought the matter over in his cold-blooded way, and hit upon a very simple, logical solution. The fellow had made his property over to his wife. Pugh proposed to reverse the process. He could be fairly certain that in such a set-up the lady would have made a will leaving everything to her husband. He had only to put her out of the way, and there would be more than enough money in the husband's hands to satisfy his little claim. That was his calculation and, as it turned out, he was dead right.

"Once having made up his mind to commit the murder, he carried it out with great simplicity and ease. He discovered by observation that his intended victim was in the habit of driving herself into Worthing every day. To get to the main road from the park she had to go through a gate across the drive which was kept shut on account of the Jersey cows. He concealed himself behind a hedge at that point, waited till she came along and then shot her through the head at close range as she got out of the car to open the gate. He used an old German pistol he had picked up years before. Then he walked quietly away, leaving the pistol in the hedge. He saw no reason why anyone should connect him with a woman to whom he had never even spoken in his life. And, indeed, there was none."

"Then how was he convicted?" asked Prothero.

"He wasn't," Hobson replied. "I never said that he was. I merely said that he was the unluckiest murderer within my recollection, and that was strictly true. You see, although he had been absolutely right in his calculations and completely successful in his crime, he never got his ten thousand pounds.

"Pugh had been so careful to avoid being suspected himself that it had never occurred to him to wonder who would be likely to be accused of the crime in his place. But of course when a rich woman with a penniless husband is murdered there is one obvious person for the police to pick on, if you don't mind my putting it that way, Mr. Wrestall. If Pugh had thought the matter out a little more carefully he would have seen that he was also the one person he couldn't afford to have convicted.

"When the authorities began to look into the case against the husband Pugh's bad luck started to operate in real earnest. It turned out that the couple had had a flaming row that very morning and that the wife was actually on her way to see her lawyer about making a new will at the moment when she was killed. It turned out, further, that the cheap revolver Pugh had used was the dead spit of one owned by the accused and—so he said—lost by him only a week or two before. That made quite a sizeable case against him, but the crucial piece of evidence arose from the unlikeliest stroke of luck you could well imagine.

"A witness was found to prove that the husband was near the scene of the crime within ten minutes or so of the critical moment. He was the prisoner's gardener, and he had no business to be there at all at that hour. His presence was due solely to the fact that his wife had scalded herself by upsetting a kettle and he was on his way to telephone for the doctor. Result: the alibi which the defence tried to set up was blown to bits, and the husband was hanged. His conviction, of course, deprived him of all his rights in the deceased's estate and he died as penniless as he had lived. You may say, then, that Pugh lost ten thousand pounds just because somebody else's gardener's wife was a bit clumsy taking the kettle off the hob. Oh, he was unlucky all right! So, when you come to think of it, was the chap who was convicted."

There was a long pause, and then Hobson's host said, "By the way, what was the husband's name? I don't think you mentioned it."

Hobson didn't seem to have heard the question. He was looking at his watch. "Heavens! I'd no idea it was so late!" he exclaimed. "I've a train to catch at Victoria. Do you mind if I rush away now, old man?"

His departure broke up the party, and as I am not fond of late hours I took the opportunity to thank Prothero for a pleasant evening and made my way out. As I went, I caught sight of Wrestall, looking, it seemed to me, distinctly thoughtful. I found Hobson outside the club hunting for a taxi. As I may have indicated, I had not taken to the man very much, but I had my car round the corner and Victoria was on my way home, so it seemed only decent to offer him a lift.

"I suppose the husband in your story was Sylvester Kemball?" I asked, as we took the corner by Marlborough House.

"Oh yes," said Hobson complacently.

"And his execution was a complete miscarriage of justice! How horrible!"

"Oh, you needn't waste any pity on *him*. He deserved all he got. His treatment of his wife alone merited hanging."

"You seem to know a lot about him," I observed.

"Well, she was my aunt. The only relation I had in the world."

I said no more until we were passing Buckingham Palace.

"When did you come to learn the truth about your aunt's murderer?" I asked him.

"About halfway through Kemball's trial," said Hobson calmly. "I knew Pugh fairly well, and I used to discuss the evidence with him. One evening we were dining together and he got a bit tight. He slipped out something that he hadn't meant to say and I broke him down. He told me the whole story."

"What on earth did you do?"

"Nothing at all. I looked at it this way: Kemball was every bit as bad as a murderer. I think he would probably have killed my aunt anyway, if Pugh hadn't got in first. And hanging Pugh wouldn't have done her any good. Besides, I couldn't afford to see him hanged."

"What do you mean?" Thank heaven, Victoria was just ahead. I could hardly bear the man's presence any longer.

"Well, I was a poor man, and I was my aunt's next of kin. If Kemball was acquitted it meant that her will leaving everything to him was good. If he was convicted, I scooped the pool. I am sure my dear aunt would have preferred to have it that way."

I stopped the car with a quite unnecessary jerk. Hobson got out.

"Thanks for the lift," he said. "Perhaps I shall see you again some day. I'm putting up for election to the Progress, by the way."

I wondered, as I drove home, whether I ought to warn Prothero about this candidate for his club. I decided not to do so. After all, I am not a member.

Guy de Maupassant

A FAIR EXCHANGE

★

M. Bontram, the celebrated Parisian advocate who for the last ten years had obtained many separations between badly matched husbands and wives, opened the door of his office and stood back to allow a new client to enter.

He was a large, red man, with close, blond whiskers, a corpulent man, full-blooded and vigorous. He bowed.

"Take a seat," said the advocate.

The client was seated and, after some hemming, said:

"I came to ask you, sir, to plead a divorce case for me."

"Speak, sir," said the advocate, "I am listening."

"I am, sir, an old notary."

"Already!"

"Yes, already. I am thirty-seven years of age."

"Continue."

"Sir, I have made an unfortunate marriage, very unfortunate."

"You are not the only one."

"I know it, and I pity the others. But my case is entirely different, and my complaint against my wife is of a very particular nature. I will commence at the marriage rite. I was married in strange fashion. Do you believe in dangerous ideas?"

"What do you mean by that?"

"Do you believe that certain ideas are as dangerous for the mind as poison is to the body?"

"Well, yes, perhaps."

"It is certain. There are ideas which enter into us, corrode us, and kill us or render us mad, if we do not know how to resist them.

They are a sort of poison to the soul. If we have the misfortune to allow one of these thoughts to glide in upon us, if we do not perceive at the beginning that it is an invader, a mistress, a tyrant, then it will extend itself hour by hour and day by day, will keep returning and finally install itself, driving out all ordinary occupation of our minds, absorbing our attention, changing our views and our judgment until we are lost.

"That is what happened to me, sir. As I have told you, I am a notary at Rouen, not poor but in straitened circumstances, full of care, forced to a constant economy, obliged to limit my tastes, yes, in everything! And it is hard, at my age.

"As a notary, I read, with great care, the advertisements on four pages of the newspapers, the wants, offers, little correspondence, etc., etc., and I had been enabled sometimes by this means to make advantageous marriages for my clients.

"One day I fell upon this:

" '*A pretty girl, fashionable, well brought up, would marry honourable gentleman and bring him two million five hundred thousand francs, clear. No agencies.*'

"On that very day I dined with two friends, one an attorney and the other the proprietor of a spinning mill. I don't know how the conversation turned to marriages, but I told them, laughing, about the pretty young lady with the two million five hundred thousand francs.

"The spinner said: 'What can these women be thinking of?'

"The attorney affirmed that he had several times seen excellent marriages made under these conditions, and gave some details. Then he added, turning to me: 'Why the devil don't you look this up for yourself? Jove! that would drive away care, two million five hundred thousand francs.'

"We all three laughed over it and then spoke of other things. An hour later I returned home.

"It grew cold that night. Besides, I lived in an old house, one of those old houses of the provinces which resemble mushroom-beds. In taking hold of the iron balustrade of the staircase, a coldness penetrated my arm, and as I put out the other to find the wall, in coming in contact with it, a second shiver enveloped me, joining with the other in my lungs, filling me with pain, with sadness, and weakness. And, seized by a sudden remembrance, I murmured: 'Gad! if only I had the two million five hundred thousand!'

"My room was dreary, the room of a bachelor in Rouen, which is taken care of by a maid who is also in charge of the kitchen. You know that kind of room! A great bed without curtains, a wardrobe, a commode, and a dressing-table; no fire. Some coats were on the chairs, papers on the floor. I began to sing, to the air of a concert-hall tune that I frequently heard about that time:

" '*Two millions, two millions*
Are fine,
With five hundred thousand
And woman divine.'

"In fact I had not yet thought about the woman, but I thought of her then as I was sliding into my bed. I even thought of her so much that I was a long time getting to sleep.

"Then next day, on opening my eyes, I remembered that I ought to be at Darnetal at eight o'clock on important business. To do this I must be up at six—and it was cold! Only think of two million five hundred thousand!

"I returned to my study about ten o'clock. In it was the odour of the red-hot stove, of old papers, with the papers of advance proceedings—nothing can equal these—and an odour of clerks—boots, overcoats, hair and skin, skin in winter, too little bathed, and all heated to seventy degrees.

"I breakfasted, as I do every day, on a cutlet and a piece of cheese. Then I put myself to work. For the first time, I then began to think seriously of the pretty young lady with the two million five hundred thousand. Who was she? Why not write to her? Why not find out?

"Finally, sir, to abridge, for two weeks this idea haunted me, possessed me, and tortured me. All my little cares and troubles, of which I had plenty but had thought little about before this time, began to sting me now like the sharp points of needles, and each of my sufferings made me think still more of the pretty young lady with the two millions.

"I ended by imagining all her history. When one desires a thing, sir, he is very apt to figure it as he hopes it to be. Certainly it was not natural that a young girl of good family, dowered in such a generous fashion, should be seeking a husband by means of the newspapers. Yet, it might be that this girl was honourable but unhappy.

"Then, at first this fortune of two million five hundred thousand had not struck me as anything fairylike. We are accustomed, we who read the offers of this nature, to propositions of marriage accompanied by six, eight, ten, or even twelve millions. The figure of twelve millions is common enough. It pleases. I know well that we can scarcely believe the validity of these promises. They, however, make us enter into the spirit of fantastic numbers, render probable, up to a certain point in our listless credulity, the prodigious sums which they represent and dispose us to consider a dowry of two million five hundred thousand as very possible and right.

"Then a young girl, the natural child of a rich man and a chambermaid, having suddenly inherited from her father, could have learned at the same time of the stain upon her birth, and in order not to have to reveal it to some man whom she might have loved, she might make an appeal to the unknown by this means, which carries in itself a sort of avowal of defect.

"My supposition was stupid. I believed in it, nevertheless. We notaries ought never to read romances, but I read one in this, sir.

"Then I wrote, as a notary, in the name of a client, and I waited. Five days later, towards three o'clock in the afternoon, when I was hard at work in my office, the chief clerk announced:

" 'Mlle. Chantefrise.'

" 'Let her come in.'

"There appeared a woman about thirty, a little stout, dark, and somewhat embarrassed.

" 'Be seated, Mademoiselle.'

"She sat down and murmured: 'It is I, sir.'

" 'But I have not the honour of knowing you.'

" 'The person to whom you wrote.'

" 'About a marriage?'

" 'Yes, sir.'

" 'Ah! very well!'

" 'I have come myself because I thought it better to attend to those things in person.'

" 'I am of your opinion, Mademoiselle. And so you desire to marry?'

" 'Yes, sir.'

" 'You have some family?'

"She hesitated, lowered her eyes, and stammered: 'No, sir. My mother and my father—are dead.'

"I started. Then I had guessed right—and a lively sympathy was suddenly awakened in my heart for this poor creature. I could not altogether spare her delicacy of feeling and I inquired:

" 'Your fortune is in your own right?'

"She responded this time without hesitating: 'Oh! yes, sir!'

"I looked at her with close attention and truly she did not displease me, only a little hard, harder than I would have liked. She was a beautiful person, a strong person, a masterly woman. And the idea came to me of playing with her a little comedy of sentiment, of becoming her lover, of supplanting my imaginary client, when I was once assured that the dowry was not illusory. I spoke to her of this client whom I depicted as a sad man, very honourable, but a little of an invalid.

"She said vivaciously: 'Oh! sir, I love people to be well.'

" 'But you will see him—only not for three or four days, because he left for England yesterday.'

" 'Oh! how annoying,' she replied.

" 'Well, yes and no. Are you in a hurry to return home?'

" 'Not at all.'

" 'Then stay here, and I will attempt to make the time pass pleasantly for you.'

" 'You are very amiable, sir.'

" 'You are at some hotel?'

"She named the best hotel in Rouen.

" 'Well, then, Mademoiselle Chantefrise, will you permit your future—notary to offer to take you to dinner this evening?'

"She appeared to hesitate, seemed disturbed, and undecided. Then she said: 'Yes, sir.'

" 'I will be at your hotel at seven o'clock.'

" 'Yes, sir.'

" 'Then until this evening, Mademoiselle?'

" 'Yes, sir.'

"And I conducted her as far as my door.

"At seven o'clock I was at her hotel. She had made a fresh toilette for me and received me in a very coquettish fashion. I took her to dine in a restaurant where I was known and ordered a troublesome *menu*. An hour later we were very friendly and she had told me her story.

"She was the daughter of a great lady seduced by a gentleman, and she had been brought up among peasants. She was rich now, having inherited large sums from her father and from her mother, whose name she would never divulge, never. It was useless to ask it of her, useless to beg, she would never tell it. As I cared little to know these things, I asked about her fortune. She spoke about it like a practical woman, sure of herself, sure of her figures, of her titles, of her income, her interest, and investments. Her understanding of these matters gave me great confidence in her, and I became gallant, with some reserve, nevertheless. But I showed her clearly that I had a liking for her.

"She affected an excessive refinement, not without grace. I offered her some champagne, and I drank some, which blurred my ideas. I then felt clearly that I was going to be entrapped, and I was afraid, afraid of myself and afraid of her, afraid that she was not moved and that she would not succumb. In order to calm myself, I began again to speak to her of her fortune, saying that it would be necessary to precisely understand matters, since my client was a man of affairs.

"She answered with gaiety: 'Oh! I know. I have brought all the proofs.'

" 'Here, to Rouen?'

" 'Yes, to Rouen.'

" 'You have them at the hotel?'

" 'Yes, I have them all there.'

" 'Could you show them to me?'

" 'Yes, indeed.'

" 'This evening?'

" 'Yes, indeed.'

"That pleased me in every way. I paid the score and we went back to the hotel. She had, in fact, brought all her certificates. I could not doubt them, for I held them in my hands, felt them, and read them. They put such a joy in my heart that I suddenly felt a violent desire to embrace her. I understood this as a chaste desire, the desire of a contented man. And I did embrace her, in fact, once, twice, ten times—so much that—with the aid of the champagne—I succumbed—or rather—no—she succumbed.

"Ah! sir, I had a head after that, and she! She wept like a fountain, begging me not to expose her or she should be lost. I promised all that she wished, and I myself got into a terrible state of mind.

"What was to be done? I had abused my client's confidence. That would not have been so bad if I had had a client for her, but I had none. I was the client, the simple client, the deceived client, and deceived by herself. What a situation! I could let her go, it is true. But the dowry, the handsome dowry, the good dowry, palpable and sure! And then, had I the right to let her go, the poor girl, after having thus surprised her? But what of the disquiet later on? How much security would one have with a woman who thus yielded?

"I passed a terrible night of indecision, tortured by remorse, ravaged by fears, buffeted by every scruple. But in the morning my reason cleared. I dressed myself with care, and, as eleven o'clock struck, presented myself at the hotel where she was staying.

"On seeing me she blushed to the eyes. I said to her: 'Mademoiselle Chantefrise, there is only one thing to do to repair the wrong. I ask your hand in marriage.'

"She murmured: 'I give it to you.'

"I married her and all went well for six months. I had given up my office and lived as a stockholder, and truly I had not a reproach, not a single fault to find with my wife.

"Then I noticed that, from time to time, she made long visits.

This happened on a certain day, one week Tuesday, the next week Wednesday. I began to believe myself deceived and I followed her. It was on a Tuesday. She went out on foot about one o'clock into Republic street, turned to the right, by the street which follows the archiepiscopal palace, and took Great-Bridge street to the Seine, followed the wharf up to Peter's bridge and crossed the water. From this moment she appeared disturbed, turning around often and looking sharply at all passers.

"As I was dressed like a coal driver she did not know me. Finally, she entered a dock on the left bank. I no longer doubted that her lover would arrive on the one forty-five train.

"I seated myself behind a dray and waited. A blow of the whistle —a crowd of passengers. She advanced, rushed forward, seized in her arms a little girl of three years, whom a large peasant accompanied, and embraced her with passion. Then she turned, perceived another child, younger, either girl or boy, it might be, carried by another nurse, threw herself upon it, drew it to her with violence, and went along escorted by the two monkeys and the two nurses towards the long, sombre, deserted promenade of the Queen's Course.

"I returned home dismayed, distressed in mind, comprehending and still not comprehending, nor daring to guess. When she returned for dinner, I threw these words at her:

" 'Whose children are those?'

" 'What children?' she asked.

" 'Those that you waited at the Saint-Sever train for.'

"She gave a great cry and fainted. When she returned to consciousness she confessed to me, in a deluge of tears, that she had four. Yes, sir, two for Tuesday, two girls, and two for Wednesday, two boys.

"And this was—what shame! this was the origin of her fortune. The four fathers! She had amassed her dowry! Now, sir, what do you advise me to do?"

The advocate replied with gravity: "Recognise your children, sir."

Louis Auchincloss

THE GREAT WORLD OF TIMOTHY COLT

★

Timothy Colt, when I first met him, was the most promising law clerk in Everett & Coates. He was then thirty-three, four years older than myself, with one foot already poised to take the final step to partnership, that goal to which our energies were consecrated and which would remove him forever from the bare, cream-painted rooms of the associates, hung with *Vanity Fair* cartoons of British judges and solicitors, to the panelled offices, albeit at first the smallest, of the members of the firm. He had the rather haggard, if handsome looks of the overworked young man who is not, however, working in vain; his face was thin, pale and cerebral, his eyes large and dark, with an appraising, noncommittal, faintly amused look. His hair was thick and shiningly black, and he had a habit of tugging at it that kept it boyishly out of place. There were moments, indeed, when he reminded me of a romantic portrait of the early last century, fragile and wide-eyed, bent over a book in a Gothic study, the fingertips of one hand resting on the head of a devoted retriever, but it was an impression soon dispelled by his own wholly sincere unawareness that his looks were any but those of a typical downtown law clerk. He had come into the firm originally under the auspices of Mr. Hazard, for whose four small daughters he had once been a summer tutor.

"It was after my second year at Columbia law," Timmy told me once, "and I really was dog-tired. But I had to have the money, and at least it was outdoors work, tennis and riding, things like that. And then Hazard discovered I'd written a note for the law review on a case he'd argued in the Appellate Division. Jesus!" He shook his head. "That really did it. We worked on a new brief for the Court of Appeals all of August, and another tutor had to be sent up for the girls. It damn near killed me, but it was worth it. It cinched me a job in Everett & Coates."

It was like Timmy to assume that he was more indebted to the chance interest of a senior partner than to his own capabilities. I knew otherwise, after six months as his principal assistant. We worked at least four nights a week and all of Saturday, and before we were through my social life had virtually ceased to exist. The outer world, in fact, had fallen away so completely that its infrequent manifestations, the letters in my mailbox at night, the occasional telegram with a holiday greeting, seemed oddly irrelevant, and I was perfectly happy of a Saturday evening simply to go to the Colts' and discuss with them over many drinks what Timmy and I had been doing all week. Of course, it was shop talk, shop talk with a vengeance, but somehow there didn't seem much point in discussing the books we hadn't had time to read or the people we hadn't seen. Fortunately for Flora Colt, she, too, had gone to law school.

"I sat next to Timmy in every class our first year," she explained to me on one such evening. "My name, you see, was Coleman, which came just before Colt. I used to think what a waste of time it was for people like me to be studying law when people like him were. I guess the only reason I lasted as long as I did was that I was afraid of losing hold of him if I busted out!"

She was certainly the perfect wife for Timmy, utterly content with the restricted life that his late hours imposed. She ran her apartment and took care of her two small noisy boys with an air of rather amiable inefficiency, filling in her spare time, when there was any, with eclectic if rather indiscriminate reading, with crosswords and double acrostics, even with radio serials. Flora could read Mauriac and *Screen Romances* almost simultaneously and, I sometimes suspected, with equal satisfaction. However late Timmy's key turned in the lock, she was never more than barely ready for him, but when she saw him and smiled, with the smile that made up so fully for her large, over-serious features, her undisciplined blonde hair, her constant habit of wearing brown, the evening was all his.

The other things, the books, the radio, even the little boys, were firmly if affectionately relegated to second place. Flora's heart was so big that it was hard to believe, as one did believe, that Timmy could occupy all of it.

On one of those Saturday nights at Timmy's, with just the three of us present, he was holding forth on the virtues of Sam Liendecker, a new client whom I had not met.

"Liendecker, Liendecker!" Flora interrupted. "All I hear now is Liendecker! I sometimes wonder," she continued, turning to me, "if I wouldn't rather lose Timmy to a blonde."

"Mr. Liendecker is a very able man, darling," Timmy reminded her. "He got American Export & Canning out of the red in five years' time. Their common was selling at ten when he took over, and it's now quoted at one thirty-five. Which I think even you will admit, Flora, is grounds for admiration."

I couldn't help glancing at the hole in the arm of the sofa that had been burned by a cigarette three months before. Or at one of the boy's trolleys under the sideboard that had been there the preceding week and would certainly be there the next. I was sure Timmy never noticed such things.

"Why do you admire success so, Timmy?" I asked him.

"Don't we all?"

"Not the way you do. No matter what sort of an ogre a man may be, you always think you can shut me and Flora up by pointing out that he's a success."

Timmy laughed quickly, rather too quickly as he was apt to when conversation became personal.

"Isn't that what's made this country great?"

"Is it? And, anyway, what of it?"

"Well, of course, Peter, if you're just going to say 'What of it' to everything——" he was beginning.

"You don't see what I mean," I interrupted. "If a thing is there, it's there. We accept it. But I thought we only admired what we wanted ourselves. What do successful men have that you want?"

"Why, he wants what everyone else wants," Flora intervened. "A bigger car and a bigger apartment——"

"But he doesn't," I protested, turning around to her, "that's just the point. And what do *you* get out of all his work, Flora? Do you have a mink coat? Or a house by the seashore? Or even a country club? Good God, woman, what do you live for?"

Flora's sense of humour, never the keenest, would desert her altogether after three drinks.

"Now just a minute, Peter Westcott," said she, pointing her finger at me, "it's going to take time before Timmy's in a position to buy me those things. But that's not the point. The point is, he gives me everything I want, right now. Everything in the world!"

"Everything?" I queried. "No nurse? No private school for the boys?"

"Timmy and I went to public school here in New York!" Flora exclaimed indignantly, moving over to her husband and putting her arm around his shoulders. "And we don't happen to feel that either of our boys is going to faint away if he finds himself sitting next to a coloured child."

Timmy joined in my happy burst of laughter.

"Flora, darling," he said, patting the hand that was on his shoulder, "he's only kidding you."

"Well, I don't like that kind of kidding."

"But I'm not criticising, Flora," I pointed out. "I think it's fine to be like you and Timmy. Never keeping up with the Joneses. Not even bothering to move out of this housing development. Which you could certainly afford to do now."

"Could we?" Timmy looked at his wife and smiled. "What *do* you do with the money, darling?"

"But if all you want," I continued, "is to be a slave at the office while Flora looks at television——"

"Television!" she exclaimed. "I wish *you* had two children to take care of, Peter!"

"What," I finished imperturbably, "can the great world offer you as a prize?"

"Does it never occur to you, Peter," Timmy demanded, "that the satisfaction of a job well done might be a sufficient reward in itself?"

Well, it might have been for him. I didn't know. But I did know what a different person he was in the office. The moment he crossed the reception hall of Everett & Coates his face assumed a grave, sometimes almost a grim expression. This was where one worked, and to confuse, even briefly, the place where one worked and the place where one played would obviously not do. None of the younger men ever dropped into Timmy's office during the day to smoke a cigarette or to gossip; he would listen politely enough to anyone who did so, for he was always polite, but his nervous, abstracted glances at the papers on his desk soon showed his visitor how little the intrusion was appreciated. At the time of our talk about success he was busier than ever before, working on the purchase by American Export & Canning of a new plant in New Jersey. It was an important deal, yet no partner had been assigned to it, and the rumour had already got around the office that it was to be Timmy's big test. Certainly I had never seen him set so stiff a pace; I was like a mountain climber lashed by a rope to my leader and uncomfortably picking my way after him as he kept disappearing into the mists above. It didn't occur to me that there was anyone else ahead of him in those regions of thin air whom he in turn might be following until one morning in his office I found him talking to a tall thin man who raised a pair of appraising eyes to examine me.

"Oh, Peter," Timmy said immediately, "this is Mr. Liendecker," He turned to the client. "Peter Westcott, sir, who is also working on the deal."

"Westcott," Mr. Liendecker repeated with a brief nod in my direction, as I sat down in the remaining chair. He made no move to shake hands, but, turning back to Timmy, simply resumed the conversation that I had interrupted. I noted with interest his long, angular, pale pink face and smooth, light grey hair. His lips were dry and almost flesh-coloured; they bore a determination that might have been half stubbornness, half pride. He was dressed in the grey which, like his eyes and hair, seemed his motif, with expensive brown suede shoes and a pink shirt. But what I couldn't take my eyes off was his tie. It was a silk tie, covered with blue and green bubbles that apparently represented the sea, for between them, in brilliant purple, were woven various manifestations of marine life, here a fin, there a tail, now even a pair of shark-like jaws, all leading the eye down from the green knot to the coiled sea monster which crouched at the wide lower section. It was not that the tie was exactly ugly; it might have been sufficiently startling as a modern chintz. It was simply that as a tie it seemed somehow defiant. It defied Timmy; it defied me; it defied even Everett & Coates and the very view of New York harbour from Timmy's window. As Mr. Liendecker sat back in his chair with the rather ominous immobility of the highly strung, I felt in his eyes and fingers, when he allowed himself to touch that tie, not only a taking it for granted that anyone who could would buy such a tie, but a challenge, faintly sneering, to any contrary-minded to tell him, Sam Liendecker, why.

"It's not as if I was asking for the final contract," he was saying in a flat voice. "It's only a draft that I want. Why can't you let me have a draft to show these people over the weekend?"

"Because once they've seen a draft they'll never let us add anything to it," Timmy explained patiently. "We'll show it to them on Monday, sir, and that's a week earlier than they expected it."

"But what's holding it up now?"

"I believe Peter's making a final check," Timmy replied, looking up at me, "on whether or not the executors need a court order before selling the plant."

Mr. Liendecker turned on me.

"Do they?"

"Well—if the will had contained the usual powers of sale——" I was beginning, startled.

"No, no," he interrupted roughly. "Don't give me that legal double talk. I want an opinion. If an executor doesn't have the power to sell a dead man's property, what *does* he have the power to do?"

"Well, he undoubtedly has the power, but if——"

"There! I thought so!"

He turned back to Timmy triumphantly. The latter, expressionless, stared down for a few moments at the blotter on his desk.

"I know all the probabilities, sir," he said quietly, without looking up. "I know perfectly well that an executor ordinarily has that power. But there are special circumstances here. Maybe I'm being overcareful, but you pay us for care. If I give it up to you now, sir, it won't be right. I can't take the responsibility."

"I see," said Mr. Liendecker, spreading his thin hands over the arms of his chair and half closing his eyes. "But is there really any reason why you *should* take such a responsibility? Isn't that a question for a member of the firm? For Hazard, himself, for example?"

Timmy flushed and looked down at his desk.

"Possibly so. You can, of course, see Mr. Hazard any time you choose."

"Naturally," Mr. Liendecker retorted, opening his eyes with a snap. "He's my lawyer, isn't he? What I want to know is whether *you* don't feel that you could profit by his advice in this matter? Whether *you* don't want to consult him?"

Timmy passed his hand over his mouth and looked across the room at me without seeming to take me in.

"I'm doing my best, sir," he said.

"You feel entirely adequate, then, to the situation?"

"I hope so."

"Then we're all set," Mr. Liendecker said, looking at me with a bland, sarcastic half-smile. "That's all I wanted to find out." He rose at this and sauntered out, carelessly picking his hat from Timmy's out-basket as he passed. I looked at Timmy for a moment, but he avoided my glance.

"Well, I'll be damned!" I exclaimed. "What's eating him?"

"He's only miffed that he doesn't have a partner on the deal," Timmy explained, almost apologetically. "I can't blame him, really. I'd feel the same way with six million bucks at stake."

"Oh, you would! Well, it so happens that you're better than any partner on this kind of deal. Anyone around here could tell him that."

"Peter," Timmy protested with a sigh, "we've got a job to do. Must we worry about the personality of the client?"

"Can't I even express an opinion? To you?"

"You don't know Liendecker, Peter. He's a man who's come up the hard way. When he took over American Export——"

"Oh, I know all that," I interrupted roughly. "When Hitler took over Germany things were in tough shape."

"Sam Liendecker is hardly a Hitler, Peter," Timmy said mildly.

"That's because you see him from the point of view of a storm trooper," I retorted. "*I* see him from the point of view of the concentration camp!"

As our work went into the drafting stage and I spent more time in Timmy's office, I became even more acutely aware of Mr. Liendecker's personality. He was one of those quiet, motionless men whose presence is as powerful as a strong scent. He would drop in at any time in the morning or afternoon and sit in the armchair, quietly smoking his gold-tipped cigarettes and reading over any documents that happened to be on Timmy's desk. He expected us to go on with our work and ignore him except when he asked questions which he would throw out, always with the same faint note of surprise, his eyes on the paper he was reading, questions that, no matter how many of us happened to be in the room, were always answered, and evidently intended to be answered, by Timmy alone. The latter's response, however disagreeable the question, however many times it had been asked before, was invariably slow, patient and exact. If he ever wanted to raise his voice or slam the door behind Mr. Liendecker's retreating back, he never gave in to the impulse. His conduct, so far as I could see, was perfect, exasperatingly perfect.

Mr. Liendecker, oddly enough, did not extend his obvious hostility to Timmy to the rest of us. He showed towards me, for example, a rather surly geniality and addressed me, when he was in one of his better moods, as "Sonny". Once he even took me out to lunch and questioned me about the office's attitude towards Timmy. At his club, high above the Hudson in an alcove of glass, he might have been showing me the kingdoms of the earth.

"Everyone thinks Timmy's doing a bang-up job," I said stoutly. "Don't you agree?"

"He's got a few things to learn," Mr. Liendecker answered coolly. "What gets a man ahead in this world is knowing how people tick and what they want. You don't learn that by holing yourself up in a two-by-four office and changing commas into semicolons."

"But Timmy's not supposed to deal with people," I pointed out. "He's supposed to draft the papers."

Mr. Liendecker grunted.

"He's supposed to deal with me, isn't he?"

I had no answer to a remark so extraordinary, but it helped me to understand how difficult a problem Timmy was up against. For what Liendecker apparently resented was the intrusion into his field of anything that he couldn't handle himself, the law, in this instance, with its requirements of paper and precautions. He should have been offered the services of a senior partner whose eminence might have done something to allay his own sense of inferiority. This way it was hopeless. There was no means except by flattery to handle the chip on Liendecker's shoulder, and the very view that he took of Timmy precluded recourse to that.

"I don't think he'll find you hard to deal with, sir," I said, "if you'll only give him half a chance."

If I had hoped, after this, that relations between Timmy and his suspicious client would be improved, I was soon disillusioned. Two days later we were summoned to Mr. Hazard's office for a progress report on the American Export deal, and as we traversed the wide corridor past the black-framed photographs of long-deceased partners, Timmy shook his head gloomily.

"It's bad news," he said. "It's always bad news when Hazard's secretary makes the call."

Henry Knox Hazard, now that Mr. Coates was dead and Mr. Everett so old, was the managing partner of the firm. He was the gentleman who told you if you got your raise each new year, calling in the associates one by one to do so, with a brief congratulatory nod of his head and the flash of a grin that had more charm than you thought it was going to. He was a big, rather magnificent man with a tremendous head and shoulders towering over a body that tapered gradually down, under richly heavy and aristocratically unpressed tweeds, to a pair of long thin legs and formidably shined shoes. He listened now to Timmy with many head noddings, his eyes fixed on the thin ankle that was resting on one knee. When he picked a cigarette out of his vest pocket, Timmy, without pausing in what he had to say, without seeming even to have noticed, casually snapped his lighter and reached it over. The gesture, simple as it was, was somehow expressive of their mutual confidence.

"I see, I see," Mr. Hazard said when Timmy had finished. "It looks as if we ought to close on schedule, doesn't it? Good. There's only one thing more." He paused, but as one pauses who has planned to isolate and emphasise his final point. "Sam Liendecker dropped in yesterday. He seems to have an idea that he's not getting the service he wants. What are you doing, Timmy? Doping off ?"

I glanced at Timmy but there was no sign of a smile on his suddenly flushed face.

"Was that his expression, sir?" he asked. "Doping off ?"

"It was certainly his implication."

"If you'll look at the time sheets," Timmy said in a choked voice, "I think they'll reassure you. Peter and I went home at three o'clock this morning."

Mr. Hazard simply nodded and then opened a blueprint on his desk. He spread it carefully over his blotter, smoothing down the corners.

"He's been having your real estate descriptions checked at American Export. Here, for example." He tapped the blueprint with his paper cutter. "He claims that this sliver, two hundred square feet, is missing from the proposed deed."

Timmy stood motionless for a moment before leaning over the desk. Then, without a word and ignoring Mr. Hazard, he handed me the deed.

"Read from there," he said, pointing to a paragraph. When I had finished he looked up and shook his head several times. Mr. Hazard smiled.

"How about it, Timmy? Is Liendecker right?"

"Apparently, sir. It looks like a hack."

"Then I take it you *have* been doping off?"

There was a heavy pause.

"Yes, sir," Timmy said in a barely audible tone. "It looks as if I've been doping off."

Mr. Hazard threw back his head and uttered a deep, gravelly laugh. Then he stood up suddenly and put an arm round Timmy's shoulders.

"Do you know what I told him, Timmy boy?" he exclaimed. "I told him if he'd complained about any other man in the office, myself included, I'd have run a check. But not on Timmy Colt. No, sir."

With his free hand he brushed the blueprint aside. "Hell, we all make mistakes. You'd have picked that one up ten times over before the final draft."

But Timmy only shook his head stubbornly.

"I think it's unwarranted to assume that, sir."

Mr. Hazard removed his protecting arm.

"What's wrong with you, anyway?" he asked with a touch of sharpness. "Have you lost your sense of humour?"

Timmy, to my horror, turned on him.

"How about Liendecker's sense of humour?" he asked, almost savagely. "He hasn't lost his by any chance, has he?"

Mr. Hazard raised his eyebrows and gave a low whistle.

"You'd better get back to your office, my boy," he said in a warning tone. "And do a little hard thinking about what happens to people who take themselves too seriously."

When I followed Timmy out of the door I knew that the job had ceased to be a job. It had become an issue of infinitely larger dimensions.

"Liendecker's got me this time," he said grimly as we retraversed the long corridor. "But I'll see him in Hell before he catches me again!"

"He's worried about his six million," I quoted back to him. "You can't blame him, really. I think I'd feel the same way."

Timmy, however, was beyond the stage of being kidded.

"I'm going to get out all the papers in this God-damn deal," he continued, "and recheck every last one of them."

The waste of it, after all we'd done, appalled me.

"What does it matter what that guy thinks of you, Timmy?" I protested. "It's what Hazard thinks that counts. You know you're square with him."

He simply looked at me as if I couldn't know what I was saying and turned off into the library. More than his humour had deserted him; his sense of proportion was gone. In the next few days he turned into a grim, driven creature who lived on sandwiches and coffee in a paper-cluttered office that he never seemed to leave. One night he didn't even go home, and when Flora came down in the morning to check up she found him asleep at his desk. After she had waked him and sent him to the washroom to shave, she came to my office.

"We've got to do something, Peter!" she exclaimed. "We've got to stop him. He's killing himself!"

"The job's almost over, Flora," I reminded her. "Take it easy."

"But this Liendecker's a fiend! Do you *know* that?"

I shrugged.

"I guess that's as good a term as any."

"And do you know *why* he's a fiend?" She leaned forward, both elbows now on my desk, her eyes glaring at me. "Because he sees Timmy the way Timmy sees himself! As sloppy and shiftless and no good!"

I stared.

"Is *that* the way Timmy sees himself?"

"Certainly it is!" she exclaimed. "The only way he gets through any job is with constant pats on the back. He's like a child, Peter. But just let one man like Liendecker get at him—well, it's the end. He'll take that man's opinion of himself against all the world!"

I sat looking out the window after she had left and pondered her concept of Liendecker as a devil especially created to prod poor Timmy at his vulnerable point. I thought of him in Timmy's office, watching him with the eye that seemed to anticipate error, dropping dry little reminders about the error in the deed and expressing and re-expressing his hope that all this "paper work" was not going to cost him his deal. It almost seemed to me that Flora might be right, that he and Timmy were like two cogged wheels, meshed to each other and moving ahead with a grim acceleration that must surely end in the destruction of one. But what could we do? It was a form of self-destruction that was eminently respectable.

Yet it ended and nothing terrible seemed to have happened. We closed on schedule, and the closing itself was as simple as the preparations had been complicated. There were twenty of us sitting about the long table in the conference room of Everett & Coates, each with a large manila envelope which we opened on a given signal, transferring the previously executed documents to and fro between ourselves in accordance with a rehearsed pattern. It was like a

Japanese comedy, a crazy pantomime as the finale of six weeks' madness. When it was over Mr. Liendecker himself walked slowly around the table and shook each of us, starting with Timmy, by the hand.

That night Liendecker gave a party for the people in his office and ours who had worked on the deal. I dined with Timmy and Flora at the Hazards', and we all went on to the Liendeckers' together. Their vast apartment, overlooking the East River, was a decorator's delight; its proprietors must have made a clean sweep of all former possessions before settling down to this harmony of grey and blue, of long low curving sofas and Mexican pottery and cream-coloured tables with tiny legs. The guests, mostly from the company, moved timidly around in couples as they had come. Mrs. Liendecker, a small, nervous woman, hurried about ineffectually, asking people what they wanted to drink, while her husband stood aloof by the fireplace surrounded by a respectful half-circle of younger men. It struck me that Mr. Hazard, with his broad teeth-baring grin, greeting the younger officers of American Export with a grip on the arm or shoulder, an approach of his large head and a snap of the eyelids, and his wife serenely following, almost a Roman matron in her plain grey evening dress, with her plain grey unwaved hair, seemed much more the host and hostess. They moved as easily through the constrained atmosphere of the room as though the Liendeckers had been their oldest friends and office parties their daily fare, yet I knew from dinner that Mrs. Hazard had only come when her husband had warned her, with just a hint of the peremptory behind his smile: "I think it might help, dear. These people are touchy." I wondered, if one's manners were good enough and one's belief in oneself sufficient, whether there might be no such thing in the world as compromise.

I walked with Timmy over to the bar table. He was extremely moody, and we had both been drinking steadily since our arrival at the Hazards' an hour before dinner.

"Well, it's over," I said.

"It's over," he agreed gloomily. "And you can say it now. Go ahead. I'm a martinet. I'm a fuss-budget."

"You're a martinet. You're a fuss-budget," I said obediently.

He gave me a bleak look.

"But we got it finished, didn't we? And finished right?"

"We got it finished," I repeated. "And finished right."

"Oh, go soak your head," he retorted.

I left him to his mood and crossed the room to where Flora was sitting alone on a beige sofa.

"Golly, what a ghastly party," she whispered. "Sit with me, Peter."

"You don't go out to sit with old friends," I reminded her.

"Don't you? I do."

"But you shouldn't. You should mingle."

"With this crowd?"

"It's good business," I said, sitting down. "Isn't this what business is?" I looked vaguely around at the looped yellow curtains, the long sofa opposite with its triangular pile of blue and white cushions. "Would you like to know what this room cost? I can tell you. I saw it in our files."

Flora looked severe. "Then you have no business telling people."

"But I *want* to tell you. I trust you." I looked at her as gravely as I could. "The responsibility of being the only one to know is too much for me."

Flora finally smiled, if a bit wearily.

"All right, Peter. How much?"

"Thirty thousand," I whispered. "Not, of course, including the flower painting in the corner. That's by Mrs. Liendecker herself and is, naturally, priceless."

"What a snob you are, Peter."

"It is you, Flora, who disdain to mingle."

"But that's different," she insisted. "These people aren't *me*. I don't understand them."

"You mean you don't like them," I corrected her.

"Well, really, Peter," she said indignantly, "what have I in common with a man who spends more on one room than I could spend on my family in three years?"

"What in common? Your husband, of course."

She puckered her brow at this, and I couldn't help smiling. It seemed so buried in the past already, the whole terrible job, and I almost felt that Mr. Liendecker's whisky made up for it, tingeing with a vaguely nostalgic quality the long rushed days behind.

"Well, we're through, anyway," she said with a sigh. "Drink to that with me, Peter. We're through with the whole damn thing." She clicked her glass against mine. "And he never blew up once, thank God."

Her tone made me look at her.

"What do you mean, Flora," I asked, "the *whole* damn thing?"

She hesitated.

"Why, the job, of course."

"Flora, I've seen you after too many of these jobs——" As I paused, staring at her, the light broke. "But of course! Timmy's been made a partner! That's it, isn't it!"

Flora turned very red and glanced quickly over in Mr. Hazard's direction.

"I never said that, Peter."

"You didn't have to! Can I congratulate him? I won't tell anyone."

"Peter!" She jumped up and put her hands on my shoulders to force me back on the sofa. "Listen, you idiot, he doesn't *know* yet! Mr. Hazard whispered it to me when we were coming up in the elevator. He promised me once that when it happened I'd be the first to know."

I stared.

"And when does he tell Timmy? Or doesn't he?"

"Tonight. After the party. Now, Peter, be an angel and hang on to your tongue. In fact, don't have any more to drink. You might leak it."

"Isn't that asking rather a lot? At a party?"

But I was not to know her answer, for at that moment we heard the sharp insistent tinkle of spoons against glasses and Mr. Liendecker's voice authoritatively calling for silence.

"Has everyone got a glass?" he demanded in the tone of a scoutmaster asking his boys if each has his knapsack. He paused to let the waiters recirculate with fresh trays. "Everyone must have a glass because it's bad luck not to join in a toast, and I want to propose one.

A toast to the boys who worked on the Jersey plant deal. They did a grand job, as I'm sure you all know—now just a second, just a second," he added testily as there were several "hear, hears" and glasses were prematurely raised. "First I want to tell you something about these fellas so you'll know what the hell you're drinking to." This reproach was followed by a mild, slightly nervous titter from the group. "It's only polite to start with the guys who aren't actually in the outfit, the lawyers and bakers and candlestick makers, and I guess the first one up to bat is Timmy Colt of Everett & Coates. I think most of you have met Timmy in the course of this deal, but I'm sure none of you have had a chance to observe him more closely than I have. We've been closeted together, Timmy and I, day after day and sometimes night after night, and I don't think I'm blowing my horn too loudly, Timmy, if I say that there were moments when even your young legal mind was glad to have the assistance of something a bit older and wiser. Isn't that so, Tim, my boy? We have to learn that theory isn't everything, don't we?"

Timmy was standing alone by the fireplace, one elbow resting on the edge of the mantel. He simply folded his arms across his chest and stared back at his host with expressionless eyes. I felt Flora's hand on my arm and the sudden intake of her breath.

"I hope we can take silence for assent," Mr. Liendecker continued briskly with an odd little gleam. "And I think I know our Timmy well enough to say that we can. I also think he knows how much we all appreciate the grand job that his firm has done and won't mind my telling you a little anecdote about how I caught him trying to save a bit of the new plant for the sellers." He paused with the tentative, anticipatory half-smile of one about to tell a funny story. "It was the kind of thing that could have happened to anyone, you understand, particularly after the pace we'd all been going at, and I'm only giving old Timmy a poke in the ribs. Well, anyway, it seems that when the deed was being drawn——"

I sat in a trance of fascinated hate as Mr. Liendecker picked his leisurely, tedious way through the tired old story of the missing fraction of an acre. My animosity, thanks to the scotch, seemed to have detached itself from my heart; it hung in the middle of the room, almost observable to myself, like a small black cloud over Mr.

Liendecker's head, as real and corporate as his malice had become to me. When I glanced about the room I could see that my reaction was not unshared; I caught the communal sense, in nervous movements and exchanged glances, of the unfitness of such an anecdote at such a time. But Liendecker, of course, didn't mind that; he might even have enjoyed it. He stood there with his small smile that had become a mixture of complacency and sarcasm, like a lion-tamer who cracks his whip with an easy, almost relaxed motion of the arm at the big demoralised cats that sit on stools around him, turning their heads away and opening their mouths in soundless snarls.

He had finished on a note that was again a jovial question to Timmy, some shabby disguise of good nature, and in the ensuing silence I heard Flora's agonised whisper in my ear.

"Dear God, this *is* the end. It really is."

And almost as she said it we heard Timmy's voice coming to us, cold and sarcastic, across the room, with only a slight tremble to show the passion behind his words.

"Mr. Liendecker has been good enough to recognise the individual nonentities behind the scenes. He shouldn't bother with them. What are they, after all, but hacks, as he has so easily demonstrated? If you must all drink toasts, drink them to Mr. Liendecker, his own financier, his own lawyer, his own priest, and if there's any justice in the after life—which I very much doubt—his own hell."

In the stupefied silence that followed this outburst Timmy marched across the room to the sofa where we were sitting.

"Come on, Flora," he said abruptly. "Let's get out of here."

She almost ran from the room ahead of him as conversation exploded nervously around their departing figures. Everybody suddenly spoke or filled a glass or lit a cigarette; they had rushed to their stations, like the disciplined crew of a suddenly foundering vessel, and could be counted on to wait, their life-jackets neatly tied, for the order to abandon ship. Above the clamour I could hear Mr. Liendecker's laugh, high and harsh, and I caught a glimpse of him, his arm around another man's shoulders, his head tilted back, surrendering to the apparent uncontrollability of his mirth and protesting, between loud gasps, that some people, particularly lawyers, could just *never* take a joke.

I turned in misery to the bar table and was well on my way through a double scotch when I heard Mrs. Hazard's voice behind me.

"Dear me, you young people must have strong heads to take those things."

I spun around and stared sullenly at her high, clear forehead. Even her husband could not have scared me now.

"Maybe I need them."

"Maybe," she said, smiling. There was no reproach, even implied, in her eyes.

"You think I should stop?"

It was wonderful how little my rudeness seemed to surprise her. "My arithmetic is simple. I think two scenes might be twice as bad as one."

"And you think I'm going to make another?"

"I think a good and loyal friend *might* make another, yes," she said with a little nod. "And I think it might be wise if we took the good and loyal friend home before he did."

She simply looked out of the window as if she cared for nothing as much as the vessels on the East River, while I stubbornly finished my drink. Then she turned towards the door, and I found myself following her, with a dumb surprise that she should so assume my obedience. In the hall we found Mr. Hazard, who had actually managed to discover my hat and coat, and in three more minutes we were moving rapidly uptown in a taxi on the East River Drive.

I must have had even more to drink than I thought, for all the way home I appealed sentimentally to Mr. Hazard.

"You've no idea, sir, what that fiend put Timmy through," I kept protesting. "You *couldn't* because you weren't there. And Timmy was so patient! I've never seen anything to equal it. Because of you, Mr. Hazard! He did it for *you*. He looks upon you as a father!"

Mr. Hazard, sitting beside me, stared out of the window and said nothing. Yet there was just the suspicion of a smile on his lips, enough, anyway, to inspire me in my intoxication with the heart-filling hope that the world, the real world, might be what it then seemed, a place of unbreakable friendships before whose high gates the jackal Liendeckers skulked in vain.

"He wants an apology, of course," Mr. Hazard said suddenly. "He told me that when we left. He made it very clear that if he doesn't get it, either Timmy goes or he goes."

"Then let *him* go!" I cried passionately, going as far as to grip his arm. "Oh, Mr. Hazard, if you only *knew* how Timmy needs backing up! His heart broke tonight. It was the last straw, before all those people! Of course, I know, sir, Mr. Liendecker's an important client, but you have lots of important clients, and Timmy will bring you plenty more. Truly, he will, sir!"

When Mr. Hazard finally turned to look at me, he was still smiling; but he was smiling, I made out with a sinking heart, only at the violence of my appeal. To him it was the scotch, of course, what but the scotch? And when I glanced suddenly at Mrs. Hazard and saw that she, too, had caught her husband's eye to exchange with him that same smile, I could only feel in a dull, defeated way that my world, scotch-inspired, was a thousand times braver and better than theirs.

"You forget something, Peter," Mr. Hazard said, putting a large hand on my shoulder and speaking in the paternal tone that I had heard him use to Timmy. "You forget that Tim treated us to a shocking breach of manners in the house of a man who was not only our client but our host. There's never any question about my backing Timmy up—I've always done that—but to back him up in the way that you suggest would be doing him a disfavour. Whatever I do, Peter, I shall be acting more for Timmy than for Sam Liendecker. You can bet on that."

We had pulled up before the old brown stone where my apartment was.

"And you won't mention this around the office tomorrow, will you, Peter?" he added.

"Oh, Mr. Hazard," I protested, getting out. "What do you take me for?"

The next morning, just before lunch, I walked down the corridor to Timmy's office. The door was closed, which was unusual in Everett & Coates, for much was made there of the advantages of an open and friendly atmosphere. When I went in I found Timmy sitting with his swivel chair turned towards the window, his feet resting on the radiator, his hands locked at the back of his head. He didn't even turn around as I entered.

"It's me," I said as the door closed behind. "What about lunch?"

He said nothing and I sat down in the chair by his desk and played with the black pen in the inkstand. When he spoke he still didn't turn around.

"They want me to apologise to that son of a bitch."

"They?"

"Hazard, of course," he answered in the same clipped tone. "The great Hazard himself. The maker of graduation addresses. The high priest of the intellect. He wants me to grovel before that psychological louse."

There was a hardness in his tone that made me wonder if he or Hazard would suffer ultimately most by what might happen.

"And, of course, you won't."

He turned at this, his feet coming off the radiator with a bang, his eyes sharp.

"Would you?"

"No." I shrugged my shoulders. "But what does that amount to? I haven't your future. I haven't Flora and the boys. I don't even have Mr. Hazard. I can afford the luxury of not apologising to men like Liendecker."

"You think it's only a luxury?"

"Fundamentally."

"You don't see the issue of personal integrity?"

"I see it. I don't see it as inevitable."

He turned away again to the window.

"I would never have thought you so slippery, Peter."

But there was no point in going into this.

"How did Hazard put it to you?" I asked. "Was it 'or else'?"

"No. He simply asked me to. But it's obvious how I'll stand here if I don't."

I nodded slowly and then sighed.

"You see too much black and white, Timmy," I said. "You forget that life can be grey, too. Even a Liendecker can be grey."

"If you're Liendecker's lawyer," he snapped, "you can sing his praises in someone else's office."

I nodded again, but only to the back of his head, and left. During the next few days none of us saw him at all. He arrived in the office in the middle of the morning and left usually in the middle of the afternoon. With his door always shut, people were quick to catch the idea that his mood, to put it mildly, was unsociable. Besides, the news of his outburst at the Liendeckers' had by now leaked from American Export and was all over the office. Associates were continually coming into my office to hear the story at first hand. I tried to minimise it, but it was the kind of story that defied minimisation. They would leave with a delighted expression of "Hot damn!"; and for all Timmy's popularity and the universal sympathy with his predicament, I found I was envied as the one who had seen the trapeze artist fall, the matador gored.

Mr. Hazard never referred to the scene in the taxicab, but he treated me very cordially now and even called me into his office one day to describe a simple codicil that his wife needed to cover a piece of jewellery that she had just inherited from an aunt. Ordinarily he would have channelled any such business through my department head, and I was flattered and pleased at such a mark of confidence. He quite took his time about the small problem involved and asked me questions with a charming deference to what he purported to consider my superior technical knowledge on the subject. It was a most satisfactory interview, and when I rose to leave he asked me about Timmy.

"How do you find him?"

"He won't talk to me," I said. "I can't help."

"I can't help either," he said with a sigh. "No one can really help Timmy but himself. He's like a stubborn child. One leaves him alone on the theory that he'll eventually come out of it. I suppose there's always the danger that he won't. But I can't understand the pleasure he gets in pounding his head against a stone wall and then rubbing it to look for blood. Can you, Peter?"

I knew that it was the wrong answer, but I couldn't help it.

"Yes, sir. I can understand it."

"Can you really?" He smiled, a touch more coolly, and then nodded to conclude our interview. "Maybe you can persuade him, then, that it's an unprofitable experience."

When I went uptown the following afternoon to Mrs. Hazard's to go over with her a draft of the codicil, I was told by the maid that she was still out, and I waited for her in her husband's dark, leathery library, walking slowly about with the awe that the room's silent, clock-ticking atmosphere induced and peering at the overframed forest scenes individually lighted with a care that seemed hardly merited. When I heard the unexpected sound of small children in the hall and went to the door, I was startled to see Timmy's two boys disappearing into the dining room. I was still staring after them when I heard a woman's heels on the stairway and, looking up, saw Flora. She was wearing a hat and coat and uttered a little cry when she saw me.

"Peter! What are *you* doing here?"

"It seems to me that I'm the one who ought to ask that question."

She hurried down the remaining steps and pushed me into the library ahead of her.

"I've had enough," she said abruptly. "I've had all I can take. I'm going away."

"And leaving the boys *here*?"

"Mrs. Hazard said I could," she said defiantly. "She's always been like a mother to me. The way he's been a father to Timmy. Who else could I go to?"

I caught her by the hand.

"Wait a second, please, Flora! You mean you're leaving Timmy. *Now!*"

She pulled her hand away.

"That's his decision!" she exclaimed. "Not mine. Mrs. Hazard will know where to find me. He can come and get me whenever he wants. Whenever he's made up his mind to stop behaving like a spoilt child."

I stared.

"You mean about Liendecker? You'll make him apologise? But this is blackmail, Flora!"

"Then I've come to blackmail," she retorted grimly. "There we are." Her expression changed, however, when she took in mine. "What else can I do, Peter?" she pleaded. "How else can I save him? He won't even talk to me about it any more, because he thinks

I'm not on his side." There were sudden tears in her eyes. "He's determined to rook his life over this foolish issue. He gets some kind of savage pleasure out of counting up the people who have deserted him, as he puts it, starting with Mr. Hazard and——"

"But there are other firms, Flora," I protested. "Timmy can always get a job. Don't make him pay a price he doesn't want to pay!"

She shook her head again, her eyes closed for a moment, as if she had been through the whole thing too many times to reopen the door.

"There aren't other firms for Timmy," she said firmly. "Not in his present mood. That firm is his life. And I'm not going to stand by and see him throw it away, just to spite Mr. Liendecker."

"But is this going to stop him?"

"As I say, that's for him to decide," she said, turning away. "It will either bring him to his senses or—or give him another jewel for that martyr's crown of his."

"But if it doesn't," I protested desperately, following her as she went down to the front door, "if he bangs out of the firm and starts drinking himself to death——"

"Then I'll come back to him, of course," she said, turning back to me and holding her hand out. "Only don't tell *him* that, Peter Westcott."

When Mrs. Hazard came in, a few minutes later, she found me still in the hall and stunned.

"Flora told me," I said at once, hurrying over to her. "I met her here. Tell me, Mrs. Hazard, do you think it's a good idea?"

Mrs. Hazard paused while she took off her hat, pulling out the long pin with the mother-of-pearl end and placing it on the table.

"Do I? Not in the least."

"Can't you do something about it?" I paused, suddenly embarrassed at my own impertinence. "Can't you make Mr. Hazard do something, I mean?"

"Well, if I leave *him*, Peter," she said, smiling at me, "where can I send my own children?"

Timmy came into my office the following morning and banged the door shut behind him. He looked as if he had not slept, and his eyes jumped at me angrily.

"I'm going over to apologise to Liendecker," he said. "I want you to come along as a witness to tell the world that I did it properly. No matter what *he* says afterwards."

All the way down in the elevator and during the two-block walk to American Export we hardly exchanged a word. Timmy walked a little bit ahead of me, pausing from time to time impatiently for me to catch up.

"Let's not be all day," he muttered once. "Let's get this damn thing over with, shall we?"

At American Export, Mr. Liendecker's secretary told us, with a tailored friendliness, that the president would see us in a few minutes. We were then kept waiting, despite Timmy's appointment, a full half-hour. I would have been almost disappointed in Mr. Liendecker had he not insisted on this final touch. His greatest strength lay in the fact that he never, no matter how regularly or at what interest a debt was paid, forgave the least portion of the unpaid balance. One knew, at least, where one stood with him. Finally I turned to Timmy.

"Is Flora back?"

He didn't look at me.

"She's back," he said briefly. "And I'm here."

"I know what this must be costing you, Timmy."

This time he looked at me, but his look was withering. A light on the secretary's desk flashed green, and she cried, as if she, too, could be happy at our good news, "Mr. Liendecker will see you now, gentlemen!"

He was leaning back in his big brown leather chair, his hands folded behind his head. When we had been seated in front of him he leaned suddenly forward and put his elbows on the desk. His eyes ran restlessly over the blotter, and he closed and opened the top of the silver inkwell. I could see the note on which he was going to play the scene, the note of faint boredom, of "what's this all about", the implication that it was we and not he who were making mountains out of molehills. And, to do even him justice, it may have been sincere. He had won, that was obvious, and it was one of the tragedies of men of his type that if defeat was unendurably galling, victory was not proportionately sweet.

"Well, gentlemen?"

Timmy went straight to the point.

"I've come to apologise, sir, for my rudeness of the other night." He gave the rug at this point a long, hard look. "Obviously, I wouldn't have come for any other reason. I won't say that I don't know what got into me. I do. I blew up at a perfectly harmless joke. I can only blame it on the nervous fatigue that followed the sale."

Mr. Liendecker glanced up at this.

"We *all* worked pretty hard on that sale, Colt."

"I know it," Timmy agreed, nodding. "You harder than anyone, Mr. Liendecker. And, after all, you had the responsibility of the whole thing. I have a lot to learn from you, sir, both in manners and in patience."

I drew in my breath and glanced out of the corner of my eye at Timmy. But he looked perfectly serious. Mr. Liendecker, who had evidently shared my suspicion, looked at him shrewdly for a moment and then grunted.

"It pays to know how to hang on to your temper, young fella," he said. "You've found that out. Okay. I wouldn't be surprised if you were the kind who only had to find it out once."

"Thank you, sir. I'll remember that."

"I guess he will, at that," Mr. Liendecker said more cheerfully now, rising and turning to me. "What about it, Westcott?"

"I'm sure he will, sir," I answered, getting up. "I'm sure that anyone who can make such a handsome apology will not forget the small slip that occasioned it."

Mr. Liendecker's grey eyes ran over me for just a moment, and then he turned back to Timmy.

"I'll call Hazard this morning, son," he said, shaking his hand, "and tell him I want our next job at Everett & Coates handled by you. Okay? Good day, gentlemen."

Outside in the lobby as we waited for the elevator Timmy looked at me sullenly.

"You almost fixed my wagon that time," he muttered. "Who asked you to stick up for me, anyway?"

"I thought if you grovelled any more you'd be under the rug," I retorted. "Did you have to go *that* far?"

"That's nothing to how far I'm going," he said roughly. "Not by a long shot, brother."

The printed card announcing that Mr. Timothy Colt had been made a member of the firm was sent out through the downtown legal world no less than two weeks after our fateful interview with Mr. Liendecker. I have known lawyers to whom the advent of partnership has been a source of almost hourly satisfaction for as much as a year afterwards, men in whose faces one could see the reflection of that bright little thought, ceaselessly reiterated like the chirp of a starling: "I'm a partner! I'm a partner!" Timmy, however, seemed to take the news very coolly. He barely smiled at us when we went to congratulate him and appeared already to have given his entire attention to the business of moving into his new office and getting started on his next job. The past was evidently not a field in which he intended to allow himself even a civilised loiter.

Such brisk efficiency, even for him, came as a surprise to the office, but what really astonished the associates was the change in his attitude towards us. He had always deplored the barrier between the partner and clerk and insisted that if he was ever promoted he would not do as so many did, cultivate old friendships for the first year and then gradually, through inertia, pressure of work and the opening up of new peaks, relax his democratic impulses and accept the "Mr." accorded him by the younger clerks as his natural due. But now, on the contrary, he seemed willing to skip even this year of laboured intimacy and to retire to an aloofness behind closed doors that made Mr. Hazard himself appear the artist of the common touch. When younger men were called to his office it was by his secretary, never himself, and it was to find a detached, distant Mr. Colt leaning over a paper on his desk, one hand propping his brow, who simply raised his eyes to acknowledge their entrance and, cutting through the usual salutations, started at once on business. In all too brief a time, the time it takes in any organisation to substitute a bad reputation for a good one, Timmy became the partner for whom we all least cared to work. It was not that he was actually disagreeable or even that he lost his temper, but he would pass his hand over his eyes when asked to explain something and pause for a moment of silence that filled the room with the atmosphere of his repressed exasperation. Then he would answer in slow, meticulous syllables that only hammered into his poor listener's head the low opinion that he had formed of his intellect. "I trust it is clear," he would say, looking up at last, "*now*?"

My first contact with this treatment came by an unhappy chance when Timmy, checking the library files on an obscure point of tax law, chanced upon an old memorandum that I had written just after I had come into the office. It was my first postwar job, and it contained a mistake which no one had picked up at the time. Timmy, of course, fell right into it.

"But I don't understand," he kept repeating to me. "Your conclusion is in direct contravention to the leading case on the subject. Direct. I don't understand."

"It's not so hard to understand," I replied. "The memorandum is simply wrong, that's all. Is that so fantastic?"

Timmy became even more the partner at this.

"In our files, Peter Westcott," he said, looking up at me sternly, "I very much hope that it *is* fantastic."

I said nothing.

"You don't even seem surprised," he pursued, "when I point out the contradiction. Are you in the habit of seeing your memoranda so easily rebutted?"

"I knew about the contradiction," I said sullenly. "It occurred to me after the memo was filed."

"Indeed? And may I ask, then, why you failed to correct it?"

"I never thought anyone would read it," I said with a sigh. "And I didn't want to stir the matter up. You know how it is, Timmy. You haven't been a partner *that* long."

He gave me a straight look.

"If you're implying that it was my habit as an associate to leave memoranda in the files which I knew to be misleading——"

"Do you know what's happening to you, Timmy?" I interrupted

angrily. "You're becoming a Scrooge! Everyone says so. But if you think I'm a Bob Cratchit, it's going to take more than a Christmas turkey to win me around!"

Timmy continued to gaze at me for a moment with faintly curious eyes and then glanced down again at the offending memorandum.

"Oh, go soak your head," he said.

It was not long after this, although in no way because of it, that I resigned from Everett & Coates to take a legal job in a publishing company that was one of their clients and where I could at least count on evenings and weekends for my own writing. Ordinarily Timmy would have been the first person whom I would have consulted before making such a decision, but as things were I allowed him to hear of it after it had become an accomplished fact. I'm afraid, indeed, that I got a perverse satisfaction out of imagining that his feelings might be hurt. He came himself to my office, which he hadn't done since his promotion, and, leaning back in a chair, put his feet up on my desk.

"This is sudden news that I heard at the partners' lunch today, Peter," he said with a little smile. "I rather thought that you and I might have discussed it."

"I saw no reason, Timmy. My mind was made up. And, besides, you're always so busy."

His little smile didn't change. It seemed to be offered up to me as a concession to his own shyness, even as a barrier against anything that I might throw.

"You don't exactly have a dim future here, you know."

"In spite of inaccurate memoranda?"

He shrugged his shoulders.

"In spite of them."

Well, it was the olive branch, of course, or as close to it as Timmy could fashion one, and maybe it was churlish of me not to have accepted it, but I was too angry at his recent neglect and too disgusted at what he seemed to have done to himself to let him off so easily. We continued to chat but in a desultory manner, and I felt that he was quietly taking in both me and my attitude as further examples of the unreasonable but utterly predictable injustice of this world.

He must have told Flora that night of my decision, for the next afternoon I had a wonderful letter from her, full of warmth and congratulation, applauding my resolution to give up the downtown world and even looking forward to the day when I should abandon my new employer and make writing my full-time occupation.

"I hope that we'll see you," she ended, "and that it won't be as it is with others who have left the firm, simply an exchange of Christmas cards. But then I've learned not to be unreasonable about what life does. Do try, however, to come and see me. As you can tell by the letterhead, we've moved to a swankier apartment. At least Timmy thinks it's swankier. He seems to be suffering these days from an acute case of mammon. Anything you want to know about us in the future you can find in the social columns. PS. I *loathe* it. PPS. So does he, only he won't admit it!"

It was several months before I found out what Flora meant by Timmy's "acute case of mammon". My new job, as it turned out, was by no means exclusively legal; I was the general assistant and handy man of the chairman of the board and as such had to go with him to various social affairs, usually cocktail parties for worthy causes and less worthy people given in the private suites of large hotels. On one such occasion I encountered Timmy. He was entirely agreeable and made no allusion to any former unpleasantness between us; he inquired politely about my new business, but instead of listening to my answers, his eyes roamed the room alertly. From time to time he interrupted me, without the least apology, to ask if I knew this or that person whom he would point out.

"Now, who is that lady?" he asked, gesturing towards a tall thin woman in black.

"That's Lorna Treadway."

"And why is she here?"

"Lorna? She goes everywhere."

Timmy frowned, the way he did at the office when somebody failed to understand the purport of his question.

"Yes, but why? I understand she writes a column on decorating. Is it for that?"

"Lord, no. That column's a joke. Lorna's just one of those people whom other people always have around. You know how it is."

He shook his head.

"Someone told me she had quite a social position."

I stared at him.

"Timmy, what's come over you? You can't start talking like that. Even if you *are* a partner."

"Clients don't grow on trees, you know."

"But you're not a client getter," I protested. "You're not even the type!"

"We'll see about that," he said coolly. "Everyone thinks I'd be perfectly satisfied to be known all my life as Hazard's helper. Well, they're wrong. You don't get to know the people who count by holing yourself up in a two-by-four office all day."

"Oh. Sam Liendecker. I see all."

"Well, Sam makes a lot of sense on these things," he retorted, obviously nettled. "I went up to Canada on a fishing trip with him last spring, and we met Harris Grant. You know, the oil man. Well, Grant didn't even know that right in Everett & Coates we happen to have one of the best legal oil specialists in the country——"

I could see, as he talked, that he had brought to his new social activities the same careful literal-mindedness that I had seen him bring to his contracts and mergers. It was a job like other jobs, wasn't it? And being done, directly or indirectly, for the firm? Which to his way of thinking, I supposed, more than took care of other issues involved.

"What does Mr. Hazard think of your new activities?" I couldn't help asking.

"Well, Hazard, of course, is an older man," he said with a slight frown. "He comes of a more secure world. And then, don't forget, he's Henry Hazard. Not an unknown like T. Colt." He turned and put his hand on my shoulder. "But to hell with this, Peter. How about coming home for a drink? Flora hasn't seen you in ages."

I went uptown with him to the east sixties where they now lived. The apartment was a good size and of good proportions, but nothing could save it from the peculiar combination of emptiness and disorder that only the Colts knew how to bestow. There were a few handsome pieces, department-store Chippendale, but theirs was a lonely show in the absence of a rug and before the bareness of walls broken only by a photograph of Timmy's wartime aircraft carrier. The children's cowboy paraphernalia lay scattered about, and beside the fireplace gleamed the wide grey vacancy of a television set.

"Flora!" Timmy called. "I've got a friend for you!"

I heard the sound of bedroom slippers in the corridor, and Flora came in, dressed in a flower-patterned wrapper, pushing her hair back. Her mouth fell open.

"Peter!" she cried and hurried over to kiss me, putting both arms around my neck. "Well, I'll be a son of a gun!"

Any other woman might have apologised for the state of the room, for her own state; not Flora. Her not doing so made it almost, if not completely, all right. Timmy went to mix drinks, and by the time he had come back I had told her more about myself and my job than I had told anyone since I had left Everett & Coates. When he handed her her whisky, however, he changed the subject.

"I looked in on the boys," he said. "Their colds seem better."

"Oh, they're much better."

"Then there's no reason you can't come with me tonight," he continued. "We might as well get some good out of that nurse."

Flora looked up in alarm.

"Oh, Timmy, I couldn't leave them! Not tonight!"

He stirred his drink slowly.

"Martha tells me their temperatures have been normal since yesterday," he observed.

"Yes, but, Timmy, you *know* how quickly they can jump!"

"Then she can call us. We'll be exactly five blocks away."

"Oh, Timmy, please! No!"

There was a pause while he looked at her steadily.

"Will you admit it's not the boys, then?" he asked quietly, glancing down again at his drink. "Will you have the fairness to admit it's because you don't want to go?"

"You *know* I don't want to go!"

"And that's your only reason?"

She took a long swallow of her drink and then looked back at him in sudden defiance.

"All right, it's my only reason. Name me a better." She turned around to me for support. "He wants me to go to the Liendeckers', Peter. You know I can't face that."

I gaped.

"Of course you can't! What are you thinking of, Timmy?"

He leaned back on the sofa and crossed his arms on his chest. He was angry now, but I could see that it was one of those rich, prepared, satisfying angers.

"What was *she* thinking of, Peter," he asked me sharply, "when she made me go on my knees to Sam Liendecker?"

"Knees?" I retorted. "Really, Timmy, you're being absurd!"

Flora had turned pale.

"So that's it," she said. "You want to get back at me for that. You've always wanted to, haven't you? Ever since?"

"It isn't a question of getting back," he said, with a rather condescending patience. "It's simply a question of the decision you made at that time. The decision of the sort of life we were going to lead."

"*I* made that decision?" she demanded.

"Most effectively," he replied. "We *had* been the kind of people who wouldn't apologise to Sam Liendecker. Now we're not. You must face that, Flora. I can't let you go on with this illusion that because you stay at home with the children you've preserved your integrity. You're in this with me. Up to the hilt."

There was a heavy silence. Flora stared into the fireplace, holding her drink close to her lips and taking, from moment to moment, quick, abstracted sips.

"I want to be in anything you're in, Timmy," she said sadly. "I'm not trying to preserve any integrity that you don't think you have. I'll admit my responsibility for the apology to Liendecker, and I'll take the consequences. But why is this party a consequence? Unless *you* make it so?"

"Because it's the life you chose," he insisted. "If I've made a pact with the devil, please don't think that he's going to get his share of me for a junior partnership. Oh, no. I want my money's worth."

Flora looked at me pleadingly.

"Does it make any sense to you, Peter?"

"None whatever."

"You want me to bring home the money," Timmy continued, angered by our exchange, "but you don't want to know where it's from. Well, I won't let you get away with it. You're going to see for yourself!"

Flora shrugged her shoulders, as one who has suddenly given up.

"All right, I'll go to the damn party," she said wearily. "But on one condition. If Peter will go, too."

"*Me?* Why drag me into it? I'm not even asked!"

"It's all right," she assured me. "We'll take you. Timmy's friend, Sam, will be delighted. Won't he, Timmy?"

He looked at her in surprise.

"As a matter of fact, he will," he agreed. "I think he liked you, Peter."

"I'm sorry I can't return the compliment."

"Oh, please, Peter." Flora got up and came over to sit on the arm of my chair. "Come for my sake. I want to have *one* friend there."

She glanced at Timmy as she said this.

"Thank you," he said grimly.

I allowed myself to be persuaded, mostly to avoid what I thought might at any moment turn into a serious row. I went home to dress and make myself a sandwich; like the other Liendecker affair, it was a late evening party. When I got back to the Colts' a little before ten Flora opened the door. She was wearing a plain evening dress, of her customary brown, and was holding an old-fashioned glass in one hand.

"I'm getting in a gala mood," she said, raising the glass. "Are you in a gala mood, Peter?"

"Well, don't overdo it," I warned her. "Remember what happened *last* time we were at the Liendeckers'."

"Don't you think it's my turn?" she demanded. "Don't you think *I* should insult him this time?"

"Maybe we'd better *not* go to this party."

She laughed, rather too loudly.

"You're afraid I will, aren't you, Peter? But why not? As long as I apologise, the way he did. Then we'll be in the same boat, won't we?" She shrugged her shoulders and turned back into the living-room. "Who knows? We might even be able to forgive each other."

Timmy appeared at the door to the bedroom corridor, buttoning the coat of his double-breasted midnight-blue tuxedo.

"Hi, Peter," he said casually, "are we about ready?" Then he saw the drink in Flora's hand and his expression changed. He crossed the room and took it from her. "What are you trying to do, anyway? Get potted?"

"It might help," she retorted and turned back into the hall to get her coat.

The Liendeckers' party was large, and I didn't know a soul there. Mr. Liendecker's social ambitions were not as specific as his business ones; he was not, as far as I could see, striking for any particular group or stratum. I suspect that to him "society" was a thing you had sent in when you gave a party, provided, so to speak, by a caterer with the little red-coated orchestra and the champagne. Where he actually got his guests I don't know; the women were pretty enough, but they had a hard manicured look and the men with them in most cases seemed to be older. I am not, however, making insinuations; they were probably mostly married just as they were probably mostly childless, the inhabitants of apartment hotels and night clubs, with big incomes consumed in evanescent luxury, the type of new-rich who abound in New York, curiously satisfied with the little that their money buys.

Mr. Liendecker greeted me enthusiastically; it was one of his characteristics that he never forgot a name. He then put a firm hand on Timmy's elbow and led him off to introduce him to Lorna Treadway. Flora and I, abandoned, sat side by side in a corner, and I noticed disapprovingly how quickly she reached for the darkest whisky on a passing tray. She looked sullen and even dowdy with her inadequately combed hair and those eyes, resentful and worried, darting from one to another of the well-dressed women who crossed and recrossed the floor in front of us. She drank off the whole glass while we made unkind comments about them. When she reached for another, however, I caught her hand.

"No, Flora. Really."

The waiter hesitated, embarrassed, and then moved off. When she looked at me I saw the tears in her eyes.

"Oh, Peter, what good am I to him now?" she asked, slumping back on the sofa. "Shouldn't I pack up and get out and let him marry one of these sleeky creatures? No, I'm not fair," she continued, shaking her head with sudden firmness, "they're not really sleeky. It's just that I'm a mess. They're beautiful, really. And so is he. Isn't he, Peter?"

"Now, Flora."

"Oh, don't comfort me for God's sake, I can't stand it." She put her hands to her eyes for a moment. "Maybe he's right. Maybe I should never have forced him. Maybe I *have* been selfish in not taking part in this new life of his. But I can't, Peter, I simply can't. Not even for love, and God knows I love him. But some things are stronger than love! Oh, Peter, how many things are stronger than love! And when you realise that and still love, you want to die, that's all."

"You can't be someone you aren't, Flora," I said.

"Oh, I could do better." Dry-eyed again, she nodded her head briskly. "I could do a lot better. I could be more careful about my clothes, and I could make small talk. And I could flatter Mr. Liendecker. But I won't. I don't know why, but I won't. Timmy's right about me, Peter. I *am* selfish. Selfish and pigheaded. I made him do what I wouldn't do myself, God help me, and now I've been paid off in kind."

She swallowed suddenly, with difficulty.

"Are you all right, Flora?"

She stood up.

"I'm going to the ladies' room."

She was gone for some time, and I was beginning to feel concerned when I saw a maid hurry out of the door into which she had disappeared and cross the living-room to whisper to Mrs. Liendecker. The latter looked startled; she drew herself up for a moment and glanced nervously about the room. Then she went over to Timmy and whispered for a moment in his ear. His expression did not change as he listened to her; he simply nodded and then turned with a firm step towards the door. I got up and hurried over to him.

"Timmy!"

He turned around.

"Yes?"

"Is Flora all right?"

"She's been sick," he said calmly and then paused for a second, adding, almost as an afterthought, "all over Mrs. Liendecker's bed."

For one wild moment I thought I was going to shriek with laughter.

"But she's okay?"

"She's okay *now*," he corrected me. "She was never a great one at holding her whisky. You remember that, Peter."

"Poor Flora."

"Poor me," he retorted. Then he glanced over my shoulder, almost curiously, at the crowded room behind me. "I think it could hardly be denied," he added in a more reflective tone, "that Flora and I are something less than assets at the Liendeckers' parties."

I had a sudden vision of her facing him later, pale and defeated, over the ruins of their evening.

"Oh, Timmy, you won't be hard on her, will you?" I begged. "You won't bawl her out?"

He gave me an odd, direct look that I couldn't interpret.

"What do you take me for?"

"Well, I simply—well——" I stopped in confusion.

"It's up to her," he explained, his eyes still fixed on me. "Don't you know that, Peter?"

I stared.

"Know what?"

"What Flora is to me," he said. "I want what she wants, Peter. Every time. But she has to make up her mind, you know. She has to make the decisions." He smiled suddenly, with the charm of the Timmy I had first known, the Timmy of romantic antecedents. "I rather imagine she's made another one just now."

But I knew, as he turned and I watched his straight back retreat down the corridor towards Mrs. Liendecker's room, that the world would not let them go back now to the old life where they had been so happy, where he with each job and she with each uneventful day had lived as if the future with its bag of small duties and lip services had not loomed before them. No, that was the past, the past of their obscurity, when they had been idealists in a vacuum. Above them, around them, in the great world, adjustments had been made, concessions granted. But none of this had even existed for Timmy and Flora; the rudeness of their awakening had shown me that. There would be nothing easy for them, as for Mr. Hazard, in compromise, nothing of grace. It was a reproach to the very world which they would live in that poor Flora's single gesture of protest should have seemed so ludicrous.

John Galsworthy

THE JURYMAN

★

I

"Don't you see, brother, I was reading yesterday the Gospel about Christ, the little Father; how He suffered, how He walked on the earth. I suppose you have heard about it?"

"Indeed, I have," replied Stepanuitch; "but we are people in darkness; we can't read."—TOLSTOI.

Mr. Henry Bosengate, of the London Stock Exchange, seated himself in his car that morning during the Great War with a sense of injury. Major in a Volunteer Corps; member of all the local committees; lending this very car to the neighbouring hospital, at times even driving it himself for their benefit; subscribing to funds, so far as his diminished income permitted—he was conscious of being an asset to the country, and one whose time could not be wasted with impunity. To be summoned to sit on a jury at the local assizes, and not even the grand jury at that! It was in the nature of an outrage.

Strong and upright, with hazel eyes and dark eyebrows, pinkish-brown cheeks, a forehead white, well-shaped, and getting high, with greyish hair glossy and well-brushed, and a trim moustache, he might have been taken for that colonel of Volunteers which indeed he was in a fair way of becoming.

His wife had followed him out under the porch, and stood bracing her supple body clothed in lilac linen. Red rambler roses formed a sort of crown to her dark head; her ivory-coloured face had in it just a suggestion of the Japanese.

Mr. Bosengate spoke through the whirr of the engine:

"I don't expect to be late, dear. This business is ridiculous. There oughtn't to *be* any crime in these days."

His wife—her name was Kathleen—smiled. She looked very pretty and cool, Mr. Bosengate thought. To one bound on this dull and stuffy business everything he owned seemed pleasant—the geranium beds beside the gravel drive, his long, red-brick house mellowing decorously in its creepers and ivy, the little clock-tower over stables now converted into a garage, the dovecote, masking at the other end the conservatory which adjoined the billiard-room. Close to the red-brick lodge his two children, Kate and Harry, ran out from under the acacia trees, and waved to him, scrambling bare-legged on to the low, red, ivy-covered wall which guarded his domain of eleven acres. Mr. Bosengate waved back, thinking: 'Jolly couple—by Jove, they are!' Above their heads, through the trees, he could see right away to some Downs, faint in the July heat haze. And he thought: 'Pretty a spot as one could have got, so close to town!'

Despite the war he had enjoyed these last two years more than any of the ten since he built "Charmleigh" and settled down to semi-rural domesticity with his young wife. There had been a certain piquancy, a savour added to existence, by the country's peril, and all the public service and sacrifice it demanded. His chauffeur was gone, and one gardener did the work of three. He enjoyed—positively enjoyed—his committee work; even the serious decline of business and increase of taxation had not much worried one continually conscious of the national crisis and his own part therein. The country had wanted waking up, wanted a lesson in effort and economy; and the feeling that he had not spared himself in these strenuous times had given a zest to those quiet pleasures of bed and board which, at his age, even the most patriotic could retain with a good conscience. He had denied himself many things—new clothes, presents for Kathleen and the children, travel, and that pine-apple house which he had been on the point of building when the war broke out; new wine, too, and cigars, and membership of the two Clubs which he had never used in the old days. The hours had seemed fuller and longer, sleep better earned—wonderful, the things one could do without when put to it! He turned the car into the highroad, driving dreamily, for he was in plenty of time. The war was going pretty well now; he was no fool optimist, but now that conscription was in force, one might reasonably hope for its end within a year. Then there would be a boom, and one might let oneself go a little. Visions of theatres and supper with his wife at the Savoy afterwards, and cosy night drives back into the sweet-smelling country behind your own chauffeur once more teased a fancy which even now did not soar beyond the confines of domestic pleasures. He pictured his wife in new dresses by Jay—she was fifteen years younger than himself, and "paid for dressing" as they said. He had always delighted—as men older than their wives will—in the admiration she excited from others not privileged to enjoy her charms. Her rather queer and ironical beauty, her cool irreproachable wifeliness, was a constant balm to him. They would give dinner parties again, have their friends down from town, and he would once more enjoy sitting at the foot of the dinner table while Kathleen sat at the head, with the light soft on her ivory shoulders, behind flowers she had arranged in that original way of hers, and fruit which he had grown in his hot-houses; once more he would take legitimate interest in the wine he offered to his guests—once more stock that Chinese cabinet wherein he kept cigars. Yes—there was a certain satisfaction in these days of privation, if only from the anticipation they created.

The sprinkling of villas had become continuous on either side of the high-road; and women going out to shop, tradesmen's boys delivering victuals, young men in khaki, began to abound. Now and then a limping or bandaged form would pass—some bit of human wreckage! and Mr. Bosengate would think mechanically: 'Another of those poor devils! Wonder if we've had his case before us!'

Running his car into the best hotel garage of the little town, he made his way leisurely over to the court. It stood back from the market-place, and was already lapped by a sea of persons having, as in the outer ring at race meetings, an air of business at which one must not be caught out, together with a soaked or flushed appearance. Mr. Bosengate could not resist putting his handkerchief to his nose. He had carefully drenched it with lavender water, and to this fact owed, perhaps, his immunity from the post of foreman on the jury—for, say what you will about the English, they have a deep instinct for affairs.

He found himself second in the front row of the jury box, and through the odour of "Sanitas" gazed at the judge's face, expressionless up there, for all the world like a bewigged bust. His fellows in the box had that appearance of falling between two classes characteristic of jurymen. Mr. Bosengate was not impressed. On one side of him the foreman sat, a prominent upholsterer, known in the town as "Gentleman Fox". His dark and beautifully brushed and oiled hair and moustache, his radiant linen, gold watch and chain, the white piping to his waistcoat, and a habit of never saying "Sir" had long marked him out from commoner men; he undertook to bury people too, to save them trouble; and was altogether superior. On the other side Mr. Bosengate had one of those men who, except when they sit on juries, are never seen without a little brown bag, and the appearance of having been interrupted in a drink. Pale and shiny, with large loose eyes shifting from side to side, he had an underdone voice and uneasy, flabby hands. Mr. Bosengate disliked sitting next to him. Beyond this commercial traveller sat a dark pale young man with spectacles; beyond him again, a short old man with grey mustache, mutton chops, and innumerable wrinkles; and the front row was completed by a chemist. The three immediately behind, Mr. Bosengate did not thoroughly master; but the three at the end of the second row he learned in their order of an oldish man in a grey suit, given to winking; an inanimate person with the mouth of a mustachioed codfish, over whose long bald crown three wisps of damp hair were carefully arranged; and a dried, dapperish, clean-shorn man, whose mouth seemed terrified lest it should be surprised without a smile. Their first and second verdicts were recorded without the necessity for withdrawal, and Mr. Bosengate was already sleepy when the third case was called. The sight of khaki revived his drooping attention. But what a weedy-looking specimen! This prisoner had a truly nerveless, pitiable, dejected air. If he had ever had a military bearing it had shrunk into him during his confinement. His ill-shaped brown tunic, whose little brass buttons seemed trying to keep smiling, struck Mr. Bosengate as ridiculously short, used though he was to cush things. 'Absurd,' he thought—'Lumbago! Just where they ought to be covered!' Then the officer and gentleman stirred in him, and he added to himself: 'Still, there must be some distinction made!' The little soldier's visage had once perhaps been tanned, but was now the colour of dark dough; his large brown eyes with white showing below the iris, as so often in the eyes of very nervous people—wandered from face to face, of judge, counsel, jury, and public. There were hollows in his cheeks, his dark hair looked damp; around his neck he wore a bandage. The commercial traveller on Mr. Bosengate's left turned, and whispered: "*Felo de se!* My hat! what a guy!" Mr. Bosengate pretended not to hear—he could not bear that fellow!—and slowly wrote on a bit of paper: "Owen Lewis." Welsh! Well, he looked it—not at all an English face. Attempted suicide—not at all an English crime! Suicide implied surrender, a putting-up of hands to Fate—to say nothing of the religious aspect of the matter. And suicide in khaki seemed to Mr. Bosengate particularly abhorrent; like turning tail in face of the enemy; almost meriting the fate of a deserter. He looked at the prisoner, trying not to give way to this prejudice. And the prisoner seemed to look at him, though this, perhaps, was fancy.

The counsel for the prosecution, a little, alert, grey, decided man, above military age, began detailing the circumstances of the crime. Mr. Bosengate, though not particularly sensitive to atmosphere, could perceive a sort of current running through the court. It was as if jury and public were thinking rhythmically in obedience to the same unexpressed prejudice of which he himself was conscious. Even the Caesar-like pale face up there, presiding, seemed in its ironic serenity responding to that current.

"Gentlemen of the jury, before I call my evidence, I direct your attention to the bandage the accused is still wearing. He gave himself this wound with his Army razor, adding, if I may say so, insult to the injury he was inflicting on his country. He pleads not guilty; and before the magistrates he said that absence from his wife was preying on his mind"—the advocate's close lips widened—"Well, gentlemen, if such an excuse is to weigh with us in these days, I'm sure I don't know what's to happen to the Empire."

'No, by George!' thought Mr. Bosengate.

The evidence of the first witness, a room-mate who had caught the prisoner's hand, and of the sergeant, who had at once been summoned, was conclusive, and he began to cherish a hope that they would get through without withdrawing, and he would be home before five. But then a hitch occurred. The regimental doctor failed to respond when his name was called; and the judge, having for the first time that day showed himself capable of human emotion, intimated that he would adjourn until the morrow.

Mr. Bosengate received the announcement with equanimity. He would be home even earlier! And gathering up the sheets of paper he had scribbled on, he put them in his pocket and got up. The would-be suicide was being taken out of the court—a shambling drab figure with shoulders hunched. What good were men like that in these days! What good! The prisoner looked up. Mr. Bosengate encountered in full the gaze of those large brown eyes, with the white showing underneath. What a suffering, wretched, pitiful face! A man had no business to give you a look like that! The prisoner passed on down the stairs, and vanished. Mr. Bosengate went out and across the market-place to the garage of the hotel where he had left his car. The sun shone fiercely and he thought: 'I must do some watering in the garden.' He brought the car out, and was about to start the engine, when someone passing said: "Good evenin'. Seedy-lookin' beggar that last prisoner, ain't he? We don't want men of that stamp." It was his neighbour on the jury, the commercial traveller, in a straw hat, with a little brown bag already in his hand and the froth of an interrupted drink on his moustache. Answering curtly: "Good evening!" and thinking: 'Nor of yours, my friend!' Mr. Bosengate started the car with unnecessary clamour. But as if brought back to life by the commercial traveller's remark, the prisoner's figure seemed to speed along too, turning up at Mr. Bosengate his pitifully unhappy eyes. Want of his wife!—queer excuse that for trying to put it out of his power ever to see her again. Why! Half a loaf, even a slice, was better than no bread. Not many of that neurotic type in the Army—thank Heaven! The lugubrious figure vanished, and Mr. Bosengate pictured instead the form of his own wife bending over her "Gloire de Dijon" roses in the rosery, where she generally worked a little before tea now that they were short of gardeners. He saw her, as often he had seen her, raise herself and stand, head to one side, a gloved hand on her slender hip, gazing as it were ironically from under drooped lids at buds which did not come out fast enough. And the word '*Caline*', for he was something of a French scholar, shot through his mind: 'Kathleen—*Caline!*' If he found her there when he got in, he would steal up on the grass and—ah! but with great care not to crease her dress or disturb her hair! 'If only she weren't quite so self-contained,' he thought. 'It's like a cat you can't get near, not really near!'

The car, returning faster than it had come down that morning, had already passed the outskirt villas, and was breasting the hill to where, among fields and the old trees, Charmleigh lay apart from commoner life. Turning into his drive, Mr. Bosengate thought with a certain surprise: 'I wonder what she *does* think of! I wonder!' He put his gloves and hat down in the outer hall and went into the lavatory, to dip his face in cool water and wash it with sweet-smelling soap—delicious revenge on the unclean atmosphere in which he had been stewing so many hours. He came out again into the hall dazed by soap and the mellowed light, and a voice from half-way up the stairs said: "Daddy! Look!" His little daughter was standing up there with one hand on the banisters. She scrambled on to them and came sliding down, her frock up to her eyes, and her holland knickers to her middle. Mr. Bosengate said mildly:

"Well, that's elegant!"

"Tea's in the summer-house. Mummy's waiting. Come on!"

With her hand in his, Mr. Bosengate went on, through the drawing-room, long and cool, with sun-blinds down, through the billiard-room, high and cool, through the conservatory, green and sweet-smelling, out on to the terrace and the upper lawn. He had never felt such sheer exhilarated joy in his home surroundings, so cool, glistening and green under the July sun; and he said:

"Well, Kit, what have you all been doing?"

"I've fed my rabbits and Harry's; and we've been in the attic; Harry got his leg through the skylight."

Mr. Bosengate drew in his breath with a hiss.

"It's all right, Daddy; we got it out again, it's only grazed the skin. And we've been making swabs—I made seventeen—Mummy made thirty-three, and then she went to the hospital. Did you put many men in prison?"

Mr. Bosengate cleared his throat. The question seemed to him untimely.

"Only two."

"What's it like in prison, Daddy?"

Mr. Bosengate, who had no more knowledge than his little daughter, replied in an absent voice:

"Not very nice."

They were passing under a young oak tree, where the path wound round to the rosery and summer-house. Something shot down and clawed Mr. Bosengate's neck. His little daughter began to hop and suffocate with laughter.

"Oh, Daddy! Aren't you caught! I led you on purpose!"

Looking up, Mr. Bosengate saw his small son lying along a low branch above him—like the leopard he was declaring himself to be (for fear of error), and thought blithely: 'What an active little chap it is!'

"Let me drop on your shoulders, Daddy—like they do on the deer."

"Oh, yes! Do be a deer, Daddy!"

Mr. Bosengate did not see being a deer; his hair had just been brushed. But he entered the rosery buoyantly between his offspring. His wife was standing precisely as he had imagined her, in a pale blue frock open at the neck, with a narrow black band round the waist, and little accordion pleats below. She looked her coolest. Her smile, when she turned her head, hardly seemed to take Mr. Bosengate seriously enough. He placed his lips below one of her half-drooped eyelids. She even smelled of roses. His children began to dance round their mother, and Mr. Bosengate, firmly held between them, was also compelled to do this, until she said:

"When you've quite done, let's have tea!"

It was not the greeting he had imagined coming along in the car. Earwigs were plentiful in the summer-house—used perhaps twice a year, but indispensable to every country residence—and Mr. Bosengate was not sorry for the excuse to get out again. Though all was so pleasant, he felt oddly restless, rather suffocated; and lighting his pipe, began to move about among the roses, blowing tobacco at the greenfly; in war-time one was never quite idle! And suddenly he said:

"We're trying a wretched Tommy at the assizes."

His wife looked up from a rose.

"What for?"

"Attempted suicide."

"Why did he?"

"Can't stand the separation from his wife."

She looked at him, gave a low laugh, and said:

"Oh dear!"

Mr. Bosengate was puzzled. Why did she laugh? He looked round, saw the children were gone, took his pipe from his mouth, and approached her.

"You look very pretty," he said. "Give me a kiss."

His wife bent her body forward from the waist, and pushed her lips out till they touched his moustache. Mr. Bosengate felt a sensation as if he had arisen from breakfast without having eaten marmalade. He mastered it and said:

"That jury are a rum lot."

His wife's eyelids flickered. "I wish women sat on juries."

"Why?"

"It would be an experience."

Not the first time she had used that curious expression! Yet her life was far from dull, so far as he could see; with the new interests created by the war, and the constant calls on her time made by the perfection of their home life, she had a useful and busy existence. Again the random thought passed through him: 'But she never tells me anything!' And suddenly that lugubrious khaki-clad figure started up among the rose bushes. "We've got a lot to be thankful for!" he said abruptly. "I must go to work!" His wife, raising one eyebrow, smiled. "And I to weep!" Mr. Bosengate laughed—she had a pretty wit! And stroking his comely moustache where it had been kissed, he moved out into the sunshine. All the evening, throughout his labours, not inconsiderable, for this jury business had put him behind time, he was afflicted by that restless pleasure in his surroundings; would break off in mowing the lower lawn to look at the house through the trees; would leave his study and committee papers to cross into the drawing-room and sniff its dainty fragrance; paid a special good-night visit to the children having supper in the schoolroom; pottered in and out from his dressing-room to admire his wife while she was changing for dinner; dined with his mind perpetually on the next course; talked volubly of the war; and in the billiard-room afterwards, smoking the pipe which had taken the place of his cigar, could not keep still, but roamed about, now in conservatory, now in drawing-room, where his wife and the governess were still making swabs. It seemed to him that he could not have enough of anything. About eleven o'clock he strolled out—beautiful night, only just dark enough—under the new arrangement with Time—and went down to the little round fountain below the terrace. His wife was playing the piano. Mr. Bosengate looked at the water and the flat dark water-lily leaves which floated there; looked up at the house, where only narrow chinks of light showed, because of the Lighting Order. The dreamy music drifted out; there was a scent of heliotrope. He moved a few steps back, and sat in the children's swing under an old lime tree. Jolly—blissful—in the warm, bloomy dark! Of all hours of the day, this before going to bed was perhaps the pleasantest. He saw the light go up in his wife's bedroom, unscreened for a full minute, and thought: 'Aha! If I did my duty as a special, I should "strafe" her for that.' She came to the window, her figure lighted, hands up to the back of her head, so that her bare arms gleamed. Mr. Bosengate wafted her a kiss, knowing he could not be seen. 'Lucky chap!' he mused; 'she's a great joy!' Up went her arm, down came the blind—the house was dark again. He drew a long breath. 'Another ten minutes,' he thought, 'then I'll go in and shut up. By Jove! The limes are beginning to smell already!' And, the better to take in that acme of his well-being, he tilted the swing, lifted his feet from the ground, and swung himself towards the scented blossoms. He wanted to whelm his senses in their perfume, and closed his eyes. But instead of the domestic vision he expected, the face of the little Welsh soldier, hare-eyed, shadowy, pinched and dark and pitiful, started up with such disturbing vividness that he opened his eyes again at once. Curse! The fellow almost haunted one! Where would he be now—poor little devil! lying in his cell, thinking—thinking of his wife! Feeling suddenly morbid, Mr. Bosengate arrested the swing and stood up. Absurd!—all his well-being and mood of warm anticipation had deserted him! 'A d——d world!'

he thought. 'Such a lot of misery! Why should I have to sit in judgment on that poor beggar, and condemn him?' He moved up on to the terrace and walked briskly, to rid himself of this disturbance before going in. 'That commercial traveller chap,' he thought, 'the rest of those fellows—they see nothing!' And, abruptly turning up the three stone steps, he entered the conservatory, locked it, passed into the billiard-room, and drank his barley water. One of the pictures was hanging crooked; he went up to put it straight. Still life. Grapes and apples, and lobsters! They struck him as odd for the first time. Why lobsters? The whole picture seemed dead and oily. He turned off the light, and went upstairs, passed his wife's door, into his own room and undressed. Clothed in his pyjamas he opened the door between the rooms. By the light coming from his own he could see her dark head on the pillow. Was she asleep? No—not asleep, certainly. The moment of fruition had come; the crowning of his pride and pleasure in his home. But he continued to stand there. He had suddenly no pride, no pleasure, no desire; nothing but a sort of dull resentment against everything. He turned back, shut the door, and slipping between the heavy curtains and his open window, stood looking out at the night. 'Full of misery!' he thought. 'Full of d——d misery!'

II

Filing into the jury box next morning, Mr. Bosengate collided slightly with a short juryman, whose square figure and square head of stiff yellow-red hair he had only vaguely noticed the day before. The man looked angry, and Mr. Bosengate thought: 'An ill-bred dog, that!'

He sat down quickly, and, to avoid further recognition of his fellows, gazed in front of him. His appearance on Saturdays was always military, by reason of the route march of his Volunteer Corps in the afternoon. Gentleman Fox, who belonged to the corps too, was also looking square; but that commercial traveller on his other side seemed more *louche*, and as if surprised in immorality, than ever; only the proximity of Gentleman Fox on the other side kept Mr. Bosengate from shrinking. Then he saw the prisoner being brought in, shadowy and dark behind the brightness of his buttons, and he experienced a sort of shock, this figure was so exactly that which had several times started up in his mind. Somehow he had expected a fresh sight of the fellow to dispel and disprove what had been haunting him, had expected to find him just an outside phenomenon, not, as it were, a part of his own life. And he gazed at the carven immobility of the judge's face, trying to steady himself, as a drunken man will, by looking at a light. The regimental doctor, unabashed by the judge's comment on his absence the day before, gave his evidence like a man who had better things to do, and the case for the prosecution was forthwith rounded in by a little speech from counsel. The matter—he said—was clear as daylight. Those who wore His Majesty's uniform, charged with the responsibility and privilege of defending their country, were no more entitled to desert their regiments by taking their own lives than they were entitled to desert in any other way. He asked for a conviction. Mr. Bosengate felt a sympathetic shuffle passing through all feet; the judge was speaking:

"Prisoner, you can either go into the witness box and make your statement on oath, in which case you may be cross-examined on it; or you can make your statement there from the dock, in which case you will not be cross-examined. Which do you elect to do?"

"From here, my lord."

Seeing him now full face, and, as it might be, come to life in the effort to convey his feelings, Mr. Bosengate had suddenly a quite different impression of the fellow. It was as if his khaki had fallen off, and he had stepped out of his own shadow, a live and quivering creature. His pinched clean-shaven face seemed to have an irregular, wilder, hairier look, his large nervous brown eyes darkened and glowed; he jerked his shoulders, his arms, his whole body, like a man suddenly freed from cramp or a suit of armour. He spoke, too, in a quick, crisp, rather high voice, pinching his consonants a little, sharpening his vowels, like a true Welshman.

"My lord and misters the jury," he said: "I was a hairdresser when the call came on me to join the army. I had a little home and a wife. I never thought what it would be like to be away from them, I surely never did; and I'm ashamed to be speaking it out like this—how it can squeeze and squeeze a man, how it can prey on your mind when you're nervous like I am. 'Tis not everyone that cares for his home—there's lots o' them never wants to see their wives again. But for me 'tis like being shut up in a cage, it is!" Mr. Bosengate saw daylight between the skinny fingers of the man's hand thrown out with a jerk. "I cannot bear it shut up away from wife and home like what you are in the army. So when I took my razor that morning I was wild—an' I wouldn't be here now but for that man catching my hand. There was no reason in it, I'm willing to confess. It was foolish; but wait till you get feeling like what I was, and see how it draws you. Misters the jury, don't send me back to prison; it is worse still there. If you have wives you will know what it is like for lots of us; only some is more nervous than others. I swear to you, sirs, I could not help it——" Again the little man flung out his hand, his whole thin body shook and Mr. Bosengate felt the same sensation as when he drove his car over a dog—"Misters the jury, I hope you may never in your lives feel as I've been feeling."

The little man ceased, his eyes shrank back into their sockets, his figure back into its mask of shadowy brown and gleaming buttons, and Mr. Bosengate was conscious that the judge was making a series of remarks; and, very soon, of being seated at a mahogany table in the jury's withdrawing room, hearing the voice of the man with hair like an Irish terrier's saying: "Didn't he talk through his hat, that little blighter!" Conscious, too, of the commercial traveller, still on his left—always on his left!—mopping his brow, and muttering: "Phew! It's hot in there to-day!" while an effluvium, as of an inside accustomed to whisky, came from him. Then the man with the underlip and the three plastered wisps of hair said:

"Don't know why we withdrew, Mr. Foreman!"

Mr. Bosengate looked round to where, at the head of the table, Gentleman Fox sat, in defensive gentility and the little white piping to his waistcoat. "I shall be happy to take the sense of the jury," he was saying blandly.

There was a short silence, then the chemist murmured:

"I should say he must have what they call claustrophobia."

"Clauster fiddlesticks! The feller's a shirker, that's all. Missed his wife—pretty excuse! Indecent, I call it!"

The speaker was the little wire-haired man; and emotion, deep and angry, stirred in Mr. Bosengate. That ill-bred little cur! He gripped the edge of the table with both hands.

"I think it's d——d natural!" he muttered. But almost before the words had left his lips he felt dismay. What had he said—he, nearly a colonel of volunteers—endorsing such a want of patriotism! And hearing the commercial traveller murmuring: " 'Ear, 'ear!" he reddened violently.

The wire-haired man said roughly:

"There's too many of these blighted shirkers, and too much pampering of them."

The turmoil in Mr. Bosengate increased; he remarked in an icy voice:

"I agree to no verdict that'll send the man back to prison."

At this a real tremor seemed to go round the table, as if they all saw themselves sitting there through lunch time. Then the large grey-haired man given to winking said:

"Oh! Come, sir—after what the judge said! Come, sir! What do you say, Mr. Foreman?"

Gentleman Fox—as who should say 'This is excellent value, but I don't wish to press it on you!'—answered:

"We are only concerned with the facts. Did he or did he not try to shorten his life?"

"Of course he did—said so himself," Mr. Bosengate heard the wire-haired man snap out, and from the following murmur of assent he alone abstained. Guilty! Well—yes! There was no way out of admitting that, but his feelings revolted against handing "that poor little beggar" over to the tender mercy of his country's law. His whole soul rose in arms against agreeing with that ill-bred little cur, and the rest of this job-lot. He had an impulse to get up and walk out, saying: "Settle it your own way. Good-morning."

"It seems, sir," Gentleman Fox was saying, "that we're all agreed to guilty, except yourself. If you will allow me, I don't see how you can go behind what the prisoner himself admitted."

Thus brought up to the very guns, Mr. Bosengate, red in the face, thrust his hands deep into the side pockets of his tunic, and, staring straight before him, said:

"Very well; on condition we recommend him to mercy."

"What do you say, gentlemen; shall we recommend him to mercy?"

" 'Ear, 'ear!" burst from the commercial traveller, and from the chemist came the murmur:

"No harm in that."

"Well, I think there is. They shoot deserters at the front, and we let this fellow off. I'd hang the cur."

Mr. Bosengate stared at that little wire-haired brute. "Haven't you *any* feeling for others?" he wanted to say. "Can't you see that this poor devil suffers tortures?" But the sheer impossibility of doing this before ten other men brought a slight sweat out on his face and hands; and in agitation he smote the table a blow with his fist. The effect was instantaneous. Everybody looked at the wire-haired man, as if saying: "Yes, you've gone a bit too far there!" The "little brute" stood it for a moment, then muttered surlily:

"Well, commend 'im to mercy if you like; I don't care."

"That's right; they never pay any attention to it," said the grey-haired man, winking heartily. And Mr. Bosengate filed back with the others into court.

But when from the jury box his eyes fell once more on the hare-eyed figure in the dock, he had his worst moment yet. Why should this poor wretch suffer so—for no fault, no fault; while he, and these others, and that snapping counsel, and the Caesar-like judge up there, went off to their women and their homes, blithe as bees, and probably never thought of him again? And suddenly he was conscious of the judge's voice:

"You will go back to your regiment, and endeavour to serve your country with better spirit. You may thank the jury that you are not sent to prison, and your good fortune that you were not at the front when you tried to commit this cowardly act. You are lucky to be alive."

A policeman pulled the little soldier by the arm; his drab figure, with eyes fixed and lustreless, passed down and away. From his very soul Mr. Bosengate wanted to lean out and say: "Cheer up, cheer up! *I* understand."

It was nearly ten o'clock that evening before he reached home, motoring back from the route march. His physical tiredness was abated, for he had partaken of a snack and a whisky and soda at the hotel; but mentally he was in a curious mood. His body felt appeased, his spirit hungry. Tonight he had a yearning, not for his wife's kisses, but for her understanding. He wanted to go to her and say: "I've learnt a lot to-day—found out things I never thought of. Life's a wonderful thing, Kate, a thing one can't live all to oneself; a thing one shares with everybody, so that when another suffers, one suffers too. It's come to me that what one *has* doesn't matter a bit—it's what one does, and how one sympathises with other people. It came to me in the most extraordinary vivid way, when I was on that jury, watching that poor little rat of a soldier in his trap; it's the first time I've ever felt—the—the spirit of Christ, you know. It's a wonderful thing, Kate—wonderful! We haven't been close—really close, you and I, so that we each understand what the other is feeling. It's all in that, you know; understanding—sympathy—it's priceless. When I saw that poor little devil taken down and sent back to his regiment to begin his sorrows all over again—wanting his wife, thinking and thinking of her just as you know I would be thinking and wanting you, I felt what an awful outside sort of life we lead, never telling each other what we really think and feel, never being really close. I daresay that little chap and his wife keep nothing from each other—live each other's lives. That's what *we* ought to do. Let's get to feeling that what really matters is—understanding and loving, and not only just saying it as we all do, those fellows on the jury, and even that poor devil of a judge—what an awful life, judging one's fellow-creatures! When I left that poor little Tommy this morning, and ever since, I've longed to get back here quietly to you and tell you about it, and make a beginning. There's something wonderful in this, and I want you to feel it as I do, because you mean such a lot to me."

This was what he wanted to say to his wife, not touching, or kissing her, just looking into her eyes, watching them soften and glow as they surely must, catching the infection of his new ardour. And he felt unsteady, fearfully unsteady with the desire to say it all as it should be said: swiftly, quietly, with the truth and fervour of his feeling.

The hall was not lit up, for daylight still lingered under the new arrangement. He went towards the drawing-room, but from the very door shied off to his study and stood irresolute under the picture of a "Man catching a flea" (Dutch school), which had come down to him from his father. The governess would be in there with his wife! He must wait. Essential to go straight to Kathleen and pour it all out, or he would never do it. He felt as nervous as an undergraduate going up for his *vivâ voce*. This thing was so big, so astoundingly and unexpectedly important. He was suddenly afraid of his wife, afraid of her coolness and her grace, and that something Japanese about her—of all those attributes he had been accustomed to admire most; afraid, as it were, of her attraction. He felt young tonight, almost boyish; would she see that he was not really fifteen years older than herself, and she not really a part of his collection, of all the admirable appointments of his home; but a companion spirit to one who wanted a companion badly? In this agitation of his soul he could keep still no more than he could last night in the agitation of his senses; and he wandered into the dining-room. A dainty supper was set out there, sandwiches, and cake, whisky and cigarettes—even an early peach. Mr. Bosengate looked at this peach with sorrow rather than disgust. The perfection of it was of a piece with all that had gone before this new and sudden feeling. Its delicious bloom seemed to heighten his perception of the hedge around him, that hedge of the things he so enjoyed, carefully planted and tended these many years. He passed it by uneaten, and went to the window. Out there all was darkening, the fountain, the lime tree, the flower-beds, and the fields below, with the Jersey cows who would come to your call; darkening slowly, losing form, blurring into soft blackness, vanishing, but there none the less—all there—the hedge of his possessions. He heard the door of the drawing-room open, the voices of his wife and the governess in the hall, going up to bed. If only they didn't look in here! If only——! The voices ceased. He was safe now—had but to follow in a few minutes, to make sure of Kathleen alone. He turned round and stared down the length of the dark dining-room, over the rosewood table, to where, in the mirror above the sideboard at the far end, his figure bathed, a stain, a mere blurred shadow; he made his way down to it along the table edge, and stood before himself as close as he could get. His throat and the roof of his mouth felt dry with nervousness; he put out his finger and touched his face in the glass. 'You're an ass!' he thought. 'Pull yourself together, and get it over. She will see; of course she will!' He swallowed, smoothed his moustache, and walked out. Going up the stairs, his heart beat painfully; but he was in for it now, and marched straight into her room.

Dressed only in a loose blue wrapper, she was brushing her dark hair before the glass. Mr. Bosengate went up to her and stood there silent, looking down. The words he had thought of were like a swarm of bees buzzing in his head yet not one would fly from between his lips. His wife went on brushing her hair under the light which shone on her polished elbows. She looked up at him from beneath one lifted eyebrow.

"Well, dear—tired?"

With a sort of vehemence the single word "No" passed out. A faint, a quizzical smile flitted over her face; she shrugged her shoulders ever so gently. That gesture—he had seen it before! And in a desperate desire to make her understand, he put his hand on her lifted arm.

"Kathleen, stop—listen to me!" His fingers tightened in his agitation and eagerness to make his great discovery known. But before he could get out a word he became conscious of that cool round arm, conscious of her eyes half-closed, sliding round at him, of her half-smiling lips, of her neck under the wrapper. And he stammered:

"I want—I must—Kathleen, I——"

She lifted her shoulders again in that little shrug. "Yes—I know; all right!"

A wave of heat and shame and of God knows what came over Mr. Bosengate; he fell on his knees and pressed his forehead to her arm; and he was silent, more silent than the grave. Nothing—nothing came from him but two long sighs. Suddenly he felt her hand stroke his cheek—compassionately, it seemed to him. She made a little movement towards him; her lips met his, and he remembered nothing but that. . . .

In his own room Mr. Bosengate sat at his wide-open window,

smoking a cigarette; there was no light. Moths went past, the moon was creeping up. He sat very calm, puffing the smoke out into the night air. Curious thing—life! Curious world! Curious forces in it—making one do the opposite of what one wished; always—always making one do the opposite, it seemed! The furtive light from that creeping moon was getting hold of things down there, stealing in among the boughs of the trees. 'There's something ironical,' he thought, 'which walks about. Things don't come off as you think they will. I meant, I tried—but one doesn't change like that all of a sudden, it seems. Fact is, life's too big a thing for one! All the same, I'm not the man I was yesterday—not quite!' He closed his eyes, and in one of those flashes of vision which comes when the senses are at rest, he saw himself as it were far down below—down on the floor of a street narrow as a grave, high as a mountain, a deep dark slit of a street—walking down there, a black midget of a fellow, among other black midgets—his wife, and the little soldier, the judge, and those jury chaps—*fantoches* straight up on their tiny feet, wandering down there in that dark, infinitely tall, and narrow street. 'Too much for one!' he thought. 'Too high for one—no getting on top of it. We've got to be kind, and help one another, and not expect too much, and not think too much. That's—all!' And, squeezing out his cigarette, he took six deep breaths of the night air, and got into bed.

1916.

Charles Dickens

BARDELL v. PICKWICK

*

"I wonder what the foreman of the jury, whoever he'll be, has got for breakfast," said Mr. Snodgrass, by way of keeping up a conversation on the eventful morning of the fourteenth of February.

"Ah!" said Perker, "I hope he's got a good one."

"Why so?" inquired Mr. Pickwick.

"Highly important; very important, my dear sir," replied Perker. "A good, contented, well-breakfasted juryman, is a capital thing to get hold of. Discontented or hungry jurymen, my dear sir, always find for the plaintiff."

"Bless my heart," said Mr. Pickwick, looking very blank; "what do they do that for?"

"Why, I don't know," replied the little man, coolly; "saves time, I suppose. If it's near dinner-time, the foreman takes out his watch, when the jury has retired, and says, 'Dear me, gentlemen, ten minutes to five, I declare! I dine at five, gentlemen.' 'So do I,' says everybody else, except two men who ought to have dined at three, and seem more than half disposed to stand out in consequence. The foreman smiles, puts up his watch:—'Well, gentlemen, what do we say, plaintiff or defendant, gentlemen? I rather think, so far as I am concerned, gentlemen,—I say, I rather think,—but don't let that influence you—I *rather* think the plaintiff's the man.' Upon this, two or three other men are sure to say that they think so too—as of course they do; and then they get on very unanimously and comfortably. Ten minutes past nine!" said the little man, looking at his watch. "Time we were off, my dear sir; breach of promise trial—

court is generally full in such cases. You had better ring for a coach, my dear sir, or we shall be rather late."

Mr. Pickwick immediately rang the bell; and a coach having been procured, the four Pickwickians and Mr. Perker ensconced themselves therein, and drove to Guildhall; Sam Weller, Mr. Lowten, and the blue bag, following in a cab.

"Lowten," said Perker, when they reached the outer hall of the court, "put Mr. Pickwick's friends in the students' box; Mr. Pickwick himself had better sit by me. This way, my dear sir, this way." Taking Mr. Pickwick by the coat-sleeve, the little man led him to the low seat just beneath the desks of the King's Counsel, which is constructed for the convenience of attorneys, who from that spot can whisper into the ear of the leading counsel in the case, any instructions that may be necessary during the progress of the trial. The occupants of this seat are invisible to the great body of spectators, inasmuch as they sit on a much lower level than either the barristers or the audience, whose seats are raised above the floor. Of course they have their backs to both, and their faces towards the judge.

"That's the witness-box, I suppose?" said Mr. Pickwick, pointing to a kind of pulpit, with a brass rail, on his left hand.

"That's the witness-box, my dear sir," replied Perker, disinterring a quantity of papers from the blue bag, which Lowten had just deposited at his feet.

"And that," said Mr. Pickwick, pointing to a couple of enclosed seats on his right, "that's where the jurymen sit, is it not?"

"The identical place, my dear sir," replied Perker, tapping the lid of his snuff-box.

Mr. Pickwick stood up in a state of great agitation, and took a glance at the court. There were already a pretty large sprinkling of spectators in the gallery, and a numerous muster of gentlemen in wigs, in the barristers' seats: who presented, as a body, all that pleasing and extensive variety of nose and whisker for which the bar of England is so justly celebrated. Such of the gentlemen as had a brief to carry, carried it in as conspicuous a manner as possible, and occasionally scratched their noses therewith, to impress the fact more strongly on the observation of the spectators. Other gentlemen, who had no briefs to show, carried under their arms goodly octavos, with a red label behind, and that underdone-pie-crust-coloured cover, which is technically known as "law calf". Others, who had neither briefs nor books, thrust their hands into their pockets, and looked as wise as they conveniently could; others, again, moved here and there with great restlessness and earnestness of manner, content to awaken thereby the admiration and astonishment of the uninitiated strangers. The whole, to the great wonderment of Mr. Pickwick, were divided into little groups, who were chatting and discussing the news of the day in the most unfeeling manner possible,—just as if no trial at all were coming on.

A bow from Mr. Phunky, as he entered, and took his seat behind the row appropriated to the King's Counsel, attracted Mr. Pickwick's attention; and he had scarcely returned it, when Mr. Serjeant Snubbin appeared, followed by Mr. Mallard, who half hid the Serjeant behind a large crimson bag, which he placed on his table, and, after shaking hands with Perker, withdrew. Then there entered two or three more Serjeants; and among them, one with a fat body and a red face, who nodded in a friendly manner to Mr. Serjeant Snubbin, and said it was a fine morning.

"Who's that red-faced man, who said it was a fine morning, and nodded to our counsel?" whispered Mr. Pickwick.

"Mr. Serjeant Buzfuz," replied Perker. "He's opposed to us; he leads on the other side. That gentleman behind him is Mr. Skimpin, his junior."

Mr. Pickwick was on the point of inquiring, with great abhorrence of the man's cold-blooded villainy, how Mr. Serjeant Buzfuz, who was counsel for the opposite party, dared to presume to tell Mr. Serjeant Snubbin, who was counsel for him, that it was a fine morning, when he was interrupted by a general rising of the barristers, and a loud cry of "Silence!" from the officers of the court. Looking round, he found that this was caused by the entrance of the judge.

Mr. Justice Stareleigh (who sat in the absence of the Chief Justice, occasioned by indisposition) was a most particularly short man, and so fat, that he seemed all face and waistcoat. He rolled in, upon two little turned legs, and having bobbed gravely to the bar, who bobbed gravely to him, put his little legs underneath his table, and his little three-cornered hat upon it; and when Mr. Justice Stareleigh had done this, all you could see of him was two queer little eyes, one broad pink face, and somewhere about half of a big and very comical-looking wig.

The judge had no sooner taken his seat, than the officer on the floor of the court called out "Silence!" in a commanding tone, upon which another officer in the gallery cried "Silence!" in an angry manner, whereupon three or four more ushers shouted "Silence!" in a voice of indignant remonstrance. This being done, a gentleman in black, who sat below the judge, proceeded to call over the names of the jury; and after a great deal of bawling, it was discovered that only ten special jurymen were present. Upon this, Mr. Serjeant Buzfuz prayed a *tales*; the gentleman in black then proceeded to press into the special jury, two of the common jurymen; and a green-grocer and a chemist were caught directly.

"Answer to your names, gentlemen, that you may be sworn," said the gentleman in black. "Richard Upwitch."

"Here," said the green-grocer.

"Thomas Groffin."

"Here," said the chemist.

"Take the book, gentlemen. You shall well and truly try——"

"I beg this court's pardon," said the chemist, who was a tall, thin, yellow-visaged man, "but I hope this court will excuse my attendance."

"On what grounds, sir?" said Mr. Justice Stareleigh.

"I have no assistant, my Lord," said the chemist.

"I can't help that, sir," replied Mr. Justice Stareleigh. "You should hire one."

"I can't afford it, my Lord," rejoined the chemist.

"Then you ought to be able to afford it, sir," said the judge, reddening; for Justice Stareleigh's temper bordered on the irritable, and brooked not contradiction.

"I know I *ought* to do, if I got on as well as I deserved, but I don't, my Lord," answered the chemist.

"Swear the gentleman," said the judge, peremptorily.

The officer had got no further than the "You shall well and truly try," when he was again interrupted by the chemist.

"I am to be sworn, my Lord, am I?" said the chemist.

"Certainly, sir," replied the testy little judge.

"Very well, my Lord," replied the chemist, in a resigned manner. "Then there'll be murder before this trial's over; that's all. Swear me, if you please, sir;" and sworn the chemist was, before the judge could find words to utter.

"I merely wanted to observe, my Lord," said the chemist, taking his seat with great deliberation, "that I've left nobody but an errand-boy in my shop. He is a very nice boy, my Lord, but he is not acquainted with drugs; and I know that the prevailing impression on his mind is that Epsom salts means oxalic acid; and syrup of senna, laudanum. That's all, my Lord." With this, the tall chemist composed himself into a comfortable attitude, and, assuming a pleasant expression of countenance, appeared to have prepared himself for the worst.

Mr. Pickwick was regarding the chemist with feelings of the deepest horror, when a slight sensation was perceptible in the body of the court; and immediately afterwards Mrs. Bardell, supported by Mrs. Cluppins, was led in, and placed in a drooping state, at the other end of the seat on which Mr. Pickwick sat. An extra sized umbrella was then handed in by Mr. Dodson, and a pair of pattens by Mr. Fogg, each of whom had prepared a most sympathising and melancholy face for the occasion. Mrs. Sanders then appeared, leading in Master Bardell. At sight of her child, Mrs. Bardell started; suddenly recollecting herself, she kissed him in a frantic manner; then relapsing into a state of hysterical imbecility, the good lady requested to be informed where she was. In reply to this, Mrs. Cluppins and Mrs. Sanders turned their heads away and wept, while Messrs. Dodson and Fogg intreated the plaintiff to compose herself. Serjeant Buzfuz rubbed his eyes very hard with a large white handkerchief, and gave an appealing look towards the jury, while the judge was visibly affected, and several of the beholders tried to cough down their emotions.

"Very good notion, that, indeed," whispered Perker to Mr. Pickwick. "Capital fellows those Dodson and Fogg, excellent ideas of effect, my dear sir, excellent."

As Perker spoke, Mrs. Bardell began to recover by slow degrees, while Mrs. Cluppins, after a careful survey of Master Bardell's buttons and the button-holes to which they severally belonged, placed him on the floor of the court in front of his mother,—a commanding position in which he could not fail to awaken the full commiseration and sympathy of both judge and jury. This was not done without considerable opposition, and many tears, on the part of the young gentleman himself, who had certain inward misgivings that the placing him within the full glare of the judge's eye was only a formal prelude to his being immediately ordered away for instant execution, or for transportation beyond the seas, during the whole term of his natural life, at the very least.

"Bardell and Pickwick," cried the gentleman in black, calling on the case, which stood first on the list.

"I am for the plaintiff, my Lord," said Mr. Serjeant Buzfuz.

"Who is with you, brother Buzfuz?" said the judge. Mr. Skimpin bowed, to intimate that he was.

"I appear for the defendant, my Lord," said Mr. Serjeant Snubbin.

"Anybody with you, brother Snubbin?" inquired the court.

"Mr. Phunky, my Lord," replied Serjeant Snubbin.

"Serjeant Buzfuz and Mr. Skimpin for the plaintiff," said the judge, writing down the names in his note-book, and reading as he wrote; "for the defendant, Serjeant Snubbin and Mr. Monkey."

"Beg your Lordship's pardon, Phunky."

"Oh, very good," said the judge; "I never had the pleasure of hearing the gentleman's name before." Here Mr. Phunky bowed and smiled, and the judge bowed and smiled too, and then Mr. Phunky, blushing into the very whites of his eyes, tried to look as if he didn't know that everybody was gazing at him: a thing which no man ever succeeded in doing yet, or in all reasonable probability, ever will.

"Go on," said the judge.

The ushers again called silence, and Mr. Skimpin proceeded to "open the case"; and the case appeared to have very little inside it when he had opened it, for he kept such particulars as he knew, completely to himself, and sat down, after a lapse of three minutes, leaving the jury in precisely the same advanced stage of wisdom as they were in before.

Serjeant Buzfuz then rose with all the majesty and dignity which the grave nature of the proceedings demanded, and having whispered to Dodson, and conferred briefly with Fogg, pulled his gown over his shoulders, settled his wig, and addressed the jury.

Serjeant Buzfuz began by saying, that never, in the whole course of his professional experience—never, from the very first moment of his applying himself to the study and practice of the law—had he approached a case with feelings of such deep emotion, or with such a heavy sense of the responsibility imposed upon him—a responsibility, he would say, which he could never have supported, were he not buoyed up and sustained by a conviction so strong, that it amounted to positive certainty that the cause of truth and justice, or, in other words, the cause of his much-injured and most oppressed client, must prevail with the high-minded and intelligent dozen of men whom he now saw in that box before him.

Counsel usually begin in this way, because it puts the jury on the very best terms with themselves, and makes them think what sharp fellows they must be. A visible effect was produced immediately; several jurymen beginning to take voluminous notes with the utmost eagerness.

"You have heard from my learned friend, gentlemen," continued Serjeant Buzfuz, well knowing that, from the learned friend alluded to, the gentlemen of the jury had heard just nothing at all—"you have heard from my learned friend, gentlemen, that this is an action for a breach of promise of marriage, in which the damages are laid at £1,500. But you have not heard from my learned friend, inasmuch as it did not come within my learned friend's province to tell you, what are the facts and circumstances of the case. Those facts and circumstances, gentlemen, you shall hear detailed by me, and proved by the unimpeachable female whom I will place in that box before you."

Here Mr. Serjeant Buzfuz, with a tremendous emphasis on the word "box", smote his table with a mighty sound, and glanced at Dodson and Fogg, who nodded admiration of the serjeant, and indignant defiance of the defendant.

"The plaintiff, gentlemen," continued Serjeant Buzfuz, in a soft and melancholy voice, "the plaintiff is a widow; yes, gentlemen, a widow. The late Mr. Bardell, after enjoying, for many years, the esteem and confidence of his sovereign, as one of the guardians of his royal revenues, glided almost imperceptibly from the world, to seek elsewhere for that repose and peace which a custom-house can never afford."

At this pathetic description of the decease of Mr. Bardell, who had been knocked on the head with a quart-pot in a public-house cellar, the learned serjeant's voice faltered, and he proceeded with emotion:

"Some time before his death, he had stamped his likeness upon a little boy. With this little boy, the only pledge of her departed exciseman, Mrs. Bardell shrunk from the world, and courted the retirement and tranquillity of Goswell Street; and here she placed in her front parlour-window a written placard, bearing this inscription —'Apartments furnished for a single gentleman. Inquire within.'" Here Serjeant Buzfuz paused, while several gentlemen of the jury took a note of the document.

"There is no date to that, is there, sir?" inquired a juror.

"There is no date, gentlemen," replied Serjeant Buzfuz; "but I am instructed to say that it was put in the plaintiff's parlour-window just this time three years. I intreat the attention of the jury to the wording of this document, 'Apartments furnished for a single gentleman'! Mrs. Bardell's opinions of the opposite sex, gentlemen, were derived from a long contemplation of the inestimable qualities of her lost husband. She had no fear, she had no distrust, she had no suspicion, all was confidence and reliance. 'Mr. Bardell,' said the widow; 'Mr. Bardell was a man of honour, Mr. Bardell was a man of his word, Mr. Bardell was no deceiver, Mr. Bardell was once a single gentleman himself; *to* single gentlemen I look for protection, for assistance, for comfort, and for consolation; *in* single gentlemen I shall perpetually see something to remind me of what Mr. Bardell was, when he first won my young and untried affections; to a single gentleman, then, shall my lodgings be let.' Actuated by this beautiful and touching impulse (among the best impulses of our imperfect nature, gentlemen), the lonely and desolate widow dried her tears, furnished her first floor, caught the innocent boy to her maternal bosom, and put the bill up in her parlour-window. Did it remain there long? No. The serpent was on the watch, the train was laid, the mine was preparing, the sapper and miner was at work. Before the bill had been in the parlour-window three days—three days—gentlemen—a Being, erect upon two legs, and bearing all the outward semblance of a man, and not of a monster, knocked at the door of Mrs. Bardell's house. He inquired within; he took the lodgings; and on the very next day he entered into possession of them. This man was Pickwick—Pickwick, the defendant."

Serjeant Buzfuz, who had proceeded with such volubility that his face was perfectly crimson, here paused for breath. The silence awoke Mr. Justice Stareleigh, who immediately wrote down something with a pen without any ink in it, and looked unusually profound, to impress the jury with the belief that he always thought most deeply with his eyes shut. Serjeant Buzfuz proceeded.

"Of this man Pickwick I will say little; the subject presents but few attractions; and I, gentlemen, am not the man, nor are you, gentlemen, the men, to delight in the contemplation of revolting heartlessness, and of systematic villainy."

Here Mr. Pickwick, who had been writhing in silence for some time, gave a violent start, as if some vague idea of assaulting Serjeant Buzfuz, in the august presence of justice and law, suggested itself to his mind. An admonitory gesture from Perker restrained him, and he listened to the learned gentleman's continuation with a look of indignation, which contrasted forcibly with the admiring faces of Mrs. Cluppins and Mrs. Sanders.

"I say systematic villainy, gentlemen," said Serjeant Buzfuz, looking through Mr. Pickwick, and talking *at* him; "and when I say systematic villainy, let me tell the defendant Pickwick, if he be in court, as I am informed he is, that it would have been more decent in him, more becoming, in better judgment, and in better taste, if he had stopped away. Let me tell him, gentlemen, that any gestures of dissent or disapprobation in which he may indulge in this court will not go down with you; that you will know how to value and how to appreciate them; and let me tell him further, as my lord will tell you, gentlemen, that a counsel, in the discharge of his duty to his client, is neither to be intimidated, nor bullied, nor put down; and that any attempt to do either the one or the other, or the first, or the last, will recoil on the head of the attempter, be he plaintiff or be he defendant, be his name Pickwick, or Noakes, or Stoakes, or Stiles, or Brown, or Thompson."

This little divergence from the subject in hand had, of course, the intended effect of turning all eyes to Mr. Pickwick. Serjeant Buzfuz, having partially recovered from the state of moral elevation into which he had lashed himself, resumed:

"I shall show you, gentlemen, that for two years Pickwick continued to reside constantly, and without interruption or intermission, at Mrs. Bardell's house. I shall show you that Mrs. Bardell, during the whole of that time, waited on him, attended to his comforts, cooked his meals, looked out his linen for the washerwoman when it went abroad, darned, aired, and prepared it for wear, when it came home, and, in short, enjoyed his fullest trust and confidence. I shall show you that, on many occasions, he gave halfpence, and on some occasions even sixpences, to her little boy; and I shall prove to you, by a witness whose testimony it will be impossible for my learned friend to weaken or controvert, that on one occasion he patted the boy on the head, and, after inquiring whether he had won any *alley tors* or *commoneys* lately (both of which I understand to be a particular species of marbles much prized by the youth of this town), made use of this remarkable expression: 'How should you like to have another father?' I shall prove to you, gentlemen, that about a year ago, Pickwick suddenly began to absent himself from home, during long intervals, as if with the intention of gradually breaking off from my client; but I shall show you also, that his resolution was not at that time sufficiently strong, or that his better feelings conquered, if better feelings he has, or that the charms and accomplishments of my client prevailed against his unmanly intentions; by proving to you, that on one occasion, when he returned from the country, he distinctly and in terms, offered her marriage: previously however, taking special care that there should be no witness to their solemn contract; and I am in a situation to prove to you, on the testimony of three of his own friends,—most unwilling witnesses, gentlemen—most unwilling witnesses—that on that morning he was discovered by them holding the plaintiff in his arms, and soothing her agitation by his caresses and endearments."

A visible impression was produced upon the auditors by this part of the learned serjeant's address. Drawing forth two very small scraps of paper, he proceeded:

"And now, gentlemen, but one word more. Two letters have passed between these parties, letters which are admitted to be in the handwriting of the defendant, and which speak volumes indeed. These letters, too, bespeak the character of the man. They are not open, fervent, eloquent epistles, breathing nothing but the language of affectionate attachment. They are covert, sly, underhanded communications, but, fortunately, far more conclusive than if couched in the most glowing language and the most poetic imagery—letters that must be viewed with a cautious and suspicious eye—letters that were evidently intended at the time, by Pickwick, to mislead and delude any third parties into whose hands they might fall. Let me read the first:—'Garraway's, twelve o'clock. Dear Mrs. B.—Chops and Tomato sauce. Yours, Pickwick.' Gentlemen, what does this mean? Chops and Tomato sauce! Yours, Pickwick! Chops! Gracious heavens! and Tomato sauce! Gentlemen, is the happiness of a sensitive and confiding female to be trifled away, by such shallow artifices as these? The next has no date whatever, which in itself is suspicious. 'Dear Mrs. B., I shall not be at home till to-morrow. Slow coach.' And then follows this very remarkable expression. 'Don't trouble yourself about the warming-pan.' The warming-pan! Why, gentlemen, who *does* trouble himself about a warming-pan? When was the peace of mind of man or woman broken or disturbed by a warming-pan, which is in itself a harmless, a useful, and I will add, gentlemen, a comforting article of domestic furniture? Why is Mrs. Bardell so earnestly entreated not to agitate herself about this warming-pan, unless (as is no doubt the case) it is a mere cover for hidden fire—a mere substitute for some endearing word or promise, agreeably to a preconcerted system of correspondence, artfully contrived by Pickwick with a view to his contemplated desertion, and which I am not in a condition to explain? And what does this allusion to the slow coach mean? For aught I know, it may be a reference to Pickwick himself, who has most unquestionably been a criminally slow coach during the whole of this transaction, but whose speed will now be very unexpectedly accelerated, and whose wheels, gentlemen, as he will find to his cost, will very soon be greased by you!"

Mr. Serjeant Buzfuz paused in this place, to see whether the jury smiled at his joke: but as nobody took it but the greengrocer, whose sensitiveness on the subject was very probably occasioned by his having subjected a chaise-cart to the process in question on that identical morning, the learned serjeant considered it advisable to undergo a slight relapse into the dismals before he concluded.

"But enough of this, gentlemen," said Mr. Serjeant Buzfuz, "it is difficult to smile with an aching heart; it is ill jesting when our deepest sympathies are awakened. My client's hopes and prospects are ruined, and it is no figure of speech to say that her occupation is gone indeed. The bill is down—but there is no tenant. Eligible single gentlemen pass and repass—but there is no invitation for them to inquire within or without. All is gloom and silence in the house; even the voice of the child is hushed; his infant sports are disregarded when his mother weeps; his 'alley tors' and his 'commoneys' are alike neglected; he forgets the long familiar cry of 'knuckle down', and at tip-cheese, or odd and even, his hand is out. But Pickwick, gentlemen, Pickwick, the ruthless destroyer of this domestic oasis in the desert of Goswell Street—Pickwick, who has choked up the well, and thrown ashes on the sward—Pickwick, who comes before you to-day with his heartless Tomato sauce and warming-pans—Pickwick still rears his head with unblushing effrontery, and gazes without a sigh on the ruin he has made. Damages, gentlemen—heavy damages—is the only punishment with which you can visit him; the only recompense you can award to my client. And for those damages she now appeals to an enlightened, a high-minded, a right-feeling, a conscientious, a dispassionate, a sympathising, a contemplative jury of her civilised countrymen." With this beautiful peroration, Mr. Serjeant Buzfuz sat down, and Mr. Justice Stareleigh woke up.

"Call Elizabeth Cluppins," said Serjeant Buzfuz, rising a minute afterwards, with renewed vigour.

The nearest usher called for Elizabeth Tuppins; another one, at a little distance off, demanded Elizabeth Jupkins; and a third rushed in a breathless state into King Street, and screamed for Elizabeth Muffins till he was hoarse.

Meanwhile Mrs. Cluppins, with the combined assistance of Mrs. Bardell, Mrs. Sanders, Mr. Dodson, and Mr. Fogg, was hoisted into the witness-box; and when she was safely perched on the top step, Mrs. Bardell stood on the bottom one, with the pocket-handkerchief and pattens in one hand, and a glass bottle that might hold about a quarter of a pint of smelling salts in the other, ready for any emergency. Mrs. Sanders, whose eyes were intently fixed on the judge's face, planted herself close by, with the large umbrella: keeping her right thumb pressed on the spring with an earnest countenance, as if she were fully prepared to put it up at a moment's notice.

"Mrs. Cluppins," said Serjeant Buzfuz, "pray compose yourself, ma'am." Of course, directly Mrs. Cluppins was desired to compose herself she sobbed with increased vehemence, and gave divers alarming manifestations of an approaching fainting fit, or, as she afterwards said, of her feelings being too many for her.

"Do you recollect, Mrs. Cluppins?" said Serjeant Buzfuz, after a few unimportant questions, "do you recollect being in Mrs. Bardell's back one pair of stairs, on one particular morning in July last, when she was dusting Pickwick's apartment?"

"Yes, my Lord and Jury, I do," replied Mrs. Cluppins.

"Mr. Pickwick's sitting-room was the first-floor front, I believe?"

"Yes, it were, sir," replied Mrs. Cluppins.

"What were you doing in the back room, ma'am?" inquired the little judge.

"My Lord and Jury," said Mrs. Cluppins, with interesting agitation, "I will not deceive you."

"You had better not, ma'am," said the little judge.

"I was there," resumed Mrs. Cluppins, "unbeknown to Mrs. Bardell; I had been out with a little basket, gentlemen, to buy three pound of red kidney purtaties, which was three pound tuppence ha'penny, when I see Mrs. Bardell's street door on the jar."

"On the what?" exclaimed the little judge.

"Partly open, my Lord," said Serjeant Snubbin.

"She *said* on the jar," said the little judge, with a cunning look.

"It's all the same, my Lord," said Serjeant Snubbin. The little judge looked doubtful, and said he'd make a note of it. Mrs. Cluppins then resumed:

"I walked in, gentlemen, just to say good mornin', and went, in a permiscuous manner, up-stairs, and into the back room. Gentlemen, there was the sound of voices in the front room, and——"

"And you listened, I believe, Mrs. Cluppins?" said Serjeant Buzfuz.

"Beggin' your pardon, sir," replied Mrs. Cluppins, in a majestic manner, "I would scorn the haction. The voices was very loud, sir, and forced themselves upon my ear."

"Well, Mrs. Cluppins, you were not listening, but you heard the voices. Was one of those voices Pickwick's?"

"Yes, it were, sir."

And Mrs. Cluppins, after distinctly stating that Mr. Pickwick addressed himself to Mrs. Bardell, repeated, by slow degrees, and by dint of many questions, the conversation with which our readers are already acquainted.

The jury looked suspicious, and Mr. Serjeant Buzfuz smiled and sat down. They looked positively awful when Serjeant Snubbin intimated that he should not cross-examine the witness, for Mr. Pickwick wished it to be distinctly stated that it was due to her to say, that her account was in substance correct.

Mrs. Cluppins having once broken the ice, thought it a favourable opportunity for entering into a short dissertation on her own domestic affairs; so, she straightway proceeded to inform the court that she was the mother of eight children at that present speaking, and that she entertained confident expectations of presenting Mr. Cluppins with a ninth, somewhere about that day six months. At this interesting point, the little judge interposed most irascibly; and the effect of the interposition was, that both the worthy lady and Mrs. Sanders were politely taken out of court, under the escort of Mr. Jackson, without further parley.

"Nathaniel Winkle!" said Mr. Skimpin.

"Here!" replied a feeble voice. Mr. Winkle entered the witness box, and having been duly sworn, bowed to the judge with considerable deference.

"Don't look at me, sir," said the judge, sharply, in acknowledgment of the salute; "look at the jury."

Mr. Winkle obeyed the mandate, and looked at the place where he thought it most probable the jury might be; for seeing anything in his then state of intellectual complication was wholly out of the question.

Mr. Winkle was then examined by Mr. Skimpin, who, being a promising young man of two or three and forty, was of course anxious to confuse a witness who was notoriously predisposed in favour of the other side, as much as he could.

"Now, sir," said Mr. Skimpin, "have the goodness to let his Lordship and the jury know what your name is, will you?" and Mr. Skimpin inclined his head on one side to listen with great sharpness to the answer, and glanced at the jury meanwhile, as if to imply that he rather expected Mr. Winkle's natural taste for perjury would induce him to give some name which did not belong to him.

"Winkle," replied the witness.

"What's your Christian name, sir?" angrily inquired the little judge.

"Nathaniel, sir."

"Daniel,—any other name?"

"Nathaniel, sir—my Lord, I mean."

"Nathaniel Daniel, or Daniel Nathaniel?"

"No, my Lord, only Nathaniel; not Daniel at all."

"What did you tell me it was Daniel for, then, sir?" inquired the judge.

"I didn't, my Lord," replied Mr. Winkle.

"You did, sir," replied the judge, with a severe frown. "How could I have got Daniel on my notes, unless you told me so, sir?"

This argument was, of course, unanswerable.

"Mr. Winkle has rather a short memory, my Lord," interposed Mr. Skimpin, with another glance at the jury. "We shall find means to refresh it before we have quite done with him, I daresay."

"You had better be careful, sir," said the little judge, with a sinister look at the witness.

Poor Mr. Winkle bowed, and endeavoured to feign an easiness of manner, which, in his then state of confusion, gave him rather the air of a disconcerted pickpocket.

"Now, Mr. Winkle," said Mr. Skimpin, "attend to me, if you please, sir; and let me recommend you, for your own sake, to bear in mind his Lordship's injunction to be careful. I believe you are a particular friend of Pickwick, the defendant, are you not?"

"I have known Mr. Pickwick now, as well as I recollect at this moment, nearly——"

"Pray, Mr. Winkle, do not evade the question. Are you, or are you not, a particular friend of the defendant's?"

"I was just about to say, that——"

"Will you, or will you not, anwer my question, sir?"

"If you don't answer the question you'll be committed, sir," interposed the little judge, looking over his note-book.

"Come, sir," said Mr. Skimpin, "yes or no, if you please."

"Yes, I am," replied Mr. Winkle.

"Yes, you are. And why couldn't you say that at once, sir? Perhaps you know the plaintiff, too? Eh, Mr. Winkle?"

"I don't know her; I've seen her."

"Oh, you don't know her, but you've seen her? Now, have the goodness to tell the gentlemen of the jury what you mean by *that*, Mr. Winkle."

"I mean that I am not intimate with her, but I have seen her when I went to call on Mr. Pickwick in Goswell Street."

"How often have you seen her, sir?"

"How often?"

"Yes, Mr. Winkle, how often? I'll repeat the question for you a dozen times, if you require it, sir." And the learned gentleman, with a firm and steady frown, placed his hands on his hips, and smiled suspiciously at the jury.

On this question there arose the edifying brow-beating, customary on such points. First of all, Mr. Winkle said it was quite impossible for him to say how many times he had seen Mrs. Bardell. Then he was asked if he had seen her twenty times, to which he replied, "Certainly,—more than that." Then he was asked whether he hadn't seen her a hundred times—whether he couldn't swear that he had seen her more than fifty times—whether he didn't know that he had seen her at least seventy-five times—and so forth; the satisfactory confusion which was arrived at, at last, being, that he had better take care of himself, and mind what he was about. The witness having been by these means reduced to the requisite ebb of nervous perplexity, the examination was continued as follows:

"Pray, Mr. Winkle, do you remember calling on the defendant

Pickwick at these apartments in the plaintiff's house in Goswell Street, on one particular morning, in the month of July last?"

"Yes, I do."

"Were you accompanied on that occasion by a friend of the name of Tupman, and another of the name of Snodgrass?"

"Yes, I was."

"Are they here?"

"Yes, they are," replied Mr. Winkle, looking very earnestly towards the spot where his friends were stationed.

"Pray attend to me, Mr. Winkle, and never mind your friends," said Mr. Skimpin, with another expressive look at the jury. "They must tell their stories without any previous consultation with you, if none has yet taken place (another look at the jury). Now, sir, tell the gentlemen of the jury what you saw on entering the defendant's room, on this particular morning. Come; out with it, sir; we must have it, sooner or later."

"The defendant, Mr. Pickwick, was holding the plaintiff in his arms, with his hands clasping her waist," replied Mr. Winkle with natural hesitation, "and the plaintiff appeared to have fainted away."

"Did you hear the defendant say anything?"

"I heard him call Mrs. Bardell a good creature, and I heard him ask her to compose herself, for what a situation it was, if anybody should come, or words to that effect."

"Now, Mr. Winkle, I have only one more question to ask you, and I beg you to bear in mind his lordship's caution. Will you undertake to swear that Pickwick, the defendant, did not say on the occasion in question, 'My dear Mrs. Bardell, you're a good creature; compose yourself to this situation, for to this situation you must come,' or words to *that* effect?"

"I—I didn't understand him so, certainly," said Mr. Winkle, astounded at this ingenious dove-tailing of the few words he had heard. "I was on the staircase, and couldn't hear distinctly; the impression on my mind is——"

"The gentlemen of the jury want none of the impressions on your mind, Mr. Winkle, which I fear would be of little service to honest, straightforward men," interposed Mr. Skimpin. "You were on the staircase, and didn't distinctly hear; but you will not swear that Pickwick did not make use of the expressions I have quoted? Do I understand that?"

"No, I will not," replied Mr. Winkle; and down sat Mr. Skimpin with a triumphant countenance.

Mr. Pickwick's case had not gone off in so particularly happy a manner, up to this point, that it could very well afford to have any additional suspicion cast upon it. But as it could afford to be placed in a rather better light, if possible, Mr. Phunky rose for the purpose of getting something important out of Mr. Winkle in cross-examination. Whether he did get anything important out of him, will immediately appear.

" I believe, Mr. Winkle," said Mr. Phunky, "that Mr. Pickwick is not a young man?"

"Oh no," replied Mr. Winkle, "old enough to be my father."

"You have told my learned friend that you have known Mr. Pickwick a long time. Had you ever any reason to suppose or believe that he was about to be married?"

"Oh no; certainly not," replied Mr. Winkle with so much eagerness, that Mr. Phunky ought to have got him out of the box with all possible dispatch. Lawyers hold that there are two kinds of particularly bad witnesses: a reluctant witness, and a too-willing witness; it was Mr. Winkle's fate to figure in both characters.

"I will even go further than this, Mr. Winkle," continued Mr. Phunky in a most smooth and complacent manner. "Did you ever see anything in Mr. Pickwick's manner and conduct towards the opposite sex, to induce you to believe that he ever contemplated matrimony of late years, in any case?"

"Oh no; certainly not," replied Mr. Winkle.

"Has his behaviour, when females have been in the case, always been that of a man, who, having attained a pretty advanced period of life, content with his own occupations and amusements, treats them only as a father might his daughters?"

"Not the least doubt of it," replied Mr. Winkle, in the fulness of his heart. "That is—yes—oh yes—certainly."

"You have never known anything in his behaviour towards Mrs. Bardell, or any other female, in the least degree suspicious?" said

Mr. Phunky, preparing to sit down; for Serjeant Snubbin was winking at him.

"N-n-no," replied Mr. Winkle, "except on one trifling occasion, which, I have no doubt, might be easily explained."

Now, if the unfortunate Mr. Phunky had sat down when Serjeant Snubbin winked at him, or if Serjeant Buzfuz had stopped this irregular cross-examination at the outset (which he knew better than to do; observing Mr. Winkle's anxiety, and well knowing it would, in all probability, lead to something serviceable to him), this unfortunate admission would not have been elicited. The moment the words fell from Mr. Winkle's lips, Mr. Phunky sat down, and Serjeant Snubbin rather hastily told him he might leave the box, which Mr. Winkle prepared to do with great readiness, when Serjeant Buzfuz stopped him.

"Stay, Mr. Winkle, stay!" said Serjeant Buzfuz. "Will your lordship have the goodness to ask him, what this one instance of suspicious behaviour towards females on the part of this gentleman, who is old enough to be his father, was?"

"You hear what the learned counsel says, sir," observed the judge, turning to the miserable and agonised Mr. Winkle. "Describe the occasion to which you refer."

"My lord," said Mr. Winkle, trembling with anxiety, "I—I'd rather not."

"Perhaps so," said the little judge; "but you must."

Amid the profound silence of the whole court, Mr. Winkle faltered out, that the trifling circumstance of suspicion was Mr. Pickwick's being found in a lady's sleeping apartment at midnight; which had terminated, he believed, in the breaking off of the projected marriage of the lady in question, and had led, he knew, to the whole party being forcibly carried before George Nupkins, Esq., magistrate and justice of the peace, for the borough of Ipswich!

"You may leave the box, sir," said Serjeant Snubbin. Mr. Winkle *did* leave the box, and rushed with delirious haste to the George and Vulture, where he was discovered some hours after, by the waiter, groaning in a hollow and dismal manner, with his head buried beneath the sofa cushions.

Tracy Tupman, and Augustus Snodgrass, were severally called

into the box; both corroborated the testimony of their unhappy friend; and each was driven to the verge of desperation by excessive badgering.

Susannah Sanders was then called, and examined by Serjeant Buzfuz, and cross-examined by Serjeant Snubbin. Had always said and believed that Pickwick would marry Mrs. Bardell; knew that Mrs. Bardell's being engaged to Pickwick was the current topic of conversation in the neighbourhood, after the fainting in July; had been told it herself by Mrs. Mudberry which kept a mangle, and Mrs. Bunkin which clear-starched, but did not see either Mrs. Mudberry or Mrs. Bunkin in court. Had heard Pickwick ask the little boy how he should like to have another father. Did not know that Mrs. Bardell was at that time keeping company with the baker, but did know that the baker was then a single man and is now married. Couldn't swear that Mrs. Bardell was not very fond of the baker, but should think that the baker was not very fond of Mrs. Bardell, or he wouldn't have married somebody else. Thought Mrs. Bardell fainted away on the morning in July, because Pickwick asked her to name the day; knew that she (witness) fainted away stone dead when Mr. Sanders asked *her* to name the day, and believed that everybody as called herself a lady would do the same, under similar circumstances. Heard Pickwick ask the boy the question about the marbles, but upon her oath did not know the difference between an alley tor and a commoney.

By the COURT.—During the period of her keeping company with Mr. Sanders, had received love letters, like other ladies. In the course of their correspondence Mr. Sanders had often called her a "duck", but never "chops", nor yet "tomato sauce". He was particularly fond of ducks. Perhaps if he had been as fond of chops and tomato sauce, he might have called her that, as a term of affection.

Serjeant Buzfuz now rose with more importance than he had yet exhibited, if that were possible, and vociferated: "Call Samuel Weller."

It was quite unnecessary to call Samuel Weller; for Samuel Weller stepped briskly into the box the instant his name was pronounced; and placing his hat on the floor, and his arms on the rail, took a bird's-eye view of the bar, and a comprehensive survey of the bench, with a remarkably cheerful and lively aspect.

"What's your name, sir?" inquired the judge.

"Sam Weller, my lord," replied that gentleman.

"Do you spell it with a 'V' or a 'W'?" inquired the judge.

"That depends upon the taste and fancy of the speller, my lord," replied Sam; "I never had occasion to spell it more than once or twice in my life, but I spells it with a 'V'."

Here a voice in the gallery exclaimed aloud, "Quite right too, Samivel, quite right. Put it down a we, my lord, put it down a we."

"Who is that, who dares to address the court?" said the little judge, looking up. "Usher."

"Yes, my lord."

"Bring that person here instantly."

"Yes, my lord."

But as the usher didn't find the person, he didn't bring him; and, after a great commotion, all the people who had got up to look for the culprit, sat down again. The little judge turned to the witness as soon as his indignation would allow him to speak, and said,

"Do you know who that was, sir?"

"I rayther suspect it was my father, my lord," replied Sam.

"Do you see him here now?" said the judge.

"No, I don't, my lord," replied Sam, staring right up into the lantern in the roof of the court.

"If you could have pointed him out, I would have committed him instantly," said the judge.

Sam bowed his acknowledgments and turned, with unimpaired cheerfulness of countenance, towards Serjeant Buzfuz.

"Now, Mr. Weller," said Serjeant Buzfuz.

"Now, sir," replied Sam.

"I believe you are in the service of Mr. Pickwick, the defendant in this case. Speak up, if you please, Mr. Weller."

"I mean to speak up, sir," replied Sam; "I am in the service o' that 'ere gen'l'man, and a wery good service it is."

"Little to do, and plenty to get, I suppose?" said Serjeant Buzfuz, with jocularity.

"Oh, quite enough to get, sir, as the soldier said ven they ordered him three hundred and fifty lashes," replied Sam.

"You must not tell us what the soldier, or any other man, said, sir," interposed the judge; "it's not evidence."

"Wery good, my lord," replied Sam.

"Do you recollect anything particular happening on the morning when you were first engaged by the defendant; eh, Mr. Weller?" said Serjeant Buzfuz.

"Yes I do, sir," replied Sam.

"Have the goodness to tell the jury what it was."

"I had a reg'lar new fit out o' clothes that mornin', gen'l'men of the jury," said Sam, "and that was a wery partickler and uncommon circumstance vith me in those days."

Hereupon there was a general laugh; and the little judge, looking with an angry countenance over his desk, said, "You had better be careful, sir."

"So Mr. Pickwick said at the time, my lord," replied Sam; "and I was wery careful o' that 'ere suit o' clothes; wery careful indeed, my lord."

The judge looked sternly at Sam for full two minutes, but Sam's features were so perfectly calm and serene that the judge said nothing, and motioned Serjeant Buzfuz to proceed.

"Do you mean to tell me, Mr. Weller," said Serjeant Buzfuz, folding his arms emphatically, and turning half-round to the jury, as if in mute assurance that he would bother the witness yet: "Do you mean to tell me, Mr. Weller, that you saw nothing of this fainting on the part of the plaintiff in the arms of the defendant, which you have heard described by the witnesses?"

"Certainly not," replied Sam. "I was in the passage 'till they called me up, and then the old lady was not there."

"Now, attend, Mr. Weller," said Serjeant Buzfuz, dipping a large pen into the inkstand before him, for the purpose of frightening Sam with a show of taking down his answer. "You were in the passage, and yet saw nothing of what was going forward. Have you a pair of eyes, Mr. Weller?"

"Yes, I have a pair of eyes," replied Sam, "and that's just it. If they wos a pair o' patent double million magnifyin' gas microscopes of hextra power, p'raps I might be able to see through a flight o' stairs and a deal door; but bein' only eyes, you see, my wision's limited."

At this answer, which was delivered without the slightest appearance of irritation, and with the most complete simplicity and equanimity of manner, the spectators tittered, the little judge smiled, and Serjeant Buzfuz looked particularly foolish. After a short consultation with Dodson and Fogg, the learned Serjeant again turned towards Sam, and said, with a painful effort to conceal his vexation, "Now, Mr. Weller, I'll ask you a question on another point, if you please."

"If you please, sir," rejoined Sam, with the utmost good-humour.

"Do you remember going up to Mrs. Bardell's house, one night in November last?"

"Oh yes, very well."

"Oh, you *do* remember that, Mr. Weller," said Serjeant Buzfuz, recovering his spirits; "I thought we should get at something at last."

"I rayther thought that, too, sir," replied Sam; and at this the spectators tittered again.

"Well; I suppose you went up to have a little talk about this trial—eh, Mr. Weller?" said Serjeant Buzfuz, looking knowingly at the jury.

"I went up to pay the rent; but we *did* get a talkin' about the trial," replied Sam.

"Oh, you did get a talking about the trial," said Serjeant Buzfuz, brightening up with the anticipation of some important discovery. "Now what passed about the trial; will you have the goodness to tell us, Mr. Weller?"

"Vith all the pleasure in life, sir," replied Sam. "Arter a few unimportant obserwations from the two wirtuous females as has been examined here to-day, the ladies gets into a very great state o' admiration at the honourable conduct of Mr. Dodson and Fogg—them gen'l'men as is settin' near you now." This, of course, drew general attention to Dodson and Fogg, who looked as virtuous as possible.

"The attorneys for the plaintiff," said Mr. Serjeant Buzfuz. "Well! They spoke in high praise of the honourable conduct of Messrs. Dodson and Fogg, the attorneys for the plaintiff, did they?"

"Yes," said Sam, "they said what a wery gen'rous thing it was o' them to have taken up the case on spec, and to charge nothing at all for costs, unless they got 'em out of Mr. Pickwick."

At this very unexpected reply, the spectators tittered again, and Dodson and Fogg, turning very red, leant over to Serjeant Buzfuz, and in a hurried manner whispered something in his ear.

"You are quite right," said Serjeant Buzfuz aloud, with affected composure. "It's perfectly useless, my lord, attempting to get at any evidence through the impenetrable stupidity of this witness. I will not trouble the court by asking him any more questions. Stand down, sir."

"Would any other gen'l'man like to ask me anythin'?" inquired Sam, taking up his hat, and looking round most deliberately.

"Not I, Mr. Weller, thank you," said Serjeant Snubbin, laughing.

"You may go down, sir," said Serjeant Buzfuz, waving his hand impatiently. Sam went down accordingly, after doing Messrs. Dodson and Fogg's case as much harm as he conveniently could, and saying just as little respecting Mr. Pickwick as might be, which was precisely the object he had had in view all along.

"I have no objection to admit, my lord," said Serjeant Snubbin, "if it will save the examination of another witness, that Mr. Pickwick has retired from business, and is a gentleman of considerable independent property."

"Very well," said Serjeant Buzfuz, putting in the two letters to be read. "Then that's my case, my lord."

Serjeant Snubbin then addressed the jury on behalf of the defendant; and a very long and a very emphatic address he delivered, in which he bestowed the highest possible eulogiums on the conduct and character of Mr. Pickwick; but inasmuch as our readers are far better able to form a correct estimate of that gentleman's merits and deserts, than Serjeant Snubbin could possibly be, we do not feel called upon to enter at any length into the learned gentleman's observations. He attempted to show that the letters which had been exhibited, merely related to Mr. Pickwick's dinner, or to the preparations for receiving him in his apartments on his return from some country excursion. It is sufficient to add in general terms, that he did the best he could for Mr. Pickwick; and the best, as everybody knows, on the infallible authority of the old adage, could do no more.

Mr. Justice Stareleigh summed up, in the old-established and most approved form. He read as much of his notes to the jury as he could decipher on so short a notice, and made running comments on the evidence as he went along. If Mrs. Bardell were right, it was perfectly clear that Mr. Pickwick was wrong, and if they thought the evidence of Mrs. Cluppins worthy of credence they would believe it, and, if they didn't, why they wouldn't. If they were satisfied that a breach of promise of marriage had been committed, they would find for the plaintiff with such damages as they thought proper; and if, on the other hand, it appeared to them that no promise of marriage had ever been given, they would find for the defendant with no damages at all. The jury then retired to their private room to talk the matter over, and the judge retired to *his* private room, to refresh himself with a mutton chop and a glass of sherry.

An anxious quarter of an hour elapsed; the jury came back; the judge was fetched in. Mr. Pickwick put on his spectacles, and gazed at the foreman with an agitated countenance and a quickly beating heart.

"Gentlemen," said the individual in black, "are you all agreed upon your verdict?"

"We are," replied the foreman.

"Do you find for the plaintiff, gentlemen, or for the defendant?"

"For the plaintiff."

"With what damages, gentlemen?"

"Seven hundred and fifty pounds."

Mr. Pickwick took off his spectacles, carefully wiped the glasses, folded them into their case, and put them in his pocket; then having drawn on his gloves with great nicety, and stared at the foreman all the while, he mechanically followed Mr. Perker and the blue bag out of court.

They stopped in a side room while Perker paid the court fees; and here, Mr. Pickwick was joined by his friends. Here, too, he encountered Messrs. Dodson and Fogg, rubbing their hands with every token of outward satisfaction.

"Well, gentlemen," said Mr. Pickwick.

"Well, sir," said Dodson: for self and partner.

"You imagine you'll get your costs, don't you, gentlemen?" said Mr. Pickwick.

Fogg said they thought it rather probable. Dodson smiled, and said they'd try.

"You may try, and try, and try again, Messrs. Dodson and Fogg," said Mr. Pickwick vehemently, "but not one farthing of costs or damages do you ever get from me, if I spend the rest of my existence in a debtor's prison."

"Ha, ha!" laughed Dodson. "You'll think better of that, before next term, Mr. Pickwick."

"He, he, he! We'll soon see about that, Mr. Pickwick," grinned Fogg.

Speechless with indignation, Mr. Pickwick allowed himself to be led by his solicitor and friends to the door, and there assisted into a hackney-coach, which had been fetched for the purpose, by the ever watchful Sam Weller.

Sam had put up the steps, and was preparing to jump upon the box, when he felt himself gently touched on the shoulder; and looking round, his father stood before him. The old gentleman's countenance wore a mournful expression, as he shook his head gravely, and said, in warning accents:

"I know'd what 'ud come o' this here mode o' doin' bisness. Oh Sammy, Sammy, vy worn't there a alleybi!"

Robert D. Q. Henriques

NO ARMS NO ARMOUR

★

The court-martial was held in a large, white room, heavily shuttered, dim, vaguely monastic. The proceedings were slow and important; they were immensely tedious. The evidence and all the submissions of prosecuting and defending officers had to be written down in full by the president, who was a general, and to whom a pen (except for the purpose of signing his name) was an unfamiliar and unfavoured instrument. There were long periods of quiet, while the pen squeaked across the buff forms and the documents on the long table rustled under the big, slow-moving fan that was fixed to the ceiling. It was grim: matter-of-fact when you expected drama; clean and antiseptic when you were ready for something rather nasty. The whole performance was ponderous and inevitable, as ruthless as machinery; and, in your membership of it, you were no more than an obscure bolt, a spindle hidden away somewhere, quite unimportant—except that the machine couldn't run without you.

The witness who was giving evidence shifted from one foot to the other, resolving to keep his testimony as short as possible, so that he could regain his chair the sooner; for him, the glamour of public appearance was already tarnished.

The staff-captain, who was prosecutor, twisted himself round, rearranging himself and leaning again on the table so as to take the weight of his head on the other elbow.

Daddy, who was defending, very delicately redistributed his papers and files, opened and shut his manual of military law, and drummed his fingers on the dome of his topi.

Tubby, the junior member of the court, looked straight to his front, looking at nothing, seeing nothing, trying in alternate waves of desperation and indifference to imbue his immediate experience with a sense of importance. But—really it was all very boring.

They were trying a man on a serious charge; so serious and so nearly proved that in a few hours (there was little doubt) he would be found guilty. In a few days, when the sentence had been promulgated, he would hear what they had decided to do to him. He might be locked up for ten years; perhaps it would be no more than five; it couldn't be less. In civil cases they gave them six months, or twelve; rarely more. But, here, a soldier's masculinity was challenged; and this most unforgivable crime must be met coldly with savage punishment. Yet there was nothing savage in their hearts—rather the reverse. They hated inflicting punishment on a fine soldier; but this was no matter of hearts, compassion, kindliness. It was the application of certain accepted standards.

And the sentence didn't matter to the sergeant-major—not yet, anyway. The pain was far too subtle to be judged by time measurements. It lay in the loss of volition, the one burning moment when the man could no longer say: "I think I'll go out; I'll come in. . ."; the quick transportation from military discipline—a discipline based on its time limitation, its cycle of contrasts from strict subjectivity to leisure hours of more than freedom, of encouraged licence—to this new and utter enslavement, this dehumanisation, this reduction to animal status.

Five years ago Tubby was at Woolwich, learning to be an officer, still a schoolboy; and in five years' time he might well be sour and withered in spirit, like Daddy. What would happen to the sergeant-major in that period? It was an unpleasant subject for thought; terrible, and—when you remembered the sergeant-major as you had known him—very tragic. But it was hard to feel distressed about it. The white walls, the heavy shutters, the ponderous ritual, denied emotion, forbade sentiment. Everything was happening in a steam-roller way, and you were part of the steam-roller and a steam-roller cannot feel but can only act as the steam directs it.

Very slowly and relentlessly the proceedings developed in their fore-ordained degrees. Tubby wiped the dampness off his forehead;

Daddy leant back and closed his eyes; the other members of the court, sitting at the head of the room behind the long table, were twisted into the most comfortable attitudes that propriety and the hard chairs permitted. The staff-captain twirled his pencil, and tried to twirl his stiff moustaches. He tapped the pencil gently on the table and stroked his ginger moustaches, running his finger down his nose until it attained its objective and continuing the stroking movement while he turned his head very slowly to the right, to survey the line of officers who comprised the court, back again to his front, to look straight past the prisoner and escort, across the room to Daddy, and finally, refocusing his eyes without the necessity for further movement, to gaze coldly at the prisoner. It was a market-day inspection, without pity and without malice. Then the eyes dropped, the ginger moustache was left to its own mutinous attitudes while, picking up again his pencil, the staff-captain drew a flat-headed, large-headed, top-heavy figure on his pink blotting paper.

The prisoner, the sergeant-major, the man who had galloped down the hill and hustled the battery into action, the fine, sturdy male with the big stomach and faded medal ribbons, the man who had come out of the darkness to stand, dark and burly, in the fringe of lamplight, sat now, quite still, with his large hands open on his knees and his eyes fixed straight before him. His head was square and stubborn, his face expressionless. He was the rock on which the waters split; he was untouched by the waters. The proceedings swept around him, tranquil, irresistible, a slow-moving river.

A score of responsible men were occupied with this business which hardly concerned the sergeant-major. He was impersonalised. It was all quiet, gentle and relentless; and only to the sergeant-major was it of any moment.

The president of the court, the General himself, wearily blotted the buff form on which he had been writing. He looked up slowly, his red, square face entirely without expression, inscrutable like an elephant or an oriental, except that—in the case of an elephant or an oriental—there is a subtle assurance that their brains are occupied. Not only his face, but all of the General was square and solid. He was kind, sure of himself and stupid. But he knew whose advice to take and whose to reject; he was a good general. He looked across to Daddy.

"Well, Captain Watson. . . ."

Daddy stood up, his sword scraping against the legs of his chair. He fiddled with the hilt and cleared his throat. He was not nervous; he was confident and yet reluctant to speak, as if he felt the atmosphere of the court was not receptive.

"Well, sir. . . ."

"One moment, Captain Watson; am I to take this down?"

"I won't trouble you, sir, just at present."

The General's voice was quiet; his words were clipped, used sparingly and not without some mental process, some reflex deliberation. It was as if their source were limited. As if, with each sentence uttered, he warned himself that one the less was left to him.

"It's not a question of trouble," he said. "You are submitting a defence?"

"Yes, sir. I was going to outline it."

"It will have to be taken down then; you must know that, Captain Watson."

"I don't think so, sir. I will put in a written statement."

The General leant towards the member of the court on his right, an old, wizened, monkey-faced, horse-dealing major. They whispered together. "Yes, yes, quite. Oh yes, quite," the major said too loudly.

"Don't you agree?"

"Oh, undoubtedly, sir, quite; undoubtedly."

Daddy stood fingering his sword knot; and Tubby saw him then, quite suddenly, as forlorn and unhappy. It was perhaps an unguarded moment; but, without a knowledge of the multiplicity of Daddy's facets, that idle figure, neatly dressed in khaki drill uniform (white and shabby at the edges from the laundry) and beautifully polished, well-worn belt and field boots and scabbard, could have no particular significance. The pink, matter-of-fact face, over-lined on the forehead for its age, and the thin, drab-coloured hair, were uninteresting. From Tubby, the man demanded affection. It was Daddy, his captain, bad-tempered, hateful, brave, clever, obstinate, kind, generous, sad, unhappy. The component elements were innumerable. Daddy himself could not have counted them; could not have known which of his many persons was in possession of his scarred soul at any particular moment.

"Oh, yes, I quite agree with you," the monkey-faced major whispered. He was clean-shaven and he pursed his thin, bloodless lips together into an expression of wisdom. He nodded his head slowly. "Oh, undoubtedly, General, undoubtedly."

"All right, Captain Watson, go on please."

Daddy looked at the president and spoke slowly and quietly. His voice gained in confidence, as if he were beginning to feel the unaccustomed part that he was playing. He identified himself with the prisoner, his sergeant-major, and yet saw him objectively, as he sometimes saw himself in moments of revealing consciousness.

"I think, sir, that the evidence against the prisoner is not only inconclusive, but strongly contestable. I should call it unreliable. The few questions I have put to the witnesses have been answered reluctantly. That would perhaps have been natural—in view of the embarrassing nature of the charge—if their answers had not materially altered the substance of their evidence . . . But I think that they did. I mean that, after I had questioned, cross-examined that is, each witness, his story was very different from the one contained in the summary of evidence. Not only that, but the stories of the different witnesses now disagree very materially. So much so that it would be very dangerous to lend credence to any of them."

"To lend *what*, Captain Watson?"

"To believe them, sir."

"Oh, I see. To believe them."

The General leant across and started whispering again. He did not turn his head but merely bent it sideways like a pendulum, looking all the time to his front, across the court, with steady, expressionless eyes.

"Oh, quite," the major said. "I see that. He says we can't believe them . . . I don't know, I'm sure . . . I must say. . . ."

"Captain Watson, I have a note of all the questions and answers you put to the witnesses."

"Yes, sir; but I thought if I just recapitulated some of them. . . ."

"Hardly necessary, is it?"

The General was not being difficult. He was anxious to help and put at ease the defending officer. The court was, of course, on the side of the defence; but nobody wanted a lot of unnecessary speech-making. Evidence and cross-examination were down in black and white, or—more holy still—in black and buff, and had acquired the sacred character that the written word has for the semi-literate.

Daddy shifted his feet awkwardly and rustled through the notes of his cross-examinations.

"What I mean, sir . . ."

"Captain Watson, are you trying to submit that there is no case to answer?"

Daddy looked up quickly. "Would you accept that submission, sir?"

"If you ask me to, the court will adjourn to consider it."

It seemed clear that a cigarette was what the General really needed; a smoke and an adjournment, when one could stretch oneself and get relief from the infernal hardness of the "chairs windsor". He spoke with the monkey-faced major, and with the short, dark, kind-looking little Richards, the other major on the court, who sat on his left. For some time they whispered together, while Daddy watched them anxiously, and the prisoner's face did not move but remained stony and indifferent.

"No, I'm afraid not," the General said regretfully. "We seem to be agreed that there is quite clearly a case for the defence to answer."

If you knew Daddy, you could see that he was winding himself up for an effort, just as he worked himself up for a bout of evil temper.

"Yes, sir," he admitted. "I see that. What I want to say is that the evidence so far is unreliable. It must, at least, leave a strong feeling of doubt. It is almost impossible for me to produce conflicting evidence. It would have to be negative evidence, you understand? I cannot prove that these alleged offences were not committed when only the witnesses and the prisoner were supposed to be present. But I *can* produce evidence of character to show that the allegations are highly improbable."

"Evidence of character—at this stage of the proceedings?"

"Well, yes, sir. I thought I'd explained it. . . ."

There was a short silence, broken sharply by the General. "Will the prisoner give evidence?"

Daddy hesitated and looked at the sergeant-major. The sergeant-major still sat with his hands on his knees. Still he stared straight in front of him and showed no interest in the proceedings. His eyes were fixed, almost in hypnosis, high up the wall at the back of the president. If the sergeant-major gave evidence, anything might come out; anything might happen. He could scarcely save himself, and the whole fort might be incriminated. It was an important moment when a decision that had been reached in advance had to be quickly reconsidered.

"No, sir. He won't give evidence."

That sounded bad for the prisoner. In the silence—the long, heavily-charged silence that followed—it was clear that the case was as good as over.

"Evidence of character," the General repeated; "at this stage of the proceedings?"

Daddy spoke urgently.

"I wish to show, sir, that the prisoner has been married five years and has four children. I suggest it indicates that his tendencies are entirely heterosexual."

"Entirely what?"

"Heterosexual, sir."

"I see. And what may that mean? We must have plain language here, Captain Watson."

"Yes, sir, of course. From the Greek . . ."

"We don't want Greek, Captain Watson."

"No, sir, of course not. . . ."

Daddy's voice was gentle in the slow drawl that betrayed his most guarded, deliberate moments. Only Tubby could detect the malice in his soft replies. Only Tubby knew the violent passion that Daddy felt at the unjustness of these scrupulously just proceedings.

"It seems necessary for me to give the court some idea of the conditions we were living in at the fort. . . ."

"One moment, Captain Watson, you appear to be giving evidence."

"I am trying to explain, sir . . ."

"You are in effect giving evidence."

"There is no one else I can call, sir, who has the same full knowledge of the conditions. . . ."

"I don't see that the defending officer can give evidence. You should have been a witness." He had a word with Richards, a word with the monkey-faced major. Richards' lips just stirred in a brief affirmative; but the monkey-faced man nodded vigorously, full of wisdom.

"Quite right," the General said. "Only a witness can give evidence."

"I'm sorry, sir. The prisoner wanted me to defend him. He has the right to choose."

"Of course. . . ."

The general turned his head to speak. He was talking again with the monkey-faced major and he looked up to say "of course" and then went back to his whispering. He was clearly anxious, not only that the prisoner should be given every benefit, but that the proceedings should contain no irregularity which might be criticised by the Judge-Advocate's department afterwards. The staff-captain's chair scraped the floor as he stood up suddenly.

"Sir?"

"Yes, Captain Higgins?"

"I don't think there can be any objection to Captain Watson giving evidence providing he appears as a witness. He should do so on oath and should, of course, be subject to my cross-examination."

The General moved his head slowly, as if controlled by a mechanism of gear wheels, back across the court to Daddy. "Do you agree, Captain Watson?"

Daddy looked down at his boots and then at his papers. The silence was just long enough to reveal his embarrassment.

"Well, Captain Watson?"

Daddy's voice was low: "I agree, sir."

He stepped round the table, his sword knocking against the legs, and stood in the well of the court next to the sergeant-major. The regimental sergeant-major on duty came from the back of the room with a Bible.

"I swear that in the evidence I shall give before this court, I shall speak the truth . . ."

The truth!

Tubby, watching Daddy and seeing his tired, grave, unrevealing face, knew how useless was the oath and how futile it was to believe that it would be not broken. In a matter of this sort, there was no truth. There were no facts which, viewed from all angles—or from more than one angle—gave the same picture. Daddy, more than anyone, discredited the hope that there was a basic, universal truth in anything.

Sitting in the shaded quiet of the court, while Daddy, in his gentle, even voice gave evidence, Tubby's mind wandered. Of all the unforeseen contradictions that had shattered his complacency, the continued revelation of Daddy had been perhaps the most startling. Discovering the multiplicity of spirits represented by that short, square and rather nondescript person had brought the final disintegration of his once happy belief in the simplicity of all that surrounded him. He knew now that things and people were not either good or bad. Life was rather more than living. He, Tubby, had progressed further than the General.

"The truth is," Daddy was saying, "that conditions at the fort were such that . . ."

No doubt it was the truth; for almost everything was the truth for someone. If Daddy, sitting in the cool of the battery office, saw a bombardier walking across the parade ground of the fort, saw him stepping with automatic precision through the evil brilliance of the midday sunlight, he saw a man who was making a useless journey. He saw someone compelled by the stupid routine of living to exert himself unpleasantly. The bombardier must walk across and make a quite unnecessary report, at a quite arbitrarily specified time, to the orderly sergeant. Then he must walk back again. It was entirely trivial and harmless, and the routine of army life demanded it. But Daddy felt bitterly about it just because he felt bitter about everything; because he saw and knew everything with a gnawing bitterness that made life sour in his mouth and acrid in his nostrils.

If Sammy, who was dead and disintegrating somewhere beneath the sands of the African desert, had been sitting in the same chair and had seen the same man perform the same entirely unremarkable journey, he would have been watching all humanity enjoying the gift of purposeful movement.

If Bert had been there, he would have stiffened instinctively. He would have seen a non-commissioned officer on duty marching across the square and not swinging his arms in the way he had been taught at the depôt.

To Lydia, the man would have been a rather attractive figure in that rather attractive light, khaki drill uniform, wearing a rather romantic topi. Very Empire-building, she would have thought, as she saw his brown arms and knees and quilted spine pad.

To Mrs. Clements, for instance, it would have been a male creature approaching her; someone to be stripped and regarded critically from the point of view of his animal potentialities; someone to be watched through the lens of her instinctive mind, which took each man, and all mankind, and viewed it as mechanically constructed for the satisfaction of woman.

But Tubby would have seen Bombardier Price of "C" subsection, a chap who had a first-class certificate of education and was due for promotion, reporting two men sick and one absent to the orderly sergeant. Was there any reason to suppose that his vision was less fallacious and more truthful than any of the others?

The whole truth!

There was someone at the door, and the sergeant on duty opened it, setting a rectangle of hard radiance at the end of the long court room. For a moment, before the door was shut again, Daddy appeared in stiff silhouette. He had turned and was facing the staff-captain, answering his questions.

"No, I can't agree to that."

The staff-captain leant forward and rested his hands on the table. His ginger moustache was aggressive; he was being clever.

"But, Captain Watson, the whole of your evidence seems to me to have been directed to one end: that is, to showing that conditions at the fort were such that this offence was inevitable."

"Not inevitable."

"Then what?"

"Explicable, perhaps."

The staff-captain raised his eyebrows very obviously. He wanted everyone to see this unspoken comment. He shrugged his shoulders and felt that he ought to have been a barrister. That was what they said to him sometimes: "You're wasted in the army, Geoffrey, you ought to have gone to the Bar or something." He raised his voice slightly and tried to affect a puzzled expression.

"Explicable, Captain Watson?"

Daddy seemed to know that he was cornered. "I'll put it this way," he said. "I consider that my cross-examination of your witnesses so shook their evidence that it cannot be relied upon. I therefore suggested that there was no case to answer. Apparently the court still believes your witnesses, in spite of the fact that they contradicted themselves and each other repeatedly."

"This seems to be rather a sidetrack," the staff-captain said softly. "We have been into this before. I think we had got to the point where, without admitting this offence, you said you considered it—er—explicable. Perhaps you would amplify that remark for us?"

"I have shown that the prisoner's tendencies are normal," Daddy said desperately. "He has a wife and four children. I am certainly not admitting that he committed this offence, much less that it has been proved against him. I am trying to say that, if the court *does* consider he committed it, conditions at the fort were such that it might almost have been expected."

Daddy turned and faced the president. He seemed to grow in stature. "In fact, sir, I am submitting that, in the circumstances, this charge—proved or not proved—is scarcely an offence at all."

"Captain Watson," the staff-captain said quickly, "you are admitting, in fact, that you believe in the guilt of the prisoner."

"Not at all."

"I must remind you that you are not at this moment defending officer. You have elected to give evidence on behalf of the prisoner."

Daddy made no answer.

"You are remembering that you are on oath?"

Daddy faced the staff-captain again and, knowing him, Tubby could read his dislike for those ginger moustaches, the ginger eyebrows, and the thin, ginger hair that was brushed back off the slightly freckled forehead. "I am remembering that," he said.

"Then I suggest to you that you believe the prisoner to be guilty?"

"My beliefs have nothing to do with it."

"Then I suggest that you have knowledge, knowledge of facts, that leads you to believe this offence was committed. Perhaps I should remind you again of your oath. You have sworn to speak the whole truth."

Daddy hesitated.

"You must answer that, Captain Watson," the General said.

Daddy looked at the staff-captain. "Will you please repeat the question?"

"Certainly . . . certainly. I suggest that you had knowledge, specific knowledge of certain facts; and that those facts lead you to suppose this offence was committed. Just yes or no, Captain Watson."

You could see Daddy bracing himself to answer.

"Yes," he said quietly.

The staff-captain had not been prepared for such success. "There are facts which lead you to believe this offence was committed?"

"Yes. But not in particular by the prisoner."

"By whom then?"

"Not by the prisoner. It is the prisoner only who is on trial."

The staff-captain looked towards the General for assistance, but the General made no sign. His hands were on the table before him, his pen laid down in front of them. His wide blue eyes were gazing placidly past everyone to the far end of the room. Finding no ally, the staff-captain returned to the final assault. "You mean that you know this offence was going on, was in fact being committed?"

"Not by the prisoner. I don't know that."

"But by others of your command?"

Daddy did not move. Except for his hand, which was resting on his sword hilt, he was standing at attention.

"Yes," he said.

"At the time did you know it was going on? Are you saying that all along you *knew* it was being committed?"

The silence in the room was terrible. Tubby looked desperately towards Daddy, praying for some means of creating a disturbance; for something that would break that dreadful quiet, that would put a stop to this long chain of inevitable questions which demanded these cruel answers. Once you were out there giving evidence, you were lost; your barriers were shattered; your innermost defences were open to exploration. There was no sure stronghold of secrecy for you to fall back upon.

The General shifted ponderously in his chair: "*Did* you know it was going on, Captain Watson?"

"Yes, sir."

"And you did nothing to stop it?"

There was a long, swelling pause.

"No!"

The word was hurled into the silence. There was either a clock somewhere in the room or Tubby's wristwatch was ticking sonorously, momentously, resisting the passage of each fatal second. The staff-captain was no longer leaning forward. His thumbs were tucked complacently into his belt and he was standing upright.

"*Could* you have stopped it, Captain Watson?"

"I daresay. Yes, I believe so."

Tubby was as surprised as anyone. In spite of what Daddy said to him, he had not believed this: that matters were so clear cut and simple; that Daddy had known all the time that this vice, this crime—the thought of which raised nausea in a decent person—had actually been prevalent; that, knowing it, he had taken no steps to stop it and that, speaking the truth with a hard integrity that few men were capable of conceiving, he must admit that it had been in his power to put an end to the practice. No less than anyone in the court, Tubby asked himself why Daddy said no more to amplify this self-accusation, to alleviate the charge, to defend himself against it.

Nothing but the truth!

Tubby waited in anguish. Why did Daddy not go on? Why did he not explain, for instance, that he could have stopped it only because his men loved him and he could control them; but that, had he suppressed this particular outbreak of vice, the evil engendered by conditions at the fort would have suppurated in some other manner. Looking back on it all, that was surely the explanation.

"Captain Watson," the General said sharply, "you admit that it was going on, that you could have stopped it. Then why in heaven's name didn't you?"

Daddy's face did not move. "I did not stop it, sir, because under the circumstances I did not believe it to be wrong."

"Did not believe it to be wrong! Did you think it right, then?"

The General spoke harshly. The staff-captain had sat down, so that now it was between Daddy and the court, between him and outraged decency.

"I did not believe it to be wrong any more than I believed it to be right. I believed it to be something quite natural."

"Will you kindly explain yourself?"

"I had to face facts, sir. I was in command of a hundred and fifty men, all of them between the ages of twenty and thirty, all of them healthy and normal. A man is an animal, for all that he is a human being. He has sexual appetites which, at that age, can only be assuaged physically. I did what I could, in the way of concerts and lectures and organised games, to keep their minds occupied and their bodies tired; but that was nothing. It is a schoolmaster's theory that physical exercise dulls physical appetites. We are not schoolmasters. We face facts and we know that the reverse is the case. Nothing dulls sexual appetites except satisfaction."

Nobody moved. They just sat, solid, resistant, while the words beat up against them, rebounded, died unacknowledged. . . .

"We all know," Daddy went on steadily, "what happened to certain units in the hill stations of India when the order was given to close the brothels. I knew that the same thing would happen in my command. If I had wanted to, I could not have opened a brothel. To be honest, I thought about it; but there were insufficient women in the village . . . Failing a brothel, I knew just what would happen; and anyone else who'd thought about it would have known the same.

"I am, of course, well aware that in England so-called unnatural vice is considered a crime. I cannot see that it is a crime in the sort of place where we were stationed, because I cannot see that it was unnatural. To my mind, it was the most natural thing in the world. In the absolute sense, the satisfaction of sexual appetites, except for purposes of procreation—I should say breeding, sir—is always unnatural; that is, if we take the behaviour of the animal world as our standard. Homosexuality has no appeal for me, and I could never indulge in it; but I am sufficiently well aware of its universal practice throughout the world for it not to sicken me. Shut up a hundred and fifty young men in a fort and give them no other sexual outlet, and they'll soon find in unnatural vice a natural enough solution to their discomforts.

"That is all I have to say, sir. I was aware that homosexuality was being practised in my command. Any experienced officer, any intelligent man in my position, would have known it. But I must insist that, beyond the evidence that has been given to-day, I have not the slightest reason to suppose that the prisoner himself indulged in it."

There was, of course, a long silence. Daddy waited, standing quite still and at attention. His face was white and strained, and he was square and upright, the dramatic, melodramatic figure of a hopeless crusader. All that he had said was true and so much more than true. Tubby knew it and knew that Daddy had sought a degree of truthfulness that belonged only to visions. You could not lecture generals and ginger-whiskered staff officers and certainly not the monkey-faced major. But Daddy had done worse than that; he had preached, not at them, but at the sky above their heads. He had exposed himself in front of men for whom his words had scarcely a superficial meaning.

The members of the court were decent, honest people; but when they met honesty, developed beyond the fœtus, they found it sheer indecency. They knew from experience that young men, imprisoned together without feminine company, indulged too often in this vice. But it was a knowledge that was rigidly abstract, that must not be particularised, that might only be admitted in retrospect. Applied to the present tense, it must be primly disregarded; eyes must be closed, consciousness shuttered.

For them, it was more than sufficient that the practice was forbidden by law, was known to be foul, unnatural. Lawbreaking demanded punishment. It was not for them to get on terms with humanity or to fashion their own code of understanding. It was easier than that. They had, they thanked God, a simple, honest, decent way of thinking.

The General's chair grated impatiently on the floor. "Captain Higgins, have you any more questions?"

"No, sir. I'll leave it at that."

"Very well, Captain Watson."

Daddy walked back to his table, his eyes traversing the court without meeting those of any of its members. His glance passed coldly over Tubby. Pale, from the reaction that followed his self-revelation, he lowered himself slowly into his chair again.

The General's voice was harsh, as though it armoured him against the dangerous atmosphere that Daddy had created. "Is there anything else, Captain Watson?"

"No, sir. That concludes the defence. If you don't mind I will put in a written statement."

"Is it ready?"

Daddy passed across a typed sheet of foolscap, handing it to Tubby who sat nearest to him, refusing to meet Tubby's eyes and to accept his sympathy. The paper was passed along to the General who glanced at it quickly.

"Do you want it read out, Captain Watson?"

"No, thank you, sir. The substance was contained in my evidence."

"Very well, then. The court is adjourned to consider the verdict."

The prisoner and escort were marched out and the court was cleared of all but its members. They pushed back their chairs and stretched themselves, and the General came slowly along the table to Tubby. He moved heavily and with the rolling gait of a sailor.

"No, no," he said. "Don't get up. Have a cigarette, will you?"

"Thank you, sir."

The General unbuttoned the pocket of his jacket and pulled out a cigarette case. Every movement that he made was deliberate, heavy and important. You could almost hear him creak as he lowered himself carefully on to the edge of the table and sat there with one leg swinging clumsily.

"Well, young feller, made up your mind about it?"

"Not entirely, sir."

"Haven't you? Well, we've half an hour or so . . . We'll run over the case in a minute, shall we?"

"Yes, sir."

"You have to give your verdict first, you know? Junior member always speaks first; you know that, don't you?"

"Yes, sir."

The General got up off the table and started to walk away. Then he turned and came back and stood, almost awkwardly, almost embarrassed, behind Tubby. He looked across the room, keeping his eyes high up and distant, and speaking in his short, clipped, jerky phrases.

"You mustn't take it amiss, young feller, what I'm going to say to you. You mustn't mind it, eh?"

"No, of course not."

"Nothing to do with me really, nothing whatever. I hear you've been seeing rather a lot of that Mrs. Clements."

"How did you hear that, sir?"

The General looked down, smiled and turned away again. There was a lot of kindness in his smile and, after it, his precise speech seemed more benevolent. "We hear these things. We hear them. Is it true, can you tell me? Nothing to do with me, mind you."

"No, sir, it's not true. I've seen her on and off at the club; at polo and so on. I've only once been to her house. I went there to dinner."

"You did, did you?" the General said, speaking very staccato but quietly, his gaze across the room, very distant. "The devil you did! And I'll bet her husband wasn't there; away on trek or something."

Tubby looked up and caught the General's eye and smiled. His conceit urged him to let the General know how things stood. His code forbade that he should put the situation into words. The smile was sufficient. The General echoed it.

"You know a lot, sir," Tubby said.

"Pretty obvious, my boy."

"Is it?"

"She's a bit that way inclined—so they tell me . . . The only trouble is the whole of Khartoum hears about it. Every man, woman and child . . . Wouldn't do for me to go there, would it? Never do for me. Wouldn't do at all, eh?"

"No, sir."

The General twisted up his face ferociously, as if he were playing with his children. "Why d'you say it like that, eh? I'm not as old as all that, am I? I daresay I'm not as old as you think, young feller."

"I didn't mean it that way, sir. I meant about everyone knowing. It wouldn't do for you, sir. . . ."

"Of course."

The General moved away a pace and then rocked himself back again. "I'm glad you found her, young feller, glad you got hold of her. Or she got hold of you—might be closer to the truth. Glad of it anyway. A young feller has to have his greens once in a way. Keep your interest below the navel, as we say in the Army. You'll come to no harm that way."

Tubby looked down and knew that he was blushing. He felt ridiculously like a child. The General's hand was on his shoulder, kneading it. "I'm glad it's that way, young feller. Your commanding officer's a good man; a splendid war record, you know, quite splendid. But a bit of a crank in some things. Whatever he may say, it's more natural to take your greens the way you and I do it. Don't you think so?" He gave Tubby's shoulder a twist. "More natural, don't you think so? More healthy, you know, anyway."

"Yes, sir," said Tubby, looking hard at the blank sheet of paper that was on the table in front of him.

The General sat down again, and everyone stopped talking, the odd remarks that finished off a conversation straying into the silence.

"Well, gentlemen, shall we make up our minds about this business?"

He started to turn over the buff forms that were covered with his own crabbed, unnatural writing. He turned to the major on his right, the one with a face like a monkey.

"How do you feel about it, Tony?"

"Well, sir . . ."

"I don't want a verdict yet."

"No, sir, of course. But it seems fairly clear to me. The witnesses didn't behave well under Watson's cross-examination. That's true enough; but I dunno that it makes a heap of difference. You don't expect it in this sort of case. Shouldn't care to be giving evidence meself, if you take me. . . ."

"I should hope not, Tony."

The major grunted. "Haven't come to that yet, have we, General?"

"Not yet," said the General. "Then you're settled in your mind about it?"

"I'm inclined to believe the witnesses, sir."

"Very well. And you, Richards?"

The General turned to his left hand.

"I'm afraid I think the same, sir," Richards said regretfully. "If we believe the witnesses, I take it there's no more to be said about it. As I see it, Watson's remarks were, well . . . er . . . interesting but a bit irrelevant."

"And you, Porter?"

"I don't know, sir. Those three or four witnesses; they didn't face the boards too well. Watson rattled 'em a bit, I thought."

"Would you like me to read over the evidence?" the General asked. "How do you feel about it, Allardyce?"

"If you'd just read the cross-examination, sir."

"Certainly."

Whilst the General was reading from his transcription, Tubby knew suddenly that his mind had been made up all along. It was quite obvious that the sergeant-major was guilty and that he had been proved guilty by the evidence that had been given that morning. The other members of the court must feel the same about it. This pretence at indecision was only to ease their consciences.

How much did they care, he wondered, one way or the other. He, himself—if he were honest about it—though he knew and admired the sergeant-major and had grown to consider him almost a friend, was unable to feel deeply about it. There was something in the atmosphere of a court martial that bred a healthy indifference, that encouraged cold, clear-headed sanity, that forbade such sentiments as pity, regret and sympathy from obtruding upon your judgment. He knew that he ought to feel more strongly about it; that humanity demanded it. Having made his mind up, he tried to hallow himself into pity through the medium of thought and imagination.

Outside the court, Higgins, bristling and self-satisfied, would be chatting with Daddy. As likely as not, Daddy would no longer be the man who half an hour ago had spoken with such tragic vehemence. The cruel cynicism of his outer folds would have closed in upon his core of utter feeling. He would be smoking, of course, and possibly joking with Higgins, his face (if you knew it) unsmiling, hiding himself beneath its mask of deliberate inscrutability. "Poor sod," he'd be saying with grim humour.

In the room next door, the sergeant-major would be sitting with an escort of his peers. They would have given him a cigarette, but the company would be silent in embarrassment and sympathy. He would be looking straight before him, his feelings tucked right down within his frozen self, curled up upon himself like an animal succumbed to terror. It was sad, all right, to think of the sergeant-major like that. But it didn't hurt personally. It was an offence against taste that the mighty should be publicly humbled. It was disillusionment; another castle broken up somewhere. But that was all. Compassion, poignant regrets, were quite absent.

"Well, young feller," the General said, "have you made up your mind yet?"

Tubby stubbed out his cigarette, feeling somehow as if he were going to church and that this moment demanded from him some symbol of respect, something of ceremony.

"Guilty, sir," he said, his voice ringing unexpectedly loud through the court room.

E. Œ. Somerville & Martin Ross

AN IRISH PROBLEM

★

Conversation raged on the long flanks of the mail-car.

An elderly priest, with a warm complexion and a controversial under-lip, was expounding his native country to a fellow-traveller, with slight but irrepressible pulpit gestures of the hand. The fellow-traveller, albeit lavender-hued from an autumn east wind, was obediently observing the anæmic patches of oats and barley, pale and thin, like the hair of a starving baby, and the huge slants of brown heather and turf bog, and was interjecting "Just so!" at decent intervals. Now and then, as the two tall brown mares slackened for a bout of collar-work at a hill, or squeezed slowly past a cart stacked high with sods of turf, we, sitting in silence, Irish wolves in the clothing of English tourists, could hear across the intervening pile of luggage and bicycles such a storm of conversation as bursts forth at a dinner-party after the champagne has twice gone round.

The brunt of the talk was borne by the old lady in the centre. Her broad back, chequered with red plaid, remained monumental in height and stillness, but there was that in the tremor of the steel spray in her bonnet that told of a high pressure of narrative. The bearded Dublin tourist on her left was but little behind her in the ardour of giving information. His wife, a beautifully dressed lady with cotton-wool in her ears, remained abstracted, whether from toothache, or exclusiveness, or mere wifely boredom, we cannot say. Among the swift shuttles of Irish speech the ponderous questions and pronouncements of an English fisherman drove their way. The talk was, we gathered, of sport and game laws and their administration.

"Is it hares?" cried the Dublin tourist, perorating after a flight or two into the subject of poachers; "what d'ye think would happen a hare in Donegal?"

His handsome brown eyes swept his audience, even, through the spokes of a bicycle, gathering in our sympathies. It left no doubts as to the tragedy that awaited the hare.

The east wind hunted us along the shore of the wide, bleak bay, rimmed with yellow sea-weed, and black and ruffled like the innumerable lakelets that lay along our route. The tall mountain over it was hooded in cloud. It seemed as threatening and mysterious as Sinai; ready to utter some awful voice of law to the brown solitudes and windy silences.

Far ahead of us a few houses rose suddenly above the low coastline, an ugly family party of squat gables and whitewashed walls, with nothing nearer them to westward than the homesteads of America.

Far and near there was not a tree visible, nor a touch of colour to tell of the saving grace of flowers. The brown mares swung the car along with something resembling enthusiasm; Letterbeg was the end of their stage; it was the end of ours also. Numb with long sitting we dropped cumbrously to earth from the high footboard, and found ourselves face to face with the problem of how to spend the next three hours. It was eleven o'clock in the morning, too early for lunch, though, apparently, quite the fashionable hour in Letterbeg for bottled porter, judging by the squeak of the corkscrew and the clash of glasses that issued from the dark interior of the house in front of which we had been shed by the mail-car. This was a long cottage with a prosperous slate roof, and a board over its narrow door announcing that one Jas. Heraty was licensed for the retail of spirits and porter.

The mail-car rolled away; as it crawled over the top of a hill and sank out of sight a last wave of the priestly hand seemed to include us. Doubtless we were being expounded as English tourists, and our great economic value to the country was being expatiated upon. The *rôle* is an important one, and has its privileges; yet, to the wolf, there is something stifling in sheep's clothing; certainly, on the occasions when it was discarded by us, a sympathy and understanding with the hotels was quickly established. Possibly they also are wolves. Undoubtedly the English tourist, with his circular ticket and his coupons, does not invariably get the best of everything. We write surrounded by him and his sufferings. An earlier visit than usual to the hotel sitting-room has revealed him, lying miserably on the sofa, shrouded in a filthy *duvet*, having been flung there at some two in the morning on his arrival, wet through, from heaven knows what tremendous walk. Subsequently we hear him being haled from his lair by the chambermaid, who treats him as the dirt under her feet (or, indeed, if we may judge by our bedroom carpet, with far less consideration).

"Here!" she says, "go in there and wash yerself!"

We hear her slamming him into a room from which two others of his kind have been recently bolted like rabbits, by the boots, to catch the 6 a.m. train. We can just faintly realise its atmosphere.

This, however, is a digression, but remotely connected with Letterbeg and Mr. Heraty's window, to which in our forlorn state we turned for distraction.

It was very small, about two feet square, but it made its appeal to all the needs of humanity from the cradle to the grave. A feeding-bottle, a rosary, a photograph of Mr. Kruger, a peg-top, a case of salmon flies, an artistic letter-weight, consisting of a pigeon's egg carved in Connemara marble, two seductively small bottles of castor-oil—these, mounted on an embankment of packets of cornflour and rat poison, crowded the four little panes. Inside the shop the assortment ranged from bundles of reaping-hooks on the earthen floor to bottles of champagne in the murk of the top shelf. A few men leaned against the tin-covered counter, gravely drinking porter. As we stood dubiously at the door there was a padding of bare feet in the roadway, and a very small boy with a red head, dressed in a long flannel frock of a rich madder shade, fluttered past us into the shop.

"Me dada says let yees be hurrying!" he gasped, between spasms of what was obviously whooping-cough. "Sweeny's case is comin' on!"

Had the message been delivered by the Sergeant-at-Arms it could not have been received with more respectful attention or been more immediately obeyed. The porter was gulped down, one unfinished glass being bestowed upon the Sergeant-at-Arms, possibly as a palliative for the whooping-cough, and the party trooped up the road towards a thatched and whitewashed cottage that stood askew at the top of a lane leading to the seashore. Two tall constables of the R.I.C. stood at the door of the cottage. It came to us, with a lifting of the heart, that we had chanced upon Petty Sessions day in Letterbeg, and this was the court-house.

It was uncommonly hot in what is called in newspapers "the body of the court". Something of the nature of a rood-screen, boarded solidly up to a height of about four feet, divided the long single room of the cottage; we, with the rest of the public, were penned in the division nearest the door. The cobwebbed boards of the loft overhead almost rested on our hats; the public, not being provided with seats by the Government, shuffled on the earthen floor and unaffectedly rested on us and each other. Within the rood-screen two magistrates sat at a table, with their suite, consisting of a clerk, an interpreter, and a district inspector of police, disposed round them.

"The young fella with the foxy mustash is Docthor Lyden," whispered an informant in response to a question, "and the owld lad that's lookin' at ye now is Heraty, that owns the shop above——"

At this juncture an emissary from the Bench very kindly offered us seats within the rood-screen. We took them, on a high wooden settle, beside the magisterial table, and the business of the court proceeded.

Close to us stood the defendant, Sweeny, a tall elderly man, with a long, composed, shaven face and an all-observant grey eye: Irish in type, Irish in expression, intensely Irish in the self-possession in which he stood, playing to perfection the part of calm rectitude and unassailable integrity.

Facing him, the plaintiff lounged against the partition; a man strangely improbable in appearance, with close-cropped grey hair, a young, fresh-coloured face, a bristling orange moustache, and a big, blunt nose. One could have believed him a soldier, a German, anything but what he was, a peasant from the furthest shores of Western Ireland, cut off from what we call civilisation by his ignorance of any language save his own ancient speech, wherein the ideas of to-day stand out in English words like telegraph posts in a Connemara moorland.

Between the two stood the interpreter—small, old, froglike in profile, full of the dignity of the Government official.

"Well, we should be getting on now," remarked the Chairman, Heraty, J.P., after some explanatory politeness to his unexpected visitors. "William, swear the plaintiff!"

The oath was administered in Irish, and the orange moustache brushed the greasy Testament. The space above the dado of the partition became suddenly a tapestry of attentive faces, clear-eyed, all-comprehending.

"This case," announced Mr. Heraty judicially, yet not without a glance at the visitors, "is a demand for compensation in the matter of a sheep that was drowned. William"—this to the interpreter—"ask Darcy what he has to say for himself?"

Darcy hitched himself round, still with a shoulder propped against the partition, and uttered, without any enthusiasm, a few nasal and guttural sentences.

"He says, yer worship," said William, with unctuous propriety, "that Sweeny's gorsoons were ever and always hunting his sheep, and settin' on their dog to hunt her, and that last week they dhrove her into the lake and dhrownded her altogether."

"Now," said Mr. Heraty, in a conversational tone, "William, when ye employ the word 'gorsoon', do ye mean children of the male or female sex?"

"Well, yer worship," replied William, who, it may incidentally be mentioned, was himself in need of either an interpreter or of a new and complete set of teeth, "I should considher he meant ayther the one or the other."

"They're usually one or the other," said Doctor Lyden solemnly, and in a stupendous brogue. It was the first time he had spoken; he leaned back, with his hands in his pockets, and surveyed with quiet but very bright eyes the instant grin that illumined the faces of the tapestry.

"Sure William himself is no bad judge of gorsoons," said Mr. Heraty. "Hadn't he a christening in his own house three weeks ago?"

At this excursion into the family affairs of the interpreter the grin broke into a roar.

"See now, we'll ask Mr. Byrne, the schoolmaster," went on Mr. Heraty with owl-like gravity. "Isn't that Mr. Byrne that I see back there in the coort? Come forward, Mr. Byrne!"

Thus adjured, a tall, spectacled man emerged from the crowd, and, beaming with a pleasing elderly bashfulness through his spectacles, gave it as his opinion that though gorsoon was a term usually applied to the male child, it was equally applicable to the female. "But, indeed," he concluded, "the Bench has as good Irish as I have myself, and better."

"The law requires that the thransactions of this coort shall take place in English," the Chairman responded, "and we have also the public to consider."

As it was pretty certain that we were the only persons in the court who did not understand Irish, it was borne in upon us that we were the public, and we appreciated the consideration.

"We may assume, then, that the children that set on the dog on wor' of both sexes," proceeded Mr. Heraty. "Well, now, as to the dog—— William, ask Darcy what sort of dog was it."

The monotonous and quiet Irish sentences followed one another again.

"That'll do. Now, William——"

"He says, yer worship, that he was a big lump of a yalla dog, an' very cross, by reason of he r'arin' a pup."

"And 'twas to make mutton-broth for the pup she dhrove Darcy's sheep in the lake, I suppose?"

A contemptuous smile passed over Darcy's face as the Chairman's sally was duly translated to him, and he made a rapid reply.

"He says there isn't one of the neighbours but got great annoyance by the same dog, yer worship, and that when the dog'd be out by night hunting, there wouldn't be a yard o' wather in the lakes but he'd have it barked over."

"It appears," observed Dr. Lyden serenely, "that the dog, like the gorsoons, was of both sexes."

"Well, well, no matther now; we'll hear what the defendant has to say. Swear Sweeny!" said Mr. Heraty, smoothing his long grey beard, with suddenly remembered judicial severity and looking menacingly over his spectacles at Sweeny. "Here, now! you don't want an interpreter! You that has a sisther married to a stationmaster and a brother in the Connaught Rangers!"

"I have as good English as anny man in this coort," said Sweeny morosely.

"Well, show it off man! What defence have ye?"

"I say that the sheep wasn't Darcy's at all," said Sweeny firmly, standing as straight as a ramrod, with his hands behind his back, a picture of surly, wronged integrity. "And there's no man livin' can prove she was. Ask him now what way did he know her?"

The question evidently touched Darcy on a tender point. He squared his big shoulders in his white flannel jacket, and turning his face for the first time towards the magistrates delivered a flood of Irish, in which we heard a word that sounded like *ullán* often repeated.

"He says, yer worships," translated William, "why wouldn't he know her! Hadn't she the *ullán* on her! He says a poor man like him would know one of the few sheep he has as well as yer worship'd know one o' yer own gowns if it had sthrayed from ye."

It is probable that we looked some of the stupefaction that we felt at this remarkable reference to Mr. Heraty's wardrobe.

"For the benefit of the general public," said Dr. Lyden, in his languid, subtle brogue, with a side-glance at that body, "it may be no harm to mention that the plaintiff is alluding to the Chairman's yearling calves and not to his costume."

"Order now!" said Mr. Heraty severely.

"An' he says," continued William, warily purging his frog-countenance of any hint of appreciation, "that Sweeny knew the *ullán* that was on her as well as himself did."

"*Ullán!* What sort of English is that for an interpreter to be using! Do ye suppose the general public knows what is an *ullán*?"

interrupted Mr. Heraty with lightning rapidity. "Explain that now!"

"Why, yer worship, sure anny one in the world'd know what the *ullán* on a sheep's back is!" said William, staggered by this sudden onslaught, "though there's some might call it the *rebugh*."

"God help the Government that's payin' you wages!" said Mr. Heraty with sudden and bitter ferocity (but did we intercept a wink at his colleague?). "If it wasn't for the young family you're r'arin' in yer old age, I'd commit ye for contempt of coort!"

A frank shout of laughter, from every one in court but the victim, greeted this sally, the chorus being, as it were, barbed by a shrill crow of whooping-cough.

"Mr. Byrne!" continued Mr. Heraty without a smile, "we must call upon you again!"

Mr. Byrne's meek scholastic face once more appeared at the rood-screen.

"Well, I should say," he ventured decorously, "that the expression is locally applied to what I may call a plume or a feather that is worn on various parts of the sheep's back, for a mark, as I might say, of distinction."

"Thank you, Mr. Byrne, thank you," said Mr. Heraty, to whose imagination a vision of a plumed or feathered sheep seemed to offer nothing unusual, "remember that now, William!"

Dr. Lyden looked at his watch.

"Don't you think Sweeny might go on with his defence?" he remarked. "About the children, Sweeny—how many have ye?"

"I have four."

"And how old are they?"

"There's one o' thim is six years an' another o' thim is seven——"

"Yes, and the other two eight and nine, I suppose?" commented Dr. Lyden.

The defendant remained silent.

"Do ye see now how well he began with the youngest—the way we'd think 'twas the eldest!" resumed Dr. Lyden. "I think we may assume that a gorsoon—male or female—of eight or nine years is capable of setting a dog on the sheep."

Here Darcy spoke again.

"He says," interpreted William, "there isn't pig nor ass, sheep nor duck, belongin' to him that isn't heart-scalded with the same childhren an' their dog."

"Well, I say now, an' I swear it," said Sweeny, his eye kindling like a coal, and his voice rising as the core of what was probably an old neighbourly grudge was neared, "my land is bare from his tastes threspassing on it, and my childhren are in dread to pass his house itself with the kicks an' the sthrokes himself an' his mother dhraws on them! The Lord Almighty knows——"

"Stop now!" said Mr. Heraty, holding up his hand. "Stop! The Lord's not intherferin' in this case at all! It's me an' Doctor Lyden has it to settle."

No one seemed to find anything surprising in this pronouncement; it was accepted as seriously as any similar statement of the Prophet Samuel to the Children of Israel, and was evidently meant to imply that abstract justice might be expected.

"We may assume, then," said Dr. Lyden amiably, "that the sheep walked out into Sweeny's end of the lake and drowned herself there on account of the spite there was between the two families."

The court tittered. A dingy red showed itself among the grizzled hairs and wrinkles on Sweeny's cheek. In Ireland a point can often be better carried by sarcasm than by logic.

"She was blind enough to dhrown herself, or two like her!" he said angrily; "she was that owld and blind it was ayqual to her where she'd go!"

"How d'ye know she was blind?" said Mr. Heraty quickly.

"I thought the defence opened with the statement that it wasn't Darcy's sheep at all," put in Dr. Lyden, leaning back in his chair with his eyes fixed on the rafters.

Sweeny firmly regarded Mr. Heraty.

"How would I know she was blind?" he repeated. "Many's the time when she'd be takin' a sthroll in on my land I'd see her fallin' down in the rocks, she was that blind! An' didn't I see Darcy's mother one time, an' she puttin' something on her eyes."

"Was it glasses she was putting on the sheep's eyes?" suggested the Chairman, with a glance that admitted the court to the joke.

"No, but an ointment," said Sweeny stubbornly. "I seen her rubbing it to the eyes, an' she no more than thirty yards from me."

"Will ye swear that?" thundered Mr. Heraty; "will you swear that at a distance of thirty yards you could tell what was between Darcy's mother's fingers and the sheep's eyes? No you will not! Nor no man could! William, is Darcy's mother in the coort? We'll have to take evidence from her as to the condition of the sheep's eyes!"

"Darcy says, yer worship, that his mother would lose her life if she was to be brought into coort," explained William, after an interlude in Irish, to which both magistrates listened with evident interest; "that ere last night a frog jumped into the bed to her in the night, and she got out of the bed to light the Blessed Candle, and when she got back to the bed again she was in it always between herself and the wall, an' she got a wakeness out of it, and great cold——"

"Are ye sure it wasn't the frog got the wakeness?" asked Dr. Lyden.

A gale of laughter swept round the court.

"Come, come!" said Mr. Heraty; "have done with this baldherdash! William, tell Darcy someone must go fetch his mother, for as wake as she is she could walk half a mile!" Mr. Heraty here drew forth an enormous white pocket-handkerchief and trumpeted angrily in its depths.

Darcy raised his small blue eyes with their thick lashes, and took a look at his judge. There was a gabbled interchange of Irish between him and the interpreter.

"He says she could not, yer worship, nor as much as one perch."

"Ah, what nonsense is this!" said Mr. Heraty testily; "didn't I see the woman meself at Mass last Sunday?"

Darcy's reply was garnished with a good deal more gesticulation than usual, and throughout his speech the ironic smile on Sweeny's face was a masterpiece of quiet expression.

"He says," says William, "that surely she was at Mass last Sunday, the same as your worship says, but 'twas on the way home that she was taking a wall, and a stone fell on her and hurted her finger, and the boot preyed on it, and it has her desthroyed."

At this culmination of the misadventures of Mrs. Darcy the countenances of the general public must again have expressed some of the bewilderment that they felt.

"Perhaps William will be good enough to explain," said Dr. Lyden, permitting a faint smile to twitch the foxy moustache, "how Mrs. Darcy's boot affected her finger?"

William's skinny hand covered his frog-mouth with all a deserving schoolboy's embarrassment at being caught out in a bad translation.

"I beg yer worships' pardon," he said, in deep confusion, "but sure your worships know as well as meself that in Irish we have the one word for your finger or your toe."

"There's one thing I know very well anyhow," said Dr. Lyden, turning to his colleague, "I've no more time to waste sitting here talking about old Kit Darcy's fingers and toes! Let the two o' them get arbitrators and settle it out of court. There's nothing between them now only the value of the sheep."

"Sure I was satisfied to leave it to arbithration, but Darcy wasn't willin'." This statement was Sweeny's.

"So you were willing to have arbithration before you came into coort at all?" said Mr. Heraty, eyeing the tall defendant with ominous mildness. "William, ask Darcy is this the case."

Darcy's reply, delivered with a slow, sarcastic smile, provoked a laugh from the audience.

"Oh, ho! So that was the way, was it!" cried Mr. Heraty, forgetting to wait for the translation. "Ye had your wife's cousin to arbithrate! Small blame to Darcy he wasn't willin'! It's a pity ye didn't say your wife herself should arbithrate when ye went about it! You would hardly believe the high opinion Sweeny here has of his wife," continued the Chairman in illuminative excursus to Dr. Lyden; "sure he had all the women wild below at my shop th' other night sayin' his wife was the finest woman in Ireland! Upon my soul he had!"

"If I said that," growled the unfortunate Sweeny, "it was a lie for me."

"Don't ye think it might be a good thing now," suggested the indefatigable doctor, in his mournful tuneful voice, "to call a few witnesses to give evidence as to whether Mrs. Michael Sweeny is the finest woman in Ireland or no?"

"God knows, gentlemen, it's a pity ye haven't more to do this day," said Sweeny, turning at length upon his tormentors. "I'd sooner pay the price of the sheep than be losin' me time here this way."

"See, now, how we're getting to the rights of it in the latter end," commented Dr. Lyden imperturbably. "Sweeny began here by saying"—he checked off each successive point on his fingers—"that the sheep wasn't Darcy's at all. Then he said that his children of eight and nine years of age were too young to set the dog on the sheep. Then, that if the dog hunted her it was no more than she deserved for constant trespass. Then he said that the sheep was so old and blind that she committed suicide in his end of the lake in order to please herself and to spite him; and, last of all, he tells us that he offered to compensate Darcy for her before he came into court at all!"

"And on top of that," Mr. Heraty actually rose in his seat in his exquisite appreciation of the position, "on top of that, mind you, after he has the whole machinery of the law and the entire population of Letterbeg attending on him for a matter o' two hours, he informs us that we're wasting his valuable time!"

Mr. Heraty fixed his eyes in admirable passion—whether genuine or not we are quite incapable of pronouncing—upon Sweeny, who returned the gaze with all the gloom of an unfortunate but invincibly respectable man.

Dr. Lyden once more pulled out his watch.

"It might be as well for us," he said languidly, "to enter upon the inquiry as to the value of the sheep. That should take about another three-quarters of an hour. William, ask Darcy the price he puts on the sheep."

Every emotion has its limits. We received with scarce a stirring of surprise the variations of sworn testimony as to the value of the sheep. Her price ranged from one pound, claimed by Darcy and his adherents, to sixpence, at which sum her skin was unhesitatingly valued by Sweeny. Her age swung like a pendulum between two years and fourteen, and, finally, in crowning proof of her worth and general attractiveness, it was stated that her own twin had been sold for fifteen shillings to the police at Dhulish, "ere last week". At this re-entrance into the case of the personal element Mr. Heraty's spirits obviously rose.

"I think we ought to have evidence about this," he said, fixing the police officer with a dangerous eye. "Mr. Cox, have ye anny of the Dhulish police here?"

Mr. Cox, whose only official act up to the present had been the highly beneficial one of opening the window, admitted with a grin that two of the Dhulish men were in the court.

"Well, then!" continued the Chairman, "Mr. Cox, maybe ye'd kindly desire them to step forward in order that the court may be able to estimate from their appearance the nutritive qualities of the twin sisther of Darcy's sheep."

At this juncture we perceived, down near the crowded doorway, two tall and deeply embarrassed members of the R.I.C. hastily escaping into the street.

"Well, well; how easy it is to frighten the police!" remarked the Chairman, following them with a regretful eye. "I suppose, afther all, we'd betther put a price on the sheep and have done with it. In my opinion, when there's a difficulty like this—what I might call an accident—between decent men like these (for they're both decent men, and I've known them these years), I'd say both parties should share what hardship is in it. Now, doctor, what shall we give Darcy? I suppose if we gave him 8s. compensation and 2s. costs we'd not be far out?"

Dr. Lyden, already in the act of charging his pipe, nodded his head.

Sweeny began to fumble in his pockets, and drawing out a brownish rag, possibly a handkerchief, knotted in several places, proceeded to untie one of the knots. The doctor watched him without speaking. Ultimately, from some fastness in the rag a half-sovereign was extracted, and was laid upon the table by Sweeny. The clerk, a well-dressed young gentleman, whose attitude had throughout been one of the extremest aloofness, made an entry in his book with an aggressively business-like air.

"Well, that's all right," remarked Dr. Lyden, getting lazily on his legs and looking round for his hat; "it's a funny thing, but I notice that the defendant brought the exact sum required into court with him."

"I did! And I'm able to bring more than it, thanks be to God!" said Sweeny fiercely, with all the offended pride of his race. "I have two pounds here this minute——"

"If that's the way with ye, may be ye'd like us to put a bigger fine on ye!" broke in Mr. Heraty hotly, in instant response to Sweeny's show of temper.

Dr. Lyden laughed for the first time.

"Mr. Heraty's getting cross now, in the latter end," he murmured explanatorily to the general public, while he put on an overcoat, from the pocket of which protruded the Medusa coils of a stethoscope.

Long before the arrival of the mail-car that was to take us away, the loafers and the litigants had alike been swallowed up, apparently by the brown, hungry hillsides; possibly also, some of them, by Mr. Heraty's tap-room. Again we clambered to our places among the inevitable tourists and their inevitable bicycles, again the laden car lumbered heavily yet swiftly along the bog roads that quivered under its weight, while the water in the black ditches on either side quivered in sympathy. The tourists spoke of the vast loneliness, unconscious of the intricate network of social life that lay all around them, beyond their ken, far beyond their understanding. They spoke authoritatively of Irish affairs; mentioned that the Irish were "a bit 'ot tempered", but added that "all they wanted was fair play".

They had probably been in Ireland for a week or fortnight. They had come out of business centres in England, equipped with circular tickets, with feeling hearts, and with the belief that two and two inevitably make four; whereas in Ireland two and two are just as likely to make five, or three, and are still more likely to make nothing at all.

Never will it be given to them to understand the man of whom our friend Sweeny was no more than a type. How can they be expected to realise that a man who is decorous in family and village life, indisputably God-fearing, kind to the poor, and reasonably honest, will enmesh himself in a tissue of sworn lies before his fellows for the sake of half a sovereign and a family feud, and that his fellows will think none the worse of him for it.

These things lie somewhere near the heart of the Irish problem.

ACKNOWLEDGMENTS

Acknowledgments are due to the following for permission to reprint these stories:

The author for the story *Mr. Portway's Practice*; the author and Messrs. William Collins, Sons & Co. Ltd. for the story *The Witness For The Prosecution*; the author and Messrs. William Heinemann Ltd. for the story *The Happy Couple* from *Creatures of Circumstance*; the author and Messrs. Hamish Hamilton Ltd. for the story *Legal Aid* from *The Stories of Frank O'Connor*; the author and Messrs. Michael Joseph Ltd. for the story *Painswick v. Gloster* from *The Painswick Line*; the executrix of the author and Messrs. Faber & Faber for the story *Murderer's Luck* from *Best Detective Stories Of Cyril Hare*; the author, Messrs. John Farquharson Ltd. and Messrs. Victor Gollancz Ltd. for the story *The Great World of Timothy Colt* from *The Injustice Collectors*; the executors of the author and Messrs. William Heinemann Ltd. for the story *The Juryman* from *Caravan*; the author and Messrs. William Collins, Sons & Co. Ltd. for the story *No Arms No Armour* from the book of that name; Messrs. John Farquharson Ltd. on behalf of the Somerville & Ross Estate for the story *An Irish Problem.*